JCK Daily News

Diamonds remain the most important resource for the government of Botswana, representing one-third of the country's gross domestic product, said Mokgweetsi Masisi, president of the Republic of Botswana, at the JCK Industry Keynote Breakfast address on May 31, 2019.

He said when Botswana first discovered diamonds in 1967, the country started what is now a five-decade association with De Beers. Eventually the pair formed Debswana, a 50-50 partnership between De Beers and the government.

"We met De Beers as equal partners, even though we were unequal to them," Masisi said. Debswana is "celebrating its 50th anniversary this year and will probably celebrate its 100th anniversary decades from now."

The success of the partnership turned Botswana from one of the world's poorest countries into an "upper-middle-income country," he said, explaining that the diamond proceeds "were used to develop not just the roads, but our people."

The president was compelled to come to JCK Las Vegas because he was "curious," he said. "Who are these people who buy our diamonds? We wanted to see what they are about. We wanted people to see us. We don't want to be a secret anymore."

Praise for Michael Stanley

"The intricate plotting, a grisly sense of realism and numerous topical motifs (the plight of the Kalahari bushmen, diamond smuggling, poaching, the homogenization of African culture, etc.) make this a compulsively readable novel. Despite a shared setting with Alexander McCall Smith's No. 1 Ladies' Detective Agency series, this fast-paced forensic thriller will resonate more with fans of Patricia Cornwell's Kay Scarpetta."
—*Publishers Weekly* Starred Review for *A Carrion Death*

"Bringing a love of Africa similar to Alexander McCall Smith's popular No. 1 Ladies' Detective Agency series, the author has created an excellent new venue for those who love to read about other cultures while enjoying a good mystery. Highly recommended."
—*School Library Journal* Starred Review for
The Second Death of Goodluck Tinubu

"*Death of the Mantis* is the best book I've read in a very long time. A fantastic read. Brilliant!"
—Louise Penny, *New York Times* bestselling
author of *Bury Your Dead*

"*Death of the Mantis* is the best book yet in one of the best series going: a serious novel with a mystery at its core that takes us places we've never been, thrills and informs us, and leaves us changed by the experience. I loved this book."
—Timothy Hallinan, author of *The Queen of
Patpong* and *A Nail Through the Heart*

"A page-turner from start to finish. Michael Stanley's enthralling series is a must-read for anyone who enjoys clever plotting, terrific writing, and a fascinating glimpse of today's Africa. Kubu—*Death of the Mantis*—Michael Stanley: the perfect mystery trifecta for any crime fan."

—Charles Todd, *New York Times* bestselling author of *A Matter of Justice*

"Impossible to put down, this immensely readable third entry... delivers the goods. Kubu's painstaking detecting skills make him a sort of Hercule Poirot of the desert. This series can be recommended to a wide gamut of readers."

—*Library Journal* Starred Review for *Death of the Mantis*

"Kubu's third recorded case is again alive with local color and detail and, refreshingly, offers his fullest mystery plot yet."

—*Kirkus Reviews* for *Death of the Mantis*

"Believable and utterly menacing. Tight plotting is seasoned with African culture."

—Steve Steinbock, *Ellery Queen Mystery Magazine* for *Deadly Harvest*

"Kubu is also hugely appealing—big and solid and smart enough to grasp all angles of this mystery. Readers may be lured to Africa by the landscape, but it takes a great character like Kubu to win our loyalty."

—*New York Times Book Review* for *A Carrion Death*

"Kubu returns with a vengeance—but what is prowling in the darkness of Botswana is more dangerous than the four-legged predators. Then there are the Chinese who just may be the most dangerous of all—I love it!"
— Charles Todd, award-winning author of the Ian Rutledge and Bess Crawford mysteries for *A Death in the Family*

"Stanley and Kubu deserve much more critical and commercial attention than they have been receiving; hopefully this latest installment will rectify that shortcoming."
— *Bookreporter* for *A Death in the Family*

"David 'Kubu' Bengu, an assistant superintendent in the Botswana CID, investigates a particularly baffling murder in his sixth, and best, outing. Stanley (the pseudonym of Michael Sears and Stanley Trollip) keeps the intriguing plot twists coming."
— *Publishers Weekly* Starred and Boxed Review for *Dying to Live*

"Stanley once again mixes strongly developed characters, puzzling plot twists and a textured African setting in an international police procedural with heart and soul that will appeal to fans of Kwei Quartey and Alexander McCall Smith."
— *Library Journal* Starred Review for *Dying to Live*

"The best yet, with both an ingenious mystery and a deeper and more textured depiction of modern Botswana and Kubu's piece of it."
— *Kirkus Reviews* for *Dying to Live*

"From Minnesota to South Africa to Mozambique to Vietnam, Michael Stanley's *Shoot the Bastards* is an extraordinary tale of the extreme measures taken to combat international poaching and smuggling."

—C.J. Box, #1 *New York Times* bestselling author of *Wolf Pack*

Also by Michael Stanley

FACETS OF DEATH

FACETS OF DEATH

A DETECTIVE KUBU MYSTERY

MICHAEL STANLEY

Poisoned Pen
PRESS

Published by Poisoned Pen Press, an imprint of Sourcebooks
P.O. Box 4410, Naperville, Illinois 60567-4410
(630) 961-3900
sourcebooks.com

Library of Congress Cataloging-in-Publication Data

Description: Naperville, Illinois : Poisoned Pen Press, [2020] | Series: A Detective
Kubu mystery |
Identifiers: LCCN 2019024149 | (trade paperback)
Subjects: LCSH: Botswana--Fiction. | GSAFD: Mystery fiction.
Classification: LCC PR9369.4.S715 F33 2020 | DDC 823/.92--dc23
LC record available at https://lccn.loc.gov/2019024149

Printed and bound in the United States of America.
SB 10 9 8 7 6 5 4 3 2 1

NOTE

The peoples of Southern Africa have integrated many words of their own languages into colloquial English. For authenticity and colour, we have used these occasionally when appropriate. Most of the time, the meanings are clear from the context, but for interest, we have included a glossary at the end of the book.

For information about Botswana, the book, and its protagonist, please visit michaelstanleybooks.com. You can sign up there for an occasional newsletter. We are also active on Facebook at facebook.com/MichaelStanleyBooks, and on Twitter as @detectivekubu.

Botswana & Surrounding Countries

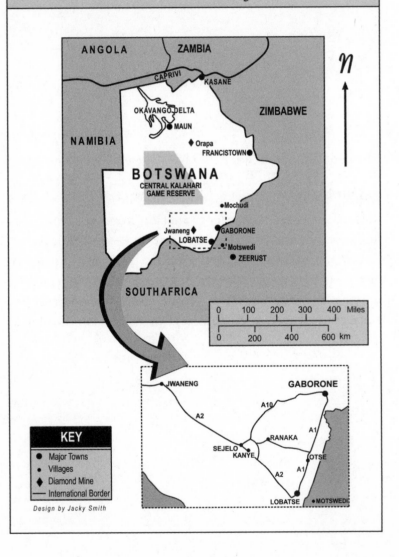

ANGOLA   ZAMBIA

n

CAPRIVI   KASANE

OKAVANGO DELTA

MAUN

ZIMBABWE

NAMIBIA

♦ Orapa
FRANCISTOWN ●

BOTSWANA
CENTRAL KALAHARI
GAME RESERVE

● Mochudi

Jwaneng ♦   ● GABORONE
LOBATSE

● Motswedi
● ZEERUST

SOUTH AFRICA

| 0 | 100 | 200 | 300 | 400 Miles |

| 0 | 200 | 400 | 600 km |

● JWANENG   GABORONE

A10

A2   A1

RANAKA

SEJELO   OTSE
KANYE

A2   A1

LOBATSE   ● MOTSWEDI

KEY
● Major Towns
● Villages
♦ Diamond Mine
— International Border

Design by Jacky Smith

CAST OF CHARACTERS

Words in square brackets are approximate phonetic pronunciations.

Bengu, Amantle: Kubu's mother [Ah-MUN-tleh BEN-goo]

Bengu, David "Kubu": Detective sergeant in the Botswana Criminal Investigation Department [David "KOO-boo" BEN-goo]

Bengu, Wilmon: Kubu's father [WILL-mon BEN-goo]

Boko, Joseph: Baggage handler at Sir Seretse Khama airport [Joseph BO-ko]

Chamberlain, Major David: Head of Jwaneng diamond mine

Dow, Luke: Inspector in the Botswana Criminal Investigation Department [Luke DOW with the OW as in HOW]

Elias: Constable at reception in the Criminal Investigation Department

Gobey, Tebogo: Director of the Botswana Criminal Investigation Department [Teh-BO-go GO-bee]

Goodman, Elijah: Head of administration at Jwaneng mine

Henkel, Pieter: Manager of Gaborone Cash in Transit company

Kamwi, Joe: Tour bus driver [Joe KUM-wi]

Katlego: Witch doctor [Cut-LEH-go]

Kenosi, Salekany: Armoured car guard [Sul-é-CAH-nee Ken-OH-si]

Letsi, Lucas: Debswana diamond trader [Lucas LET-see]

Mabaku, Jacob: Assistant superintendent in the Botswana Criminal Investigation Department [Jacob Muh-BAH-koo]

MacGregor, Ian: Pathologist for the Botswana police

Murewa: Constable in Otse [Moo-REH-wuh]

Naledi, Sheila: Armoured car guard [Sheila Nuh-LEH-di]

Neo, Mathew: Detective sergeant in the Botswana Criminal Investigation Department [Mathew NEE-o]

Nari, Phineas: Manager of the Jwaneng airport [Phineas NUH-ree]

Oteng, Jake: Armoured car guard [Jake OH-teng]

Pono, Happy: Inspector at the police station in Sejelo [Happy POH-noh]

Roberts, Tony: Pilot for Debswana

Samkoa, Nelson: Detective sergeant in the Botswana Criminal Investigation Department [Nelson Sum-KOH-uh]

Serome, Joy: Clerk in the Botswana Police Service Records Department [Joy Sé-ROE-meh]

Tau, Eddie: Head of security at Jwaneng mine [Eddie TOW with the OW as in HOW]

Tshane, Peter: Guard at Jwaneng mine [Peter TSHUH-neh]

Tuelo, Vusi: South African criminal [VOO-si TWEH-loh]

Venter, Piet: Colonel in the South African Police Service [Piet FEN-ter]

Zuma, Alfred: Baggage handler at Sir Seretse Khama airport [Alfred ZOO-muh]

MONDAY
Chapter 1

The early-morning sun promised a scorcher of a day, and David "Kubu" Bengu's clothes were already damp with sweat—not unusual for a man of his size in a hot climate. He was standing in front of the Criminal Investigation Department on Queens Road, excited and nervous about walking through the front door—excited because it was his first day as a detective in the Botswana Police; nervous because he'd been hired to the position without having had any time as a constable on the beat. In fact, he'd never even been in uniform. He was expecting to take some heat for that.

Kubu pulled a handkerchief from his pocket. He leant over and cleaned his shoes, which were covered in dust from his long walk to work. When he was satisfied, he took a deep breath and squared his shoulders. "Here goes," he said out loud and strode towards the door. "I'll always remember the thirtieth of November, 1998—my first day at work."

"Detective Sergeant Bengu reporting for work," he told the man at reception, who looked him up and down with a frown.

"Bengu?" The man shuffled through a stack of papers. "Bengu?"

A few moments later, he found what he was looking for. "David Bengu?"

"Yes, but everyone calls me Kubu."

The man snorted, taking in Kubu's bulk. "I can see why."

Kubu didn't react. He was used to that sort of response. After all, he'd had the nickname for over five years, ever since he first met Angus Hofmeyr, a rich white boy, at Maru-a-Pula School.

"You're David?" Angus had exclaimed in disbelief when they first met. "*David* Bengu? That's not right. You aren't a David. Not even a Goliath! You're a *kubu*. That's what you are—a big, friendly hippopotamus."

Kubu remembered being upset at first, but he'd come to like the special familiarity of the name. The other kids had laughed, of course, but soon Kubu was his name. Now he was sure that some of his friends didn't even know his real name.

Miffed that his snide comment had failed to raise even one of Kubu's eyebrows, the receptionist ordered Kubu to go immediately to Assistant Superintendent Mabaku's office. "He's going to be your boss! I don't envy you because he eats nails!"

———

"Sit down. I'll be with you in a minute."

Mabaku waved at one of the chairs in front of his desk. Kubu lowered himself, carefully maintaining some of his weight on his legs until he was sure the chair wouldn't collapse. He waited patiently while Mabaku growled at a letter he was reading.

Mabaku's office was small and very hot. The window air conditioner was on, judging by the strained noises, but very little cool air was being pushed into the room. There were stacks of files on every horizontal surface, and on top of one filing cabinet was a colour photo of a woman whom Kubu took to be Mabaku's wife.

Eventually Mabaku looked up and glared at Kubu. He shook the letter in the air. "It's your fault. The director wants me to file all the paperwork so that you get paid, that you have health insurance, and that you start contributing towards your pension. I thought that's why we have secretaries—to do all the tough work."

Kubu didn't respond.

"Do you have a driver's licence?"

"Yes, sir."

"And a car?"

Kubu nodded and smiled. "An old Land Rover, sir."

He was still amazed that he'd been able to buy it. It was mainly due to the generosity of one of his lecturers at the university, who had wanted to sell it and had told him to pay it off as he could afford to. At his police salary, it wasn't going to be paid off anytime soon.

Mabaku glanced up, surprised. "How old?"

The smile vanished. "Um…quite old, sir."

Mabaku picked up a sheet of paper from his desk and handed it to Kubu. "Fill this out and take it to Miriam, the director's assistant. It authorizes you to take a car from the pool if you need one. Use one of them for business rather than your Land Rover. There are usually two or three pool cars at the back of the building. Check they haven't been reserved before you take one."

Mabaku scratched his head. "I'm sure I've missed something, but it'll come to me, probably at an inconvenient moment."

There was a long silence, something that Kubu was good at maintaining.

"Do you fit into your office?" Mabaku asked at last. "I'm sorry it's so small, but it's the only one we've got. Have they stocked it with pens, notebooks, the usual forms, and so on?"

"Nobody's shown me my office, sir."

"Goddamn it." Mabaku pounded the top of his desk. "That Elias at reception is already trying to cause trouble for you."

"I don't understand."

"It's my fault! I just hope it doesn't become too much of a problem for you."

Kubu frowned.

"You impressed the right people at the university. They persuaded me you'd be wasted spending several years in uniform on the beat, so we took a chance and hired you as soon as you graduated. We've never done that before. Just ignore Elias and others like him. That's my advice. They're just jealous."

"I was expecting something like that." Kubu shrugged.

Mabaku looked through the papers on his desk. "I think that's all for now. Any questions?"

"Yes, sir. What's my first job? I'm keen to get to work."

"We meet every Monday in the room at the end of the passage. We're meeting in fifteen minutes to be exact. We'll find out then what's happened over the weekend. That's all. Go and tell Elias that he's to show you to your office and to make sure you have the supplies you need."

With that, Mabaku lifted a file from one of his stacks, opened it, and started reading.

"Yes, sir. Thank you, sir."

Kubu heaved himself out of his chair. He closed the door quietly as he left the room and walked back to reception.

"What do you want now?" Elias asked.

"Assistant Superintendent Mabaku would like you to show me to my office and to make sure I have all the supplies I need."

"I'm busy right now."

"The assistant superintendent wants me to be settled in my office before the staff meeting in fifteen minutes," Kubu responded, stretching the truth a little. "But if you are too busy, I'll go and ask him who can help me."

Elias glared at Kubu, knowing he'd lost the round. "Follow me," he barked.

As they walked down the corridor, Kubu made a mental note to double check anything Elias did for him. He was sure Elias would try to even the score.

"That's your office." Elias pointed to a door. "I'll bring the stuff you need in a few minutes."

"Thank you for your help." Kubu wasn't quite able to keep the sarcasm from his tone.

Sure enough, Elias walked into Kubu's office a few minutes later with a box full of supplies.

Again, Kubu thanked him, but Elias just glowered.

With only a few minutes left, Kubu grabbed a notebook and pencil from the box and headed to the meeting room, where Director Tebogo Gobey would preside.

At last, Kubu thought. He was about to start doing what he'd wanted to do for such a long time—be a detective.

Chapter 2

A hundred miles to the west, Phineas Nari, the manager of Jwaneng's small airport, spotted the pilot driving up to the gate. He knew Tony Roberts well, and once he'd pulled open the gate, he waved him through with only a cursory glance at his Debswana identification. Then he locked the gate and followed the car up to the parking lot. The pilot was grabbing his bag from the boot of the car.

"How are you, Phineas? Nice morning for flying."

Nari nodded. The weather was clear, and the early-morning air was still.

"Where are you headed today, Tony?"

"Off to Orapa to pick up some De Beers engineers and fly them back to Joburg. I'd best be off."

He headed for the apron. The plane had been refuelled the day before and was ready to go. Nari stood watching him as he went through his checks and climbed into the plane. Jwaneng had no tower, so Roberts would call Gaborone once he was airborne and activate a flight plan he'd already filed by phone.

At last the engines started up, and the plane moved onto the runway. It would taxi to the far end, turn, and then take off towards the east. Nari lit a cigarette. His job was hardly demanding. There would be nothing else to do until the diamond transport plane arrived a few hours later.

When the plane was about halfway to the end of the runway, he saw flames and smoke coming from the right engine. The plane stopped, the propellers stopped turning, and Roberts jumped out and walked around to where the fire was. Suddenly a fireball burst from the right wing. Roberts staggered back, clutching his face.

"Shit!" Nari exclaimed and ran across the apron to where the emergency fire vehicle was parked. He jumped in and raced towards the burning plane and immediately realised that there was little he could do to save it. He drove as close as he thought was safe, jumped out, and ran to Roberts.

"Tony! Oh God, I've got to get you to hospital." The pilot's hair was gone, and his skin was black. He took Roberts's arm and led him to the vehicle. He opened the passenger door and helped the pilot in. "We'll be at the hospital in five minutes."

Chapter 3

When Kubu walked through the door of the meeting room, the hubbub of idle conversation quietened, and heads turned to look at him. But no one greeted him.

"Good morning," he said as he looked around for a seat. There were only four left—three at one end of the table and one at the other. He headed to the single one, thinking he had probably been channelled there so he would be facing the director.

He pulled the chair back from the table, sat down—cautiously—and smiled.

A few moments later, the director walked in, followed by Mabaku and another man Kubu didn't recognize.

"Morning, everyone." Director Gobey put a stack of folders on the table. He looked down the table at Kubu. "I take it you are Detective Sergeant Bengu?"

"Yes, sir. But everyone calls me Kubu."

A snicker ran around the table.

"I couldn't care what people call you. In the CID, you are Detective Sergeant Bengu. Understood?"

"Yes, sir."

Gobey looked around the table. "Anyway, I'd like you all to welcome our newest detective sergeant, David Bengu. He has a lot to learn, so please help him out wherever you can." He glared around at the group of men.

"Right. First, old business. Samkoa, what's the status of your investigation into the theft at the garage on Molepolole Road?"

"We arrested a suspect last Friday, sir. We had a good CCTV image, and it didn't take long to identify him when we showed his picture around to some of our informers. Of course, he says he's innocent, but the video is conclusive."

"Excellent. Tiro, how are you doing with the pickpockets on the Mall?"

"Not as well as Detective Sergeant Samkoa, sir. We had some of our male and female employees shop along the Mall in their everyday clothes, hopefully looking like tourists. All we achieved was to waste department money for tourist trinkets that are now on the shelves by the coffeepot. Our next move is to put up some CCTV cameras around the areas where we've had the most problems. We're trying to get the city to pay for them but haven't succeeded yet."

And so Gobey went around the room, with each detective reporting how things were going with their individual investigations. Some had been successful; some were stalled. Kubu listened carefully, trying to imagine how he would approach each case.

"Now, new business," Gobey said, getting ready to take notes. "Mabaku, what did the weekend bring?"

Mabaku cleared his throat and read from notes he'd prepared.

"Two things, sir. There were several more incidents of rustling at Ramatlabama over the weekend. Almost certainly cross-border from South Africa. The border is so damned porous. I've spoken to the South African Police Service at Mahikeng. They're looking into it. I've no idea when or if we'll hear back from them.

"Then, for the second item, an unusual number of suitcases belonging to tourists leaving the country seem to have gone missing. Of course, they were only missed at their destinations, some in London and some in Paris. British Airways and Air France are blaming Air Botswana. All of the suitcases should have been offloaded from Air Botswana flights arriving in Joburg and loaded on the relevant outgoing flights to Europe."

"How many cases in all?" Gobey asked.

"Fifteen."

"Fifteen? We'd better get to the bottom of that quickly. Otherwise we'll start to see tourism drying up."

"Yes, sir. We've already contacted the airlines in question."

Kubu put up his hand.

"Yes, Detective Sergeant?"

"Did I hear the assistant superintendent say that all the lost suitcases left Sir Seretse Khama on Air Botswana flights rather than on South African Airways flights?"

"That's correct," Mabaku answered. He turned to one of the detectives sitting next to Kubu. "Neo, what've you found out?"

"Not much so far, sir. We were only told about these suitcases on Saturday afternoon. We do know that they were all properly tagged before they left, but we haven't heard back from Joburg about what happened there."

"Okay. Bengu, you work with Neo on this. A good one to get your feet wet on."

"Yes, sir," Kubu responded.

Gobey looked around the room. "Anything else?"

Nobody raised their hands, and the meeting adjourned

Kubu turned to Neo and held out his hand. "I'm Kubu. Pleased to meet you." The man looked a little taken aback but stammered a response. "Neo. Mathew Neo."

Kubu stood up. "Let's go to your office and get started."

Chapter 4

Two hours after the plane had caught fire, Elijah Goodman, head of administration at the Jwaneng diamond mine, ended his phone call to civil aviation with a muttered curse. The major wasn't going to be happy.

Well, there's no time to waste, he thought. *I'd better get on with it.*

He left his office, told his secretary he was going to see Major Chamberlain, and crossed the corridor to Eddie Tau's office. Tau was head of security and was always available for urgent matters.

"Is he in?" he asked Tau's secretary.

"Yes, Rra Goodman. But he has a meeting coming up and—"

Goodman didn't wait to hear the end of her sentence. He opened Tau's door and walked in.

Tau gave his usual easy smile. "Dumela, Elijah. What's up?"

Goodman's news wiped the smile off his face.

"Shit! Will the pilot be okay? We need to inform the major right away."

He jumped up, and they made their way to the boss's more imposing office at the end of the corridor.

David Chamberlain's personal assistant looked up with surprise. She wasn't expecting the heads of administration and security, and the major liked to operate by appointment.

"We need to see him right away," Tau said. "It's urgent."

The PA saw their expressions and immediately went into her boss's office. A moment later, she returned and signalled them in.

Major Chamberlain's desk was positioned in front of a large corner window overlooking the sprawling Jwaneng diamond-mine complex. The size of the open pit always astonished Goodman—a thousand metres across and much deeper than the country's tallest skyscraper. And the ore trucks! Even the tyres dwarfed a man. Goodman was convinced the office was deliberately positioned there to remind a visitor of how big the operation was and who was in charge of it. He thought the large photograph of the major's wife on his desk was there for the same reason. She was a cousin of the chairman of De Beers, one of the mine's owners.

"Yes, what is it, Elijah, Eddie?" He didn't invite them to sit. "What's so urgent?"

"Major," Goodman began, "we've got a big problem. They've closed the airport. There's been a fire. It could be out of service for a couple of days."

"What! When did that happen?" He waved them to seats in front of his desk.

"Earlier this morning. A plane going up to Orapa caught fire in the middle of the runway. It's a write-off. The pilot's in hospital. He managed to get out, but the airport manager says he got burnt when the petrol exploded. He has no idea what could have happened. The civil aviation people are sending a team to investigate, but in the meantime, they've closed the airport completely."

"But it's our airport!" The major's voice rose. "What right do they have to tell us that it's closed?"

"It still comes under their authority, Major," Tau explained.

"And that will be several days? Why can't they just tow the plane out of the way? Did you explain to them how urgent it is?"

Goodman nodded. "I just spoke to them in Gaborone. Nothing can be disturbed till they've done their investigation.

They said we could bring in a chopper and land it at the end of the runway if we wanted to."

Tau shook his head at once. "We don't have any of our own, and we can't bring in an outside team at short notice for this sort of job. It's much too risky."

The major nodded in agreement.

Goodman had an idea. "Shall we try the military? The president owes us a favour or two. Maybe they can help us out?" It seemed a sensible option to him, and because of Chamberlain's army background, he thought the major would like it. But Tau didn't look happy, and the major was already shaking his head.

"I'm not going crawling for help!" he said angrily. "It won't look good."

Goodman knew he meant that the directors in Gaborone wouldn't like it. But the reality was that the voracious processing plant in Gaborone would be expecting a delivery today—a larger delivery than usual because the plane they used to take the diamonds to Gaborone had spent the past two days being serviced at Lanseria in South Africa. The plant would probably need to start processing the stones as soon as they arrived if it was to keep on schedule. He checked his watch. About one hundred thousand carats of mainly gem-quality, raw diamonds needed to be on their way within the next few hours. Failing that, Debswana's total diamond exports for the week would be well below target, and the directors wouldn't like that at all.

"We have a backup plan." Chamberlain waved at them. "You two had better get off your backsides and implement it, hadn't you? Sort out this mess we're in."

Goodman chewed his lip. He wasn't really keen on the backup plan. They'd never used it before, and he felt it was too complicated. Complicated things could go wrong. But the major had designed it, so there was no point in even raising that.

"Sir, this shipment is much bigger than usual. Perhaps we should consider waiting a day. Maybe the runway—"

"It's all set up, isn't it?" Chamberlain interrupted. "Is the security company on standby?"

Goodman frowned. "Yes sir, but—"

"Well, then, get on with it."

———

They went back to Goodman's office, and he found the contract with Gaborone Cash in Transit and tossed it to Tau.

"It's all in there. You remember when we negotiated it with them? It stipulates immediate response."

Tau nodded and flipped through the document.

Goodman hesitated. "Eddie, I think we should delay this. At least until tomorrow. Check with Gaborone first. I'm nervous about doing this on zero notice." As head of security, Tau was much more likely to persuade the major than Goodman was. And Tau was usually the cautious one.

Tau didn't look up from the contract. "The major wasn't interested in a delay. We'll just have to make this work."

Goodman sighed, grabbed the phone, and called Gaborone Cash in Transit. He insisted on speaking to the managing director and then put him on speakerphone.

"Rra Henkel? This is Elijah Goodman at Jwaneng. I'm here with Eddie Tau. You'll remember that he's our head of security here at the mine. We have a problem." He explained the situation at the airport and that they needed to implement their backup plan. Tau chipped in with details of what would be required.

There was silence on the line for a few seconds before the man responded. "I understand. When do you want all this to happen?"

"Right now," Tau replied. "We were expecting to load the plane in a couple of hours."

"*Today*? You can't be serious! You want three armoured vehicles—each with an experienced three-man team—and backup vehicles—at half an hour's notice? We have a schedule, you know. We can't just drop all our other customers."

Goodman had sympathy with the man's point of view, but it wasn't his problem.

"I have the contract in front of me." His voice left no room for disagreement. "It says 'immediate response.' That means now, not tomorrow or next week."

"It can't be done! You'll have to give me until tomorrow at least."

Goodman sighed. He could imagine what the major would say if he was having this conversation.

"You simply have to make this happen, Rra Henkel. Today. You've had good money from us on this contract for nearly two years, and you've never had to lift a finger or spend a pula to earn it. You didn't have to sign it, but you jumped at it. Now it's payback time. I really don't think you want to make an enemy of Debswana."

"Let me take a look at the contract," Henkel replied. "Please hold on." He was quiet for almost a minute. "It does say immediately," he conceded eventually. "But I assumed *some* notice." When neither Debswana official commented, he continued. "I'll look at the options and see what can be done. I'll call you back."

"I expect to hear from you within fifteen minutes."

Goodman hung up and gave a sigh of relief. He hoped it wasn't premature.

Chapter 5

"You shouldn't have volunteered to help me," Detective Sergeant Mathew Neo said as they walked into his office after the meeting.

"I didn't," Kubu responded. "All I asked was whether I'd heard the assistant superintendent correctly. The director volunteered me."

"Are you totally stupid, Bengu? Asking a question is the same as volunteering. Nobody does that if they can help it."

"Please call me Kubu. I really prefer it to David or to Bengu. Can I call you Mathew?"

Neo squirmed in his chair. This newcomer, whom everyone despised, had put him on the spot by being friendly and suggesting they address each other informally.

"I suppose so," he replied reluctantly. "But only in private."

"Why's that? I don't understand."

Neo didn't have the courage to tell Kubu that he didn't want to be mocked by his colleagues for becoming Kubu's first friend.

"The director is a stickler for the rules," he stammered. "Let me fill you in on what I know about the suitcases."

Kubu pulled out his notebook. "Go ahead."

"All the suitcases were properly tagged here in Gabs and then scanned as they were loaded on the planes. I've just received a fax from Joburg. They've confirmed that the bags were scanned when they were put on their next flight, either to London or Paris."

"So they must have disappeared at the destination cities, right?"

"That's what I think," Neo mumbled. "But…"

"But what?"

"The English and French baggage handlers insist that the bags were not on the planes when they landed."

Kubu shrugged. "Well, I'm sure they didn't fall out somewhere over the Sahara. Somebody's not telling the truth. Let's go to the airport and talk to the Air Botswana people to make sure we understand how their tracking works. Can you drive?"

Neo wasn't used to things happening quite so quickly, but he couldn't think of a reason not to head out to the airport. On the way, he and Kubu discussed various possibilities for how the suitcases had disappeared.

"From what I've read," Kubu said, "most criminals are pretty stupid, which means they often leave clues or haven't thought their plans through carefully. I'd be surprised if this was any different."

"Well, I don't know how the bags disappeared," Neo responded. "I stick by my first conclusion that they were stolen at the destination airports."

When they arrived at the Air Botswana counter, they asked to speak to the manager and were escorted to her office. After introductions were made, Kubu asked her to explain exactly how the tracking system worked. Neo was put out that Kubu had jumped in and taken the lead.

"It's a very good system," she explained. "When a passenger checks in, we generate a paper tag that is attached to the handle. It's designed to hold together if left outside in any sort of weather. It has a bar code for easy scanning, as well as flight and connection information and the name of the passenger. There's a small version of the bar code on the tag that we remove and stick on the bag. That's an extra precaution in case the tag is torn off. And, of course, we give the passengers a receipt for their bags, which is also taken from the baggage tag. It's a very efficient process, and very few bags disappear. The worst that usually happens is that a bag is late or sent to the wrong destination. But almost always, a missing bag finds its way back to its owner."

Kubu scratched his head. "Okay. So, what happens next?"

"When the bag is loaded onto the plane, the baggage handler scans the tag. That way, we know it's on board and headed to its first destination. The same process is followed each time the bag is loaded onto a plane."

"And the missing bags were scanned all the way to their destinations?" Neo jumped in. "But didn't arrive on the carousels?"

"Yes. We confirmed that this morning."

"And you're sure they were scanned here and when they were loaded in Joburg?" Kubu asked the manager.

"I'm certain of that. It showed up on our system each time. It's a complete mystery to us how it could have happened."

"Just a few last questions: first, which flights did the bags leave on?"

"Two oh three and two two seven to Joburg. Eight of the bags were on two oh three and seven on two two seven."

"And do you have any CCTV footage of the area where the bags are put on the carts to be taken to the plane?"

"Yes. I've loaded it on a bunch of CDs for you, from the time the plane landed until it took off."

"Any footage of the bags being loaded on the plane?"

"No. Only of the baggage area."

"And finally, I'm sure the passengers have given you descriptions of the missing bags. We'd like a copy of that too."

"We thought you'd want those, so we've already made a list for each flight." She handed an envelope to Kubu.

"Thank you. Very efficient!" Kubu smiled. "We won't take much more of your time, but could we walk through the baggage area? It's always good to see things for yourself."

———

"Well, that was very helpful, don't you think?" Kubu said as Neo drove them back to CID headquarters.

Neo frowned. "What do you mean? There wasn't any new information different from what I knew already."

"That may be true, but at least with the CCTV footage, we should be able to confirm that the bags left Botswana. Or not!"

"But we know that already!"

"No, Neo, we only have the manager's word that they left, but we haven't checked whether that's actually the case. We'll do that when we get back."

What an interesting first day, Kubu thought as Neo pulled into the police parking lot. *And it's not even lunch.*

Chapter 6

Jake Oteng was already tired. He and his partner had done a morning shift in Gaborone, and then had driven their Cash in Transit vehicle for nearly three hours to Jwaneng. With the journey back to Gaborone with the cargo still ahead of them, he was going to be exhausted when he got home. Debswana had demanded only reliable, experienced teams, so there was no one who could substitute for them. And a fast-food lunch that he'd swallowed before they left was causing his stomach to complain.

Salekany Kenosi was driving and was even more dour than usual, hardly saying a word. Oteng had never felt really comfortable with him. He wasn't sure if he could rely on his partner to get his back if the chips were down.

Just as well we seldom run into trouble with armoured vehicles in Botswana, he thought. *Lucky we aren't in South Africa!*

He wondered how Sheila Naledi was doing in the cargo section. Even when it was empty, they followed procedure. Only she could open the back door when they were in transit. Oteng had become used to having a woman on the team, even if she was the only one in the whole security industry. She was impossible to fault, but most of his workmates felt riding shotgun wasn't a suitable job for a woman. She agreed with them. Her ambition was to own a security company, but she was willing to learn the ropes by starting at the bottom.

They reached Jwaneng, turned right to the mine, and checked through the security gate. The guard directed them, and they parked on the apron outside the packing plant. Two more Gaborone Cash in Transit vehicles joined them after a few minutes, and finally the backup vehicle pulled in behind them.

Three identical metal cases were waiting on the apron, with two armed guards standing next to them.

A man met them, introduced himself as Eddie Tau, head of security at the mine, and explained what they had to do. Each vehicle would take just one of the boxes, and then they would leave at fifteen-minute intervals, with the backup vehicle bringing up the rear.

"Which one do we take?" Oteng asked. "They all look the same."

Tau shrugged. "Doesn't matter. They are all the same. Just choose one." He handed Oteng a clipboard and a ballpoint pen. "You need to fill out these forms first."

Without waiting for Oteng to work his way through the paperwork, Kenosi went over to inspect the boxes. They were black metal cases, about fifty centimetres long and fifteen by fifteen in cross section. The lids had three heavy hinges on one side and two top-security padlocks on the other, impossible to open with a bolt cutter. There were solid, padded handles on each end.

The security guard told them to wait for the paperwork, and Kenosi nodded. But then he walked around the boxes, tugging at each lock. Immediately the guard rushed over.

"I just told you! You can't touch anything till the paperwork is done. You stupid or something?"

"I was just checking they're all secure. That's all," Kenosi replied.

Oteng walked up with the paperwork for the guard. He shook his head, wondering why Kenosi was in such a rush.

The guard signed the paperwork and watched as Kenosi lugged a case to his vehicle. From the way he handled the box as he lifted it into the cargo compartment, Oteng thought it must be heavy.

Well, raw diamonds are rocks, he thought. *That case is full of rocks.*

His mind whirled at how much that many gemstones would be worth. He had no idea, but it would be millions of pula. And there were three boxes of them!

Naledi climbed in the back and closed the door. She locked it from the inside. It couldn't be opened now unless she released it herself. That was a standard security feature.

The two men climbed into the vehicle to wait their turn. The first vehicle departed and headed for the security gate and on towards the A2 to Gaborone. They would be the second to leave.

"I wonder why they insisted on three vehicles," Oteng said to Kenosi. "One could have taken all three boxes, no problem. Then there wouldn't have been the panic about how to cover the deliveries in town and all the rest of it."

His partner shrugged. "None of our business."

Oteng sighed. Probably they wanted to spread the risk, he thought. Better to lose a third of their gems than the whole lot. He felt another twinge of indigestion.

Precisely fifteen minutes later, they pulled off and headed out of the mine. This time Oteng drove, and Kenosi contacted Control on the two-way radio and confirmed the time of departure and the lat-long coordinates displayed on the GPS—a backup procedure in case the satellite link failed.

Their estimated arrival time in Gaborone was just over three hours. Oteng sighed again. That would get them back around six. His wife wasn't going to be happy. He was about to make a comment to Kenosi but noticed he was sitting with his jaw set and staring straight ahead, so he kept his thoughts to himself.

Oteng swallowed. He'd been in security a long time, and his

instincts were honed. He was getting a bad feeling about this trip. Maybe the twinges in his stomach weren't coming from the food after all.

Chapter 7

When Kubu returned to his office after lunch, again wet through with sweat, he felt drowsy. He was beginning to regret having two bowls of pap and nyama. And that ice cream cone. He closed the door, sat down, and put his feet on his desk for one of his favourite pastimes—a ten-minute power nap.

He was startled awake by the door opening. "First day and already sleeping on the job!" Elias sneered. "You're not going to last long." He dumped a pile of files on Kubu's desk.

Kubu grimaced as he pulled the files towards him. Of course, it would have to be Elias who caught him napping. No doubt he'd make it his business to tell anyone who would listen.

The top file was a collection of APBs. None were recent, and many were long out of date, but a few were interesting. There was one from a month ago for a twenty-seven-year-old house breaker in Francistown, Nomedi Moseki, who'd been arrested and then managed to escape from the courtroom during his trial. He was 1.8 metres tall and of medium build.

Kubu shook his head. How could they have let that happen?

He looked carefully at the grainy photograph of the man and tried to memorise it, but the man had no distinguishing features.

Then there was an older APB from the South Africa Police

Service for an expert safe cracker, Vusi Tuelo, who was wanted for murder and armed robbery. He was armed and dangerous and believed to have fled the country. He was thirty-eight years old, 1.7 metres tall, and of medium build. The photograph showed a man with a narrow face with eyes that were too close together.

Kubu flipped through a few more sheets, stopping when he saw one alerting the police to look for a black Cadillac hearse that had been used as a getaway car in a bank robbery in Molepolole. He laughed as he remembered the news coverage of the case—the hearse had been stopped less than an hour after the robbery, minutes after the APB had been circulated. The headline in one of the newspapers was "A Dead Giveaway."

He shook his head again. He hoped all the criminals he was going to look for were that stupid.

He closed the file and went on to the next one, which contained the procedures specific to the Botswana Police Service. He'd covered most of the material at university, but in a more generic way. Mabaku had told him he needed to know what to do and what specific paperwork to file for all cases, so he paid close attention to the details.

"And," Mabaku had said, "you'd better know the mission of the police service inside out and backwards and forwards. The director and the commissioner both expect you to honour it throughout your career. And so do I."

Kubu looked up at the poster on the wall. The mission was embossed in gold:

BOTHO
EXCELLENCE
INTEGRITY
TEAMWORK

Kubu was pleased that the mission included a Setswana word—BOTHO. It described well his parents' view of the world and consequently his own upbringing: living a life of humility, dignity, courtesy, and respect for others, regardless of their status in life.

Kubu also knew it had an even deeper meaning, one to which he fully subscribed: Motho ke motho ka batho, meaning "I am because you are," and was a social contract of earning respect by first giving it. It was at the heart of Botswana culture and in Kubu's heart also.

As for EXCELLENCE, INTEGRITY, and TEAMWORK, Kubu believed in those too.

Kubu was committed to living up to the mission, whatever it took.

Chapter 8

Oteng and Kenosi's journey proceeded smoothly for the first hour, and Kenosi reported in and confirmed their position at regular intervals. As he drove along the two-lane A2, flanked on each side by a cattle fence, Oteng thought there had to be something wrong with the road's design, judging by the number of decomposed cows lying on the side.

He laughed. "The fence is better at keeping cows on the road than away from it. Must be hard to see a cow on the road in the middle of the night."

Kenosi didn't respond.

He's in one of his moods, Oteng thought and concentrated on the road ahead.

The traffic was light, and what there was passed them at the first opportunity, so it wasn't hard for Oteng to spot the white SUV behind them. It kept its distance, dropping out of sight from time to time, but then it would appear again in the distance. *Maybe it's just travelling at the same speed as we are,* he thought, but he was suspicious. It didn't seem right.

He glanced at Kenosi, who was staring straight ahead.

"I think maybe we're being followed. There's a white SUV behind us. It's been just keeping pace with us for five minutes or so."

Kenosi checked his watch. "We're right on schedule. Slow down and see if it passes."

Oteng slowed down, and the SUV dropped back again.

"You'd better alert Control," Oteng said. "It's just about time to report in anyway."

At first there was no reply. Then Kenosi said in a voice harsh with tension, "Slow down, Jake. Keep both your hands on the wheel. If you try anything, I promise I'll kill you."

Aghast, Oteng glanced at him. Kenosi had his automatic pointed straight at Oteng's head. Although it was almost impossible to believe, Oteng knew at once what was going on—Kenosi was hijacking the vehicle and the diamonds. The white SUV must be his support.

Kenosi reached over and yanked Oteng's gun from its holster.

Oteng's mind was racing. What could he do? Very quickly he decided that he shouldn't do anything. The rules were clear—if you were in a life-threatening situation, cooperate. An agent's life was worth more than the valuables being transported, even if it was a crate full of diamonds.

"Why are you doing this, Salekany? You know you can't get away with it. Everyone will know it was you. This is *Debswana* you're robbing. They'll hunt you down like a jackal!"

"Shut up! Shut up and just do what I say."

Oteng could see in the mirror that the SUV was tailing them now, just a few vehicle lengths behind.

"Slow down. We'll turn off to the left just ahead here. Slow down!"

Even with the warning, Oteng nearly missed the turn. It was just a dirt track leading off the main road into the scrub, probably heading to a cluster of homes too small even to be called a village. As he bumped off the main road, Oteng glanced at the control panel. Surely Naledi had realised by now that something was wrong? But there was no alert from her emergency alarm. With a sinking feeling, he realised it must have failed, or more likely, been disabled somehow. So, no alert had gone to Control. He could feel sweat breaking out on his forehead. He glanced at Kenosi and saw his face was also damp.

Oteng drove down the track, through a gate in the cattle fence that hung open, and then had to wrestle with the steering wheel for a hundred metres or so of soft sand. When the track forked, Kenosi directed him to the right, where he was forced to stop by the wreck of a bakkie that had been dragged across the road. The SUV pulled up behind, and four men wearing ski masks and carrying automatic weapons jumped out. They'd covered any possible escape route. Kenosi released the door locks, and Oteng was pulled roughly out of the driver's side.

At once Kenosi called the control room and, after identifying himself, read off coordinates from a piece of paper. His voice sounded strained, but Oteng doubted Control would notice over this sort of radio connection. As soon as Kenosi disconnected, a man with a device that looked like a transistor radio climbed into the cab.

It's a blocker, Oteng realised, blocking the radio signals that would alert Control that the vehicle was being tampered with.

Sure enough, after a few minutes, the man gave the thumbs-up to one of the others who had been pushing a putty-like substance around the cargo door. Everyone headed away from the vehicle, and there was a loud crack and smoke as the plastic explosive did its job. One of the men yanked the door open just enough to throw in a stun grenade, and a few minutes later they pulled Naledi out. She was unconscious at best, but Oteng had an awful feeling it might be worse than that. A few minutes later, the case of diamonds had been transferred to the SUV.

And what happens now, Oteng wondered. His stomach lurched. This time he was certain it had nothing to do with the food.

Chapter 9

The duty officer at the Control desk at Gaborone Cash in Transit was worried after the call from Kenosi came in. The coordinates Kenosi had given him looked about right, but the blip showing vehicle two on his screen had stopped moving. He wondered if there was a technical problem. However, the other two vehicles were both moving along as expected.

The problem isn't at our end, he thought. *It's at the vehicle.* And that thought made him very uncomfortable. He tried to raise unit two on the radio but received no response. He tried again with the same result. He grabbed his handset and dialled his boss's office. This was a shipment for Debswana, a big deal. Rra Henkel would want to know.

A few minutes later, Pieter Henkel ran into the control room.

"What's happening? Any change?"

The duty officer shook his head.

"Get them on the radio."

"I've tried. There's no reply."

"Try again."

"Unit two, come in for Control."

There was no response.

"Unit two, come in."

Nothing.

Henkel cursed. He knew he should have had a backup vehicle with each unit, but he just hadn't had the resources.

He took the microphone. "Backup unit. Come in."

"Standing by."

"Head up to unit two. Check it out."

"Roger. Out."

Chapter 10

"Why shoot them?" Kenosi demanded as they moved off in the SUV. "I was told there would be no violence! No one gets hurt. That's what he said!"

The leader just looked at him. "They knew what you did. How could we leave them alive? Your share is a million pula. You think that would be enough to keep you safe from Debswana?"

"But the woman? She knew nothing."

The leader ignored that. "We have a new plan, Kenosi, so listen carefully. When we've passed Kanye—in about fifteen minutes—you call in and tell them you're having electrical problems, but all is well. Then we drop you off, rough you up a little. You say we made you call in and then threw you out of the car. You go find someone. Tell them what happened. Take your time. You'll be a hero. Okay?"

"And the money?" Kenosi asked, now doubtful if he'd ever see it.

"You get it as soon as we move the stones. Just like we agreed."

Kenosi nodded. He realised he had no choice. The original plan had called for him to go with them, to hide out in South Africa. But now he had a strong suspicion the new plan was quite different from what the leader had just spelt out. He wished he'd kept his gun or Oteng's, but the leader had taken them both—to get rid of the evidence, he'd said.

They turned onto the main road and picked up speed. After about a kilometre, they came upon a large herd of cattle milling around at the side of the road. The leader told the driver to pull over. He opened his window and shouted for the herd boys. They ran up, and he shoved a handful of pula notes at them.

"You know what to do," he told them, and they nodded. "Do it now!"

As the vehicle started forward, the leader looked over his shoulder. The boys were herding the cattle onto the road, hitting them with thin sticks if they tried to stray. The leader grinned, and his men started to relax.

They weren't expecting any trouble, but at the intersection of the A10 to Gaborone and the A2 to Kanye, they came to a police roadblock.

As they approached, the leader heard his men readying their guns.

"Wait! The Sejelo police station is right here. This must be just a regular roadblock, checking licences and so on. They can't know about us yet. And we've picked up nothing on the police band. Keep cool. Let me handle this." He turned to the driver. "You've got your licence?"

The man nodded. He'd need a new one after this.

The leader glanced behind him. "Keep your pistols out of sight. But be ready. Are the AKs and the box properly covered up in the back? And get that bullet-proof vest off, Kenosi. I hope he doesn't ask about your uniform. I don't want to explain why we have a security man in the car."

A policeman waved them down.

"Dumela, rra. Driver's licence, please."

He took it and studied it carefully. "Where are you heading today?"

"Gaborone," the leader told him. "To talk about lobola for my niece."

The policeman nodded. All the male members of the immediate

family would be expected to take part in discussing the bride price. "I hope they treat you well." However, he didn't give back the licence. He walked around the car and looked in the back. Kenosi held his breath, unsure what side he was on now. Eventually the policeman walked all the way around and handed the driver his licence. Then he waved them on. "Travel safely."

They drove on and, a few minutes later, turned off the main road and headed east on the minor road towards Ranaka. Shortly after, the leader called a halt. One of his men fiddled with some equipment and gave Kenosi a microphone. Trying to keep his voice steady, Kenosi called in.

"What happened? We couldn't raise you, and the satellite feed shows you stationary at the point where you last called in."

"We're having electrical problems. This bucket needs an over-haul. The lights and indicators are dead. We've no idea what's going on. Here are our coordinates." He read them off from the scrap of paper he'd been given.

There was a moment's silence from the other end. They weren't buying it, and if he was going to be dumped out here, he needed to cover himself.

"Everything's cool," he said. Then he repeated it. "Everything's cool."

He signed off, and the leader took back the microphone. "Okay, Kenosi. Get out of the car."

Kenosi did as he was told and immediately backed away.

The leader raised his gun.

"I'm sorry, Kenosi," he said. "There's been another change of plan."

Chapter 11

"Where the hell's the backup vehicle?" Henkel yelled. Now they knew the second vehicle was in trouble because Kenosi had used the alarm phrase "Everything's cool." And the story about electrical problems was nonsense—that wouldn't freeze the satellite position.

The duty officer raised the backup vehicle on the radio. "Unit two's in trouble! They used the emergency code phrase—"

Henkel interrupted him. "The satellite track for unit two stops right about where you should be. Can you see anything?"

A few seconds later, the response came that unit two was nowhere to be seen.

"Okay, we'll give you the coordinates Kenosi just gave us. I'm sure they're false, but you need to take a look."

A few minutes later, the backup vehicle called in again.

"We're stuck in a cattle jam. They're all over the place. I swear the herd boys are keeping them on the road instead of getting them off!"

"Push through the bloody cows!" Henkel shouted. "Get moving! Right now."

A few moments later they reported they were through, and the duty officer gave them the coordinates.

After that, he checked with units one and three, but they were fine and their satellite feeds matched their positions. He warned them that there was a problem, and they should be on high alert.

After about ten minutes, the backup vehicle reported they'd reached a roadblock, and there was no sign of unit two.

"We've checked with the guys here. One armoured vehicle's been through. Only one."

Henkel shook his head. "We've lost them." The day had been a nightmare from the moment Goodman had called. Now it had become a disaster.

"Okay. I'm going to alert the police. And Debswana. I need to get the contacts and the protocol in my office." As he turned to go, the duty officer tried again to raise unit two on the radio, but there was no reply. Henkel shook his head again and walked out.

Chapter 12

The station commander of Sejelo police station was about to head home for dinner when the deputy commissioner reached him on the phone. By the time he hung up, he knew he wouldn't be going home for quite some time, and dinner would be long delayed—if he had any at all.

He jumped up from his desk and walked quickly to the main office, yelling for the sergeant on duty. The man met him halfway, but the commander didn't break his stride.

"We think there's been an attack on a Gaborone Cash in Transit vehicle," he told the man as they reached the sergeant's desk. "The company says the vehicle's in trouble. How many squad cars can you get out there right now?"

The sergeant didn't hesitate. "Two vehicles are out on patrol." He grabbed the police-network microphone as he continued talking. "And we've got six men running a routine roadblock at the intersection of the A2 with the A10. Should we pull them in?"

The station commander shook his head. "A roadblock could be just what we need. Get me the two patrol vehicles on the radio."

Moments later he was addressing them. "Attention, men. This is the station commander speaking. We believe there's an attack in progress on an armoured cash-in-transit vehicle on the A2 towards Jwaneng. The security company has given us the position where they believe it is—that's between the fifty-two point four and fifty-two point five markers. Get going. And use extreme caution—the attackers are likely to be heavily armed. Don't try to take them down yourselves. Your job is to keep them under surveillance till we get backup there. Clear?"

The vehicles confirmed. They were already on their way, sirens blaring.

"Who's being robbed, Superintendent?" the sergeant asked.

The station commander hesitated. "Debswana. But keep that to yourself. The deputy commissioner doesn't want the newspapers hounding him right now. He's arranging helicopter support from the air force, and he's also arranging a roadblock just outside Jwaneng with the police there. Then we'll have the road controlled at both ends. Tell our men at the roadblock to stop every vehicle and search it. Every one. And to be careful."

The sergeant nodded. "Yes, sir. What are they looking for?"

"A box. About fifty centimetres long, secured with heavy-duty padlocks. And weapons. Definitely weapons. Tell them to get the occupants out of each vehicle and cover them while they search. And you need to get reinforcements there as well."

The sergeant looked flustered. "I haven't got the men. We'll need—"

"Find them, Sergeant! Get on to it. And keep in touch with our two vehicles all the time. I need to report to the deputy commissioner, but I'll be back in a minute."

As the station commander headed back to his office, the sergeant called the roadblock and relayed the station commander's instructions. The constable there had news of his own. "Only one of their vehicles has been through, so the second vehicle must still be on the road from Jwaneng."

Next, the sergeant sent off the two constables still in the building to pick up weapons, take a squad car, and join the other two heading to the scene. Then, he checked with the patrol cars already on the way there. They were still a few minutes away. Finally, he made a quick phone call.

"We need you at the station. Right away," he told the person who answered.

"Come on, Sergeant! It's my day off. And I'm with a girlfriend. There must be someone else on call."

"Everyone is coming in, Constable. Get over here *now*."

"I've had a few drinks," the man said slyly.

"You sound fine. You better be able to shoot straight though. You may need to. There's a heist of an armoured vehicle underway!"

"Oh. Okay, I'm on my way."

The station commander came back to the desk and demanded a report.

"I've alerted the roadblock, sir. They say only one Gaborone Cash in Transit vehicle has been through. And another patrol car will be heading to the scene in a few minutes."

"Well done, Sergeant. We've got them trapped between here and Jwaneng. The deputy commissioner is arranging help for us from Gaborone too. Those bastards are going to be sorry!"

Chapter 13

At the CID, Kubu had spent the afternoon brooding about his case. It was a real puzzle.

He and Neo had watched the CCTV footage and saw the missing bags—at least the ones they could positively identify—being put on the baggage carts that would take them to the plane, where they would be scanned as they were loaded. And they had been scanned.

And the records showed that they'd been scanned again in Johannesburg as they were loaded for the next leg of their journey.

He frowned. How could a piece of luggage be scanned in Gaborone, scanned again in Johannesburg, yet not arrive at its destination? It didn't make sense.

Unless Neo was right—that they'd been stolen by the baggage handlers in London and Paris.

But the baggage handlers were adamant that they'd put all of the bags from the two aircraft in question onto the carousels. The bags that were missing had not been on those flights.

Kubu could accept that the handlers at one airport were lying. But at two different airports a long way apart, in different countries? No way. That wasn't possible.

He thought back to what his childhood Bushman friend,

Khumanego, had once told him—that black men couldn't see what was in front of their eyes.

So what was he missing? What was in front of him that he couldn't see?

He shook his head.

Let me go through everything again, he thought. *Carefully. One step at a time.*

Chapter 14

The police squad car with constables Boi and Kabo was the first to reach the section of the A2 indicated by the security company. They were delayed by cattle milling around the road at one point, but the herd boys drove the cows off the road as soon as they spotted the police vehicles.

They drove slowly between the designated road markers.

There was nothing there.

Both of them felt the tension, guessing that the robbers would be better armed than they were, and there might be more of them.

"They probably forced the vehicle off the road into the bush," Boi said. "I'll go on a little farther, then turn around."

They drove on another few hundred metres before they did a U-turn and slowly made their way back, checking for where a vehicle could have turned off the road. Kabo spotted a small track heading off into the bushes on the left.

"They could have gone down there. But how would they have forced the driver to turn off the road?"

"Should we take a look?" Boi asked. "They could be in those bushes over there."

"We should wait for the other vehicle. They must be close behind us."

Boi nodded. Neither man was in a hurry to take on whatever was waiting up that track. He radioed for instructions. It was the station commander who answered.

"We've got a helicopter on the way. You can check out the track, but don't get too close. Okay?"

"Yes, sir," Boi responded. At that moment the second vehicle drove up. "We're going in now, sir," he added.

They edged off the main road and proceeded cautiously down the track. They could see nothing unusual.

"It must be over," Kabo said. "If this is the right place, they're gone."

Boi hoped that was true, but he wasn't betting on it.

Again, they edged forward. Then Boi slammed on the brakes. "There it is! The armoured vehicle. Through those trees there."

Kabo grabbed the mic and reported back to the station. The second vehicle pulled up behind them.

"Any sign of anyone?" the station commander asked.

"Nobody. And there's no other vehicle. They've gone."

"Okay, take a look. But don't assume that the vehicle is abandoned. Stay on high alert."

Kabo and Boi took out their guns and climbed from their vehicle, taking cover behind it. The men from the other patrol car joined them.

"Police! Come out with your hands up. Right now!" Boi shouted.

There was no response, only the usual summer sounds of the bush. He shouted again, and again there was no reply. Then the four men spread out and approached the vehicle.

There was no sign of life, and soon they could see that the back of the cash-in-transit vehicle had been blown open.

It was Kabo who spotted a body lying a few metres away in the brush with flies buzzing around the head. Still alert, he moved towards it. "Here's one of the guards," he called. "He's dead. Looks like he's been shot in the face."

Boi walked over. "God! That's not the result of a shoot-out. That's a shot in the face at close range. And it's not a man, it's a woman."

Kabo realised he was right.

Then one of the other men discovered Oteng's body, and the story there was the same.

Disgusted and angry, Kabo headed back to the squad car to report.

Chapter 15

Kubu had just started listing all he knew about the case of the disappearing suitcases when the phone rang. It was Miriam, the director's assistant.

"Detective Sergeant Bengu? The director wants everyone in the meeting room in five minutes." Without waiting for an acknowledgement, she rang off.

Kubu grabbed his notebook and headed to the meeting room. One or two detectives were already there, and the others came in quickly.

Director Gobey joined them after a few minutes, looking grim. He dropped into his seat and got to the point at once.

"We believe a Gaberone Cash in Transit vehicle transporting diamonds from Jwaneng for Debswana was attacked just over half an hour ago. Right now, police from Sejelo are heading for the scene, and—" He broke off as Miriam came in and whispered something to him.

"I'll be back in a minute."

There was a murmur around the room. Cash-in-transit heists were uncommon in Botswana; one involving a load of diamonds from Debswana was unheard of.

Gobey returned after a couple of minutes looking even more

serious than before. "That was the deputy commissioner," he began. "Police from the Sejelo station have found the cash-in-transit vehicle." Anger filled his voice. "Two of the security guards were murdered. Shot in the face at close range. The vehicle was blasted open, and the cargo stolen. A large amount of rough diamonds, apparently. Here are some other points you need to know. Debswana used three armoured vehicles. Two were carrying dummies—boxes containing stone chips. The third had all the diamonds, although the armoured vehicle guards didn't know that. We don't yet know which of the vehicles had the diamonds—it was chosen at random. The vehicles travelled from Jwaneng fifteen minutes apart, and it was the middle vehicle that was attacked. The others are progressing normally and now have police escorts.

"There are already some clues. It appears that the security system of the van they attacked was tampered with. The guard in the back should have been able to alert the company of the attack, but didn't, and the front doors seem to have been unlocked, not forced. Also, this isn't the way Debswana normally transports diamonds. They usually fly them from their airport at Jwaneng, but there was an explosion on the runway this morning when a plane took off. It's an obvious possibility that that was engineered. There's a lot more to this than an opportunistic heist."

Mabaku put up his hand, and Gobey nodded to him. "So, the robbers would have needed to know about the plan to go by road?"

"Clearly," Gobey responded. "The backup plan was approved at the highest levels in Debswana, as well as the police service. In fact, I approved it also. So, it looks like inside information leaked from Jwaneng. And there was someone with access to Gaborone Cash in Transit's vehicles. Any other questions?" He glared at the group. "Good. Assistant Superintendent, I'd like you to head out to Jwaneng mine right away. We'll tell them to expect you this evening. Take someone with you to help—maybe Samkoa.

Where is he anyway?" No one seemed to know, so he continued. "I'm going out to the security company myself. Detective Sergeant Neo will accompany me. We also need to liaise with the Sejelo detectives. They had a roadblock set up before the heist, so it's possible the robbers may have gone through it. Inspector Dow will handle that. Inspector, you probably need to get out there right away. You can check out the crime scene also."

Kubu put up his hand. "How can I help, sir?"

"By being on standby till further instructed. Now everyone get going." As they got up, he held up his hand. "One more thing. No comments to the press. The commissioner wants to announce the capture of the robbers at the same time as the heist. So, we've got our work cut out for us."

As Mabuku turned to leave, Gobey stopped him. "I'd like a word with you before you go, Assistant Superintendent. I'll walk with you."

Mabaku was puzzled but nodded, and they headed off together.

"This business stinks, Jacob. You know I've been liaising with Debswana and the Diamond Police, and we were reviewing the plan that was put into action today. Let me explain how it was meant to work. You'll need to know that."

Gobey took a few minutes to outline the contingency plan and answer a couple of questions Mabaku had.

"I think someone found out that we were going to tighten security," Gobey continued, "and took their chance while they could. The question is who told them. Keep your wits about you at Jwaneng, Jacob. The bad smell may be coming from there."

Chapter 16

Mabaku was left with Detective Sergeant Robert Samkoa to accompany him to Jwaneng. He wouldn't have been Mabaku's choice. He wasn't the CID's smartest detective—in fact, he fell short of that by quite a long way. But he was solid, if lacking imagination. Mabaku wished he had an experienced detective who had a real spark, someone who would surprise him and come up with an angle that he hadn't thought of himself. Talking to Samkoa was more or less the same as thinking aloud.

As he walked back to his office, he almost bumped into Kubu coming from the coffee room holding a brimming cup. He was the only detective who hadn't received an assignment. Mabaku hesitated. The young man was certainly intelligent and seemed smart enough to do what he was told and not get in the way. At worst, he would learn something about procedure; at best, he might have a useful insight or two.

"Bengu, dump that coffee. You're coming with me to Jwaneng. There could be a lot to do there. Hurry up."

Kubu instantly threw the coffee in the sink, checked that he had his notebook, and then hurried to catch up.

That's about the fastest I've seen him move, Mabaku thought with amusement.

Mabaku stuck his head into Samkoa's office. "Go home and get a change of clothes. Be back here in thirty minutes."

"Yes, sir."

"You too, Bengu."

Kubu hesitated. "Sir…"

"Yes, Bengu. What is it?"

"I walked here this morning. It'll take me more than half an hour—"

"Come with me. I'll get some clothes, then swing by your place." Mabaku strode towards the parking lot.

"Yes, sir," Kubu gasped as he struggled to keep up.

———

Closer to forty minutes had passed when the three of them headed out to Mabaku's Land Rover. Kubu climbed into the back, and they joined the traffic leaving the city after the workday.

"Normally Debswana transports the diamonds by private plane from Jwaneng to Gabs," Mabaku told Samkoa. "The Debswana processing plant here in Gabs is practically at the airport, and they have strong security around it. But this morning the Jwaneng airport had to be closed after a plane caught fire on the runway. I'm sure that wasn't a coincidence."

Kubu nodded—he'd heard this at the meeting. Samkoa didn't respond.

"Anyway, when the airport closed, Jwaneng used their backup plan. They called out three armoured vehicles from Gaborone."

Now Samkoa did have a question. "Why take the risk? Why not just wait until the airport reopened?"

"We'll ask them that. Anyway, the plan was to send three boxes to the processing plant. The security company men would have thought that each box contained a third of the consignment, but actually one box had all the diamonds, and the other two were full of gravel."

"So, even if one armoured vehicle was hit, they would have a two-thirds chance of keeping the diamonds," Kubu ventured.

Mabaku nodded. "Right. The question is whether the robbers knew about that part of the plan. If they did, they would want to know which vehicle the gems were in. They wouldn't go through all this for a one-third chance of getting the diamonds."

"Yes, Assistant Superintendent. You're right," Samkoa responded.

"And that means someone inside Jwaneng is working with them."

Samkoa nodded. After a moment he asked, "What happened to the men in the armoured vehicle that was hit?"

"Two were shot dead. One was a woman. We don't know where the third is."

They drove on in silence.

Chapter 17

Time dragged at Jwaneng. Major Chamberlain, Goodman, and Tau were in the major's office, waiting for news of what had happened to the missing armoured vehicle and its cargo. Tau was doodling on a pad, looking unhappy. The major seemed calm, but Goodman knew him better than that.

"I've been thinking about the fire on the plane," he wondered out loud. "How did the hijackers even know there was something to hijack? They didn't just hang around for two years waiting for us to use our backup plan."

"You think it was deliberate? That the plane was sabotaged?" the major growled. "I thought you said it was an accident?"

"That's what they thought this morning. But now…" He shrugged.

Tau nodded. "Of course, they could have been tipped off. Several people knew we were using ground transport as a backup plan. Still, we'd better get the police to work with the civil aviation people to follow up Elijah's idea. He could be right."

"You mean it was a setup? Goddammit!"

"It's just a possibility." Goodman wished he'd raised the possibility just with Tau. Now he'd only worsened the major's already foul mood.

"One good thing," Tau put in. "They can't know which vehicle has the diamonds since no one knows that. It's two to one that we still have the diamonds."

Goodman checked his watch again. Five fifteen. By his reckoning the lead vehicle should be arriving at Debswana's processing plant in Gaborone in about fifteen minutes. If it had the diamonds, all would be well. If not, it would be fifty-fifty the robbers had them. He had a bad feeling that they'd lost the middle vehicle and its cargo with it. He put his hand in his pocket and rubbed his good-luck charm.

The phone rang, and the major grabbed it.

"Yes, Deputy Commissioner. What news? I'll put you on speaker."

They listened to a summary of the discovery of the armoured vehicle and of the two murdered Gaborone Cash in Transit guards.

The major said nothing, but his face registered shock.

"They killed the security guards?" Tau's voice was unsteady. "Why? They're always instructed not to resist… Was there a shoot-out?"

"We don't know that yet," the deputy commissioner replied. "The third guard is missing. He was probably abducted and forced to give a false position of the vehicle to confuse us, but he managed to slip in a phrase that alerted the company that something was wrong. I don't have much hope that we'll find him alive."

"Three men killed. That's terrible. Simply awful," Goodman put in, shaking his head.

"One was a woman."

There was silence for a few moments.

"What about the cargo?" the major asked.

"It's gone. The back of the armoured vehicle was blown open."

"Hardly a surprise," the major said dryly. "What's your plan?"

"We have roadblocks and army helicopters patrolling the border fence with South Africa, and the regular border crossings are on alert. They're searching all vehicles going through."

"Too little, too late. They'll be down some side track by now and will slip across the border at night somewhere."

"It's been less than an hour since we discovered what was happening!" the deputy commissioner pointed out sharply.

Chamberlain ignored that and turned to the others. "Either of you have any questions? Any input that could help the police?"

Goodman shook his head, but Tau told the deputy commissioner their thoughts about the plane.

There were a few moments silence before the response. "We also thought of that. We're looking into it."

"Nothing more from our side then, Deputy Commissioner," the major said. "Please keep us in the picture."

"We've the best detectives from CID Headquarters on the job. Assistant Superintendent Mabaku should be there in about two and a half hours. He'll need to interview you all as soon as possible. Will you still be at your office at the mine?"

"Interview us? This evening?"

"We need all the information we can get as soon as we can get it."

"We'll be here," the major assured him, and then hung up.

Time dragged on again.

Chapter 18

Just before 5:30 p.m., the first of the cash-in-transit vehicles pulled up to the Debswana complex in Gaborone. It now had a police escort, and there was another police vehicle with flashing lights waiting for it at the security gates. The guard waved it through, and the vehicle headed straight into the loading shed at one side of the processing complex. Two policemen, armed with automatic weapons, covered it.

The two men in the front of the armoured vehicle climbed out, obviously relieved that their trip was finally over without incident. They greeted the policemen and then gave the man in the back the all clear. He opened the back door, and the police told the two waiting Debswana personnel that it was safe to approach. One signed off the paperwork, and the two of them carried the box into the facility.

Once it was in a secure room, they opened a sealed envelope and took out six keys—each one would open one of the six locks on the total shipment. The first key they tried didn't work for either of the locks, but the second key opened one. It was eventually the sixth key that opened the other. They lifted the lid and stared down at a mass of gravel.

"That means there's an even chance that the robbers got the

diamonds," one said finally. The other nodded. He dug his hands into the gravel, but there was nothing else below the surface. "I thought maybe they'd camouflaged them."

The other shook his head. "They would have told us. Let's go and tell the boss. The next vehicle is only due in half an hour."

They closed the lid and locked the box again. Then they headed into the building to report the bad news.

Chapter 19

Director Gobey and Detective Sergeant Neo reached the main office of Gaborone Cash in Transit around 5:30 p.m. It was a large complex, sporting a tall aerial construction on the roof. A high-security fence ringed it, and an armed guard stood at the gate.

"It looks well secured," Gobey commented with approval. "But that doesn't help if someone on the inside is working for your enemies."

They were immediately taken to the office of the managing director, Pieter Henkel, who rose to shake hands and offer seats at his small conference table. Everything in the office was functional. No framed certificates or pictures of family. The desk was tidy, apart from a file, which lay open with its contents spread around the desk.

"Is that the Debswana protocol, Rra Henkel?" Gobey asked.

Henkel nodded. "And the contract and so on."

"And you followed all the steps as approved?"

Henkel nodded. "As soon as we received the alert that one of the vehicles was in trouble, we contacted the nearest police station—Sejelo in this case, then the deputy commissioner's office, and finally Debswana itself."

Neo jotted it all down in his notebook. Then Gobey asked,

"Who has access to the protocol documents? Are there other copies around?"

Henkel looked up, surprised, but then he understood where Gobey was going. "You're worried someone here may have leaked the protocol. No, this is the only copy, and it's normally locked in one of those cabinets." He indicated a bank of filing cabinets opposite his desk.

"And who has keys to the cabinets?"

"Just me. And my secretary. Sometimes she needs to get to documents when I'm not in the office." He hesitated and then added, "She's been with me for nearly ten years. I built this business. She helped."

Gobey shook his head. "That doesn't take her off the suspect list. I've had cases with staff working at companies for far longer than that before they turned to crime. And you are the only person here who knows about the Debswana plan?"

"Yes. None of my guards knew that only one of the vehicles had the diamonds." He paused for a moment and looked down at the table. "Now two of them are dead and a third, Salekany Kenosi, is missing. I'll have to visit their families and explain what happened. Once I know that myself."

Gobey knew only too well what sort of job that was. "We'll send a senior officer to inform them, Rra Henkel. But I'm sure they'll appreciate a visit from you also."

Henkel just nodded, and Gobey changed the subject.

"When exactly did you discover that something was wrong?"

"I can get you the exact time, but it was close to four fifteen p.m. The operator who was in contact with the convoy and tracking the vehicles noticed that the satellite feed giving the second vehicle's location had stopped moving. He called me, and we tried to contact the vehicle, without success. We had a fourth vehicle for backup, and we called it to investigate."

"You didn't contact the police at that point?"

"It was just the satellite tracking. Nothing from the driver or the guard in the back with the cargo. She was able to alert us independently of the driver. That was Sheila Naledi. She was the best person in the team. Now she's dead." He shook his head. "What a waste of a young life."

"But she didn't alert you. Although a robbery was underway."

Henkel looked upset. "Something must've failed with the backup system. We'll have to—"

"Does that happen?"

"Well, the vehicles are checked and serviced and the systems tested. Usually before they go on an assignment, but…"

"But?"

"I had to pull in these vehicles urgently to meet Debswana's demand for immediate support. We didn't have time to test everything first."

"So, the vehicle could have been tampered with some time before."

"In theory, yes. But who would know that that particular vehicle was going to be used? And that I'd get that call from Jwaneng? It was all completely unexpected. No, it must have been an unfortunate equipment failure."

"Maybe so. We'll know more once we've had some time with the vehicle." Gobey glanced at Neo to be sure he was noting everything. Then he turned back to Henkel. "How does the tracking work?"

"It's a state-of-the-art system, and we're the only company in Botswana that has it. It's expensive, and it's only used if the client is willing to pay a big premium for it. Debswana wanted it, of course. The idea is quite simple—it's a GPS with a transmitter that pushes updates to a satellite about the vehicle's location every few seconds. The satellite sends the info to our control room, and then a computer plots the vehicle's location on a map display, so we can see exactly where the vehicle is."

"Exactly?"

Henkel shrugged. "Within twenty or thirty metres."

"So, when the signal stops at a single point, it means that the vehicle has stopped there?"

Henkel hesitated. "Well, yes...except that if we lost the satellite feed, the map would indicate the last known position. I thought that might have happened."

"And do you sometimes lose the signal?"

Henkel looked down at the table again. "It's never happened in my experience."

"But you didn't alert the police for another twenty minutes. That twenty minutes could have been critical in catching the robbers."

"I suppose so. We were concentrating on trying to find the vehicle. We didn't even know where it was. Then we got a call from Kenosi. Have you found him yet?" Gobey shook his head. "Well, he used the emergency phrase that alerts us that he's talking under duress. After that, we followed the protocol at once."

"Can you tell where that call came from?"

"We discovered that it was picked up by our office in Kanye and then relayed to us. So all we know was that it was from that general area."

Gobey frowned. "That's disappointing. I'd hoped that it would give a clue to which way the robbers had headed." He climbed to his feet. "Thank you, Rra Henkel. I know you have a lot to deal with right now, but we'll need to ask you some further questions as the case develops. For now, we'd like to talk to the operator concerned and have him show us the tracking system."

"He's still tracking the third vehicle. The first one made it safely to its destination just before you arrived. But I'll show you the system, and you can talk to the operator as soon as he's finished." He checked his watch. "In about ten minutes."

Chapter 20

Kubu couldn't believe his luck. He'd resigned himself to pushing on with the suitcase puzzle at the CID while the others solved one of the most exciting cases in the CID's history. Now he was right in the centre of it with the assistant superintendent himself. He wondered why Mabaku had decided to include him. He didn't know Samkoa, so it was unlikely to be his suggestion. Could it have been the director when he grabbed Mabaku after the meeting? Kubu didn't think so. The director had much too much on his mind right now to worry about a new detective. Whatever the reason, Mabaku had decided to include him in the trip, and Kubu was determined not to let him down.

As Mabaku negotiated the traffic, Kubu thought about what he knew about the heist. He was sure Mabaku was right about the robbers knowing which vehicle had the diamonds, and in that case, the detectives needed to determine who'd provided inside information from the mine. But he suspected that there was a twist involved somewhere. He hoped he would be the one to spot it.

Mabaku concentrated on the driving, and there wasn't much conversation, but Kubu found it an interesting trip anyway. He hadn't been to this part of the country before, and the hills they passed through reminded him of Mochudi. For the rest, it was typical Botswana semi-desert, with lots of sand and clusters of small bushes bravely trying to survive the harsh conditions.

After about an hour, they came to the roadblock near the Sejelo police station. Mabaku pulled over and spent a few minutes talking to the officer in charge. As he climbed back into the vehicle, he said, "They've found nothing new. He said we'd see a police vehicle on the main road when we come to the scene."

They drove towards Jwaneng on the A2, and the country became flatter. After about fifteen minutes they spotted a police vehicle on the verge of the road.

"This is it." Mabaku pulled over. A few minutes later, they were being shown around. There was little to learn since forensics and the pathologist hadn't arrived yet from Gaborone. But all Kubu's ideas of neatly solving a puzzle were shattered by the sight of the bodies. The man was bad enough, but the woman was even worse. She lay collapsed on the ground like a crushed doll, her face unrecognisable through the mess of congealed blood. Only a few hours before, these had been people with lives and aspirations. Now they lay in the veld with flies buzzing greedily around them. There was no stink as yet, but there was a smell of death.

Mabaku noticed Kubu's expression. "You okay, Bengu? This is bad, but you'd better get used to it."

Kubu nodded. He wasn't feeling sick. He was angry.

Chapter 21

Henkel led Gobey and Neo from his office to the control room. They gathered behind one of the workstations and watched the operator as he tracked the last vehicle. Every few seconds, the indicator dot jumped a short way on the screen, following the road heading to the Debswana processing plant. After about five minutes, the dot became stationary at its destination.

The last vehicle was home.

"Thank God," Henkel exclaimed.

"It'll take a few minutes before we know if the diamonds are in the box. They have to take it to the secure area before they open it. I've asked them to phone me immediately with the news, and I'm sure they'll let the mine know as well."

———

At just after six, the phone rang in the major's office. He picked it up, gave a couple of grunts in response to the news, thanked the caller, and hung up. Goodman held his breath.

"So that's it then," Chamberlain told the others. "The first and third boxes were the ones with the gravel. The robbers got the diamonds. All one hundred thousand carats of them."

He pushed his chair back from his desk. "I'm going to get something to eat. We'll meet back here at nineteen hundred hours to talk to the detectives. Waste of time if you ask me."

Chapter 22

After Mabaku, Kubu, and Samkoa left the scene of the hijacking, they continued in silence on the A2 towards Jwaneng. Eventually Samkoa burst out, "Why kill them? The guards. What could they do?"

"Do? Nothing," Mabaku responded. "But maybe there were things they could tell."

Samkoa nodded. "I suppose so. I'd like to get my hands on the bastards!"

"So would I. And we will, sooner or later."

The detectives at the scene had been helpful with what information they'd gleaned, but they were sensitive about turf. This was their crime scene, their murder investigation. They had been polite, but there was an undercurrent that they didn't like the implications of Gaborone CID taking over the case. But they did what Director Gobey had instructed, which was to cooperate fully.

Mabaku switched on the car radio, and they caught the evening news. There was the usual discussion about what the president and his ministers had been up to, but at the end there was a short piece that caught their attention.

"Just in, we have a report that the Botswana Police Service is investigating the heist of a cash-in-transit vehicle. There are no details as yet, but there is a major police presence along the A2 outside Kanye. However, traffic is still flowing smoothly. We'll keep you updated on this breaking story!"

"I knew they would never keep this quiet," Mabaku commented. "So much for that idea."

———

When they reached the mine at Jwaneng, they were met by Eddie Tau, who immediately took them to the office of the head of the mine. The man introduced himself as Major David Chamberlain. That didn't impress Mabaku. He wasn't going to call any civilian "major."

"You've already met Eddie, our head of security, and this is Elijah Goodman, the head of administration for the mine. We can chat here in my office if you like."

Mabaku introduced himself and the others, but then he made it clear that he wanted to talk to each of them separately.

He started with Chamberlain. They sat around the major's conference table, and as instructed, Samkoa and Kubu took notes while Mabaku asked the questions.

"Mr. Chamberlain, when did you first realise there was a problem with your usual delivery method to Gaborone?"

"When Mr. Tau and Mr. Goodman informed me about the accident at the airport. I think that was about ten a.m."

"Do you believe the plane catching fire at the airport was an accident?"

"That's what we all thought at the time. Now, I'm not so sure. Do you have any information on that?"

"Not yet. So, you decided to use a security company to transport the diamonds?"

"That's right. As you probably know, we have a detailed contingency plan in place, approved by senior management and the police. So we went ahead with that."

"Why didn't you just wait for the airport to be cleared?"

"The authorities wouldn't allow us to move the burnt-out plane that was blocking the runway. We were told it could be several days."

When the major didn't elaborate, Mabaku prompted, "And that was a problem?"

"It certainly was. The plane we normally use for transporting the diamonds had just been out of commission for two days for routine servicing, so we've slipped behind with deliveries. We couldn't afford to wait several days to get the diamonds out to be processed. That's exactly why we have the contingency plan in the first place."

As Kubu noted that down, he thought that he'd have tried to find out more about the aircraft fire before he committed to the ground transportation plan, but he kept that to himself.

Mabaku took a deep breath. "Can we back up a bit? I know nothing about your operation. Could you give us a very brief summary of how you end up with a box full of diamonds?"

"Okay. As you probably know, this is the richest diamond mine in the world. It's an open-pit mine covering about forty hectares and is about three hundred metres deep. The first step is blasting at the kimberlite pipe to get transportable chunks of rock. They're brought in from that pit on huge trucks." The major waved at the now-dark window behind him. "Then they're put through a crusher and separated from the rock in a cyclonic separator. Next, they go to the acid cleaning plant. Finally, they're packed in our special, locked transport boxes and sent to Gaborone." He paused, then continued. "We have to mine nearly a tonne of ore to produce one carat of raw diamond, and we produce about ten million carats a year. That gives you an idea of the size of the operation."

"That's amazing. So what's the usual way the diamonds get from the mine to Gaborone?"

"The boxes are taken to the airport in our armoured car.

After that, they're flown to Gaborone and again collected by an armoured vehicle and taken to the sorting and polishing facility near the airport."

"So, having the runway out of service triggered the backup plan. Who knew the details of the contingency plan?"

"Here at the mine? Just the three of us. It was strictly confidential. Need-to-know basis. The senior Debswana management in Gaborone approved it, of course, and the police who were involved in setting up the strategy knew the details. Your director was one of them. And the owner of Gaborone Cash in Transit, of course. They were under contract to provide immediate response if it was required."

Kubu wrote down all the names. That was already quite a few people, he thought. And each may have mentioned it to others despite the strict confidentiality. They would have to follow up with every single one.

"Mr. Chamberlain, did you mention the plan—even casually—to anyone else?"

"Absolutely not! I just told you it was strictly confidential."

"And where are the documents kept?"

"You'll have to ask Mr. Goodman about that. I don't do the filing."

Mabaku nodded. "Please explain the plan to us in detail, and tell us exactly what happened after you decided to implement it."

The major did so, and Mabaku asked for clarity on a couple of points, but it soon became clear that having made the decision to go ahead, Chamberlain had left the implementation to the others.

Eventually Mabaku said, "Thank you, Mr. Chamberlain. That was very helpful. I'm sure I'll need to follow up with you on some points as they come up."

"Of course." The major got to his feet.

Mabaku rose as well and added, "I'll also have to get a set of fingerprints from you, to eliminate them if they turn up on the boxes or something like that."

The major stiffened. "I can assure you I don't handle any of that stuff. I'm a manager."

"Nevertheless, it's the procedure."

The major pouted. "Can I ask you something, Assistant Superintendent? How is all this helping to catch the robbers and recover our diamonds?"

"I believe the robbers knew about your plan, Mr. Chamberlain, and I suspect they knew which vehicle had the diamonds as well. They were behind the fire at the airport and the sabotaged security van. This was all carefully planned and executed. I must also remind you that they murdered at least two people, not in a shoot-out, but to silence them. That's our top priority now. Don't you think it's important that the police know at least as much about your strategy as the robbers did?"

The major nodded but didn't meet Mabaku's gaze.

"Now, I have one more question for you. Why didn't you just split the diamonds into thirds between the three vehicles? That way you would still have two-thirds of them."

The major hesitated and looked uncomfortable. "We don't normally have such a large shipment. I told you we were behind. This shipment was more than double the normal one."

"How big was it?"

"About a hundred thousand carats."

That made Mabaku pause and Kubu look up from his notebook.

"So why not split them?" Mabaku prompted after a moment.

"It wasn't the plan," Chamberlain replied, still not meeting Mabaku's eye.

Chapter 23

As the white SUV neared the A1, it passed the Botswana Police College on its right. The men were in high spirits and made jokes about how they could teach the recruits a thing or two. Then they turned south on the A1. The hills of Otse surrounded them, and they slowed as they searched for a minor road to the left into the village. Finding it, they swung onto the dirt road and picked their way between the houses. The road crossed the Nywane River that supported the farms to the east, and then skirted Manyelanong Hill. After that, they turned off onto a bush track and bumped their way towards a farmhouse.

They stopped at a rusty farm gate. The leader told one of his men to open it. *No lock*, the leader thought. *But the Otse people know the doctor lives here. They keep away.*

A few hundred metres farther on, they came to a ramshackle farmhouse and pulled up outside. A grizzled old man, dressed in slacks and a jacket despite the heat of the day, was waiting at the door. A younger man, wiry with a pinched face, was with him. He watched them without smiling.

The leader jumped out of the vehicle and walked up to the older man. "It is done, Ngaka," he said, addressing the man as Doctor.

The man nodded. "You have the box? The guards are dead?"

"It is so."

"Good. You will rest here tonight. We will eat pap and goat seswaa and have some beer. Not too much." He indicated the man next to him. "This is my son, Vusi. Tomorrow night, when it is dark, he will show you the way."

The leader hesitated. "Why not tonight?"

The doctor shook his head. "The police are everywhere, and helicopters are flying along the border with search lights. Tomorrow night is better."

"Will your son come with us into South Africa? It will be hard to find our way there in the dark."

Vusi shook his head. "I'll take you to the border and make sure you're on the right path. Then I'll return. That's the arrangement." The doctor nodded.

The leader didn't like it, but it seemed he had no choice. "We get our money now."

The doctor nodded. "When I have checked what is in the box."

"You know what is in the box!"

"There were three boxes," Vusi reminded him. "We must check you have the right one."

The leader said nothing. He hadn't told his men what they'd stolen, although they'd surely guessed. He signalled for one of them to take the box out of the vehicle. He thought how easy it would be to kill the old man and his son and have both the money and the box of diamonds, but he dismissed the thought at once. They were being very well paid, and he had no idea what he'd do with a box of raw diamonds in any case. But most of all he was scared of the doctor and his dark spells and potions. It was better not to take on those forces.

"I must weigh everything," the doctor told him. "They will want everything exact. You will wait here. Then we will eat." Vusi lifted the case with ease and strode into the house, followed by the doctor.

There were some plastic chairs pulled up under a large acacia tree, where a woman was stirring bubbling samp in a large, three-legged pot over a small fire. The four men went over and greeted her politely, but she ignored them and went on with her work. So they sat in the shade and waited. The leader was used to waiting.

After half an hour, the doctor came out alone.

"It is all as it should be," he told the leader and passed him a carry-all bag. "Here is the money. It is all there. You can count it."

The leader did just that.

The doctor waited until he was satisfied and then pointed at the SUV. "There is a hidden compartment in the front seat of your vehicle. Hide the money there. No one will know."

———

They dined on the shredded goat with samp and vegetables. Although the doctor had warned them not to drink too much, there was plenty of Shake Shake sorghum beer to be had. When they'd eaten their fill and were enjoying a few more beers, the doctor said to the leader, "There are too many police. It is too dangerous to keep the diamonds here."

"They will never look here, Ngaka."

The doctor shrugged. "People talk. People listen."

"They won't dare come here." The leader paused. "I've done my part. It's finished. Tomorrow we go home, and as far as anyone knows, we've never been in Botswana."

"You must take the diamonds with you across into South Africa."

The leader shook his head. "Ngaka, you are mad. The SA Police will also be looking for the diamonds!"

"The same again," the doctor said. "You will be paid the same again when you deliver the diamonds in Johannesburg."

The leader was amazed by the offer. It was a lot of money. "So much? And you will trust me with the diamonds?"

The doctor smiled, but there was no warmth in it. "I already have. But I know where you are always. I can always find you. I can always reach you." He said it as though he was mentioning an obvious fact that everyone knew, but the leader felt the hair rise on the back of his neck.

Chapter 24

Eddie Tau was waiting for the detectives in his office. He jumped up when they entered and offered seats at his conference table. There was a platter of sandwiches and a tray with a flask of hot water and tea bags and instant coffee laid out.

"You must be hungry. It's been a long day for all of us, but you had the drive from Gaborone as well. I asked the canteen to put something together when I heard you were coming out. Cheese and tomato and some beef." He pulled off the cling wrap. "Please help yourselves."

"That's thoughtful, Rra Tau. Thank you. We'll need to talk while we eat, I'm afraid. We're pushed for time."

Tau nodded, and the three men helped themselves to a couple of sandwiches each and poured a hot drink. Kubu was pleased to see that there was plenty of food, so he took two more.

"We've spoken to Rra Chamberlain, and he's filled us in on the contingency plan. Can you tell us exactly what happened after he gave the go-ahead for it?"

Tau nodded. "First Elijah and I went to his office and contacted Gaborone Cash in Transit. As you can imagine, they weren't pleased about providing the transport on essentially no notice, but we persuaded them because Elijah had the contract in front of him. We set the pickup for three p.m. After that, I went and arranged things."

Mabaku swallowed a mouthful. "Please tell us step-by-step exactly what that entailed."

"Well, I called the cleaning plant and confirmed that the case of diamonds would be packed and ready at two that afternoon. Then I set up the guards to be ready for collection at that time. We normally use our own vehicle—in convoy with armed guards—to take the diamonds to the airport. This time it would be the security company's vehicles, and there would be three cases instead of one. I needed to explain the arrangements to the men at the main gate also."

"Did they know what to expect?" Mabaku took a sip of coffee.

Tau shook his head. "No, they were surprised. But they don't ask questions. They follow instructions."

"Did any of the people you talked to give an indication that they were expecting your call or weren't surprised?"

Tau took a few moments before he responded. "I don't think so. I would have picked up anything out of the ordinary, I'm sure."

"Where were the dummy boxes at this point? Did you prepare them on the spot?"

"No. We have them ready, stored in an annex off the cleaning plant. But once I knew how big the shipment was, I had to get some more gravel to fill them up. We wanted the weight of the dummy boxes to be as close as possible to that of the box with the diamonds."

"And what actually goes on in this cleaning plant?"

"Let me give you some background. The plant is where the diamonds are cleaned up, washed, dried. Small chips are set aside and dealt with separately. Jwaneng is a very rich mine. More than two-thirds of our diamonds are gem quality, and the rest are good for industrial use. The final sorting and cleaning happens in Gaborone. Here the diamonds are cleaned of the host rock, called kimberlite, and packed for transport.

"The plant is where we have the greatest risk of loss. So, anything that goes in or out of the plant is searched and x-rayed. People go through scanners both ways and change into work overalls when they go in and back into their own clothes only when they leave. In addition, they can be and often are body searched. You wouldn't believe where people hide stones on their bodies. It's my biggest headache. We're actually planning to have a completely automated plant in the future, but that's still a way off."

"So, what exactly happened at two p.m.?"

"I went over to the cleaning plant and supervised the transfer of the diamonds. I took Peter Tshane with me. He's one of the guards. No one is ever alone with diamonds. No one. Always in pairs. Two of the men from the plant brought the box to us. We took it through to an annex off the main plant, where I weighed it and gave it a final check before locking it with two heavy-duty padlocks. After that, we got out the two dummy boxes and topped them up with granite chips until their weights were within a few grams of the diamond box."

"Do the boxes look identical?"

Tau nodded. "They look exactly the same and weigh the same. No one can tell them apart."

"So only you and the guard knew which box was which."

"We knew at that point. But after that, I asked Tshane to arrange the boxes any way he liked. Then I locked up, and we went and had a coffee together. At two forty-five, three different guards—I don't even know who they were—collected the three boxes and took them out through the plant security gates to the collection point. They set them out next to each other, again in no particular order, and went back to their other duties as soon as they saw Tshane and me approaching."

Kubu caught on at once and blurted out, "So *no* one knew which box was which at that point?"

Tau smiled. "That was exactly the plan. No one knew. None of us. And not the security guards from Gaborone Cash in Transit or the people at Debswana in Gabs. There was no way anyone could tip off an attacker. The major dreamt it up, and everyone went along with it. He was very proud of it."

"Pity it didn't work though, isn't it?" Mabaku commented dryly.

Tau's face fell. "No. There was always the chance they would hit the right vehicle. It was unlucky."

"Especially for the people who are now dead."

"Yes."

"Who else had keys to the annex room?"

"There are only two. I had one when I went in with Tshane. Three guards went to my office, and my secretary gave them the other. I collected that one from them afterwards."

"We'll need to talk to those guards."

"No problem. I'll find out who they were and let you have their names."

"And what about the keys to the padlocks? Who had them?"

"Again, there are only two for each lock—a total of twelve keys in all. I have six here, one for each lock, and the other six are at Debswana in Gabs."

"So the keys weren't with the boxes."

"That's right."

Mabaku considered that for a moment, then stood up. "I need to check in with Director Gobey. Is there a phone I can use?"

"You can use the one in my secretary's office. Just dial nine to get an outside line."

Mabaku thanked him, and Samkoa and Kubu remained in the office while Mabaku made his call in private.

He returned after about five minutes. "Thank you for your time and the sandwiches, Rra Tau. We'll need a set of your fingerprints for elimination purposes." He paused, and Tau nodded.

"We've still got a lot to do, so I told the director we'll stay over. I'd like to look around and interview this Peter Tshane and the other guards. Can you arrange that for tomorrow morning?"

"Of course. And I can organise accommodation for you. We have a guesthouse for visitors."

"Thank you. We'll see Rra Goodman now. He's had a long wait."

Chapter 25

Almost from the word go, Inspector Dow had difficulty with Inspector Pono, his counterpart from the Sejelo CID. It wasn't that the man was particularly unhelpful, or that he wasn't competent. The problem was that he was dour to the point of pessimism, while Dow's nature was completely the opposite.

When Dow arrived in Sejelo from Gaborone, Pono shook his hand and then said, "Waste of time you coming out here, you know. Everything's going to Gabs anyway. They'll take the bodies to the mortuary there, and you can read the forensics report there as well as you can here."

"I'm just here as liaison for Director Gobey," Dow soothed, "but of course I'll help any way I can."

"Well, I'll take you out to the crime scene in the morning. I've just come back from there. We're not going to find out anything new until forensics and the pathologist provide their results."

Dow wanted to go right away to see the damaged vehicle and the bodies of the two guards for himself. Also, he wanted to take pictures so he would have his own record of the scene. He sighed. He badly wanted to catch the men who'd done this, but he wondered if they would if there was little sense of urgency.

Pono seemed to read his thoughts. "We won't catch them,

you know. They'll be safely across the border into South Africa by now, and the police there have plenty of their own issues. But you can go out to the scene with the forensics people when they get here if you really want to."

Dow nodded. That would have to do.

At that moment, a constable hurried over and told Pono he was wanted urgently on the phone. The inspector returned after about five minutes looking sombre. He carried a curled-up sheet of fax paper. "Someone's found a body out on the Ranaka road. It's about ten kilometres out of town. The man who found it thinks the person was shot."

"That a picture of the missing guard?"

Pono nodded and smoothed the fax so that Dow could see the grainy, monochrome image. "There's a patrol vehicle on the way there already, and I'm going out there now. You want to come?"

Dow did. He grabbed his notebook and camera. Neither man had much doubt that it was the body of the missing guard.

As they walked quickly to Pono's vehicle, the inspector pointed at the camera. "Forensics does all that, you know."

"I find taking pictures myself helps me later with the case. And it's digital, so I get the pictures immediately." Dow was rather proud of the camera that he'd bought with his own money. He believed that technology was the future of detection. Having pictures instantly with no delay or cost was a step on that road, but he doubted Pono would share that view, so he said nothing more.

"Suit yourself. Here's the car."

Chapter 26

Elijah Goodman was sitting at his desk when the detectives walked in.

He didn't get up but waved the detectives to seats opposite him.

"I feel really bad about those guards," he said. "We didn't think it through well enough."

"Why do you say that, Rra Goodman?" Mabaku asked. "The plan was set up a long time ago and approved by senior people."

Goodman shook his head. "We should have worried more about the plane. Why did it suddenly catch fire? We've never had an accident with the planes before, and Debswana is mad on safety. It was quite a coincidence that it happened on the day we had a double shipment."

Mabaku leant forward, and Kubu could see that he was suddenly more interested in the interview.

"You realise you're saying that information was leaked from here, both about the backup plan and about the large order."

Goodman nodded. "What else could have happened?"

"Couldn't it just have been a lucky hit for the robbers?"

"I don't believe that. Do you?"

Mabaku didn't answer that. Instead he asked, "I've been told you have charge of the documents. Apart from yourself, Rra Tau, and Rra Chamberlain, who else would have had access to the plan?"

Goodman thought for a moment. "No one here. They are marked as strictly confidential, and the secretaries don't have access to those. But the security company? Debswana management? Even the police? I can't say how careful or circumspect they are."

"And who might know about the larger than usual consignment?"

Goodman shrugged. "Not the actual amount, but it was common knowledge that we were behind with deliveries and trying to catch up."

"What was your involvement with this afternoon's activities?"

"Not much. I set up the arrangements with Gaborone Cash in Transit with Eddie and then did other work." He hesitated. "I did ask both Eddie and the major to consider delaying for a day or so. They didn't want to."

Mabaku thought about that for a few seconds but didn't pursue it.

"When did you hear about the fire on the runway at the airport?"

"It was about ten this morning. I was alerted by the airport manager, a Phineas Nari. He insisted on speaking to me, and I'm glad he did. As one of our Cessnas was taxiing for takeoff for Orapa, the right engine caught fire, and then there was an explosion. He saw it happen and took the pilot to the hospital. I was really worried and called the hospital. I was relieved when they said that he'd be okay, even though he had some bad burns.

"That's when I started to worry about the shipment. I contacted the civil aviation authorities, and they said the plane couldn't be moved until a full investigation had been done. That it could be several days. When I heard that, I took the news to Eddie and the major."

Mabaku decided he was too tired to explore this any further.

"Thank you, Rra Goodman. We'll pick up on a number of points tomorrow. And we'll need a set of your fingerprints also."

Goodman looked alarmed. "Am I a suspect, then?"

"It's just for elimination purposes."

"But I didn't touch anything, I—"

"Nothing to worry about," Mabaku interrupted. "Rra Tau said he'd organise accommodation for us."

"Yes, of course. I'll show you the way. It's in the town."

Mabaku thanked him, and they headed out. But at the door, Goodman paused.

"Assistant Superintendent, those guards who were killed. Did they have families?"

Mabaku didn't know the answer to that.

Chapter 27

The sun was setting behind them as Inspectors Dow and Pono drove, and the fiery light drenched the plateau overlooking the Ranaka valley, turning everything orange.

The uniformed officers had already secured the scene by the time they arrived. The body was lying under a large knobthorn tree, whose upper canopy was covered by a sprawling sociable-weaver nest.

Dow used his camera to take close-ups of the dead man's face, as well as of the body and surroundings from different angles. It looked as though the man had been shot three times in the chest and then was left where he fell.

Pono compared the man's face to the faxed image from the security company. The image was blurred, but it appeared to be a match. More convincing still, the man's shirt had the Gaborone Cash in Transit logo on the pocket. He nodded. "I'm pretty sure it's him."

Dow went on taking pictures.

Pono slipped his hand into the dead man's shirt pocket and pulled out an ID. He glanced at it. "It's Kenosi, all right."

He went back to the road. "Looks like they pulled off here. Probably threw him out of the car and shot him."

"Why in the chest? You'd think he'd make a run for it."

"Maybe they said they were just dumping him."

Dow grunted, unconvinced. "Who found the body?"

"Chap heading home to Kanye. He reported it in town. He spotted the body as he was driving past, went to investigate, then drove like crazy to the police station when he realised what he'd found."

"Where does this road go?" Dow asked.

"In about fifty kilometres it joins up with the A1, which runs..."

"Along the border with South Africa," Dow finished for him.

Pono nodded. "They'll be comfortably settled in some kraal on the other side by now. Probably having a few beers."

Dow frowned. Unfortunately, even four years after the democratic elections there, the South African police were in transition, and it wasn't easy to get their attention. "We need to report back to CID headquarters," he said.

"Okay, we can radio in from the vehicle. It's getting too dark to see much now anyway. We'll need some lights, and we want forensics out here as soon as possible. And it's going to be a busy evening for your pathologist too."

Dow nodded. It was going to be a busy evening for everyone.

———

When they returned to the Sejelo police station, Pono said he needed to report to the station commander. Dow asked him if there was somewhere he could get something to eat because he'd left Gaborone without supper. Pono directed him to the canteen. "You may find a stale sandwich or something if you're lucky."

In fact, there was some pap and sausage left over from lunch, which they heated in the microwave. He took it to one of the tables and settled himself to eat. The warm food cheered him, and an instant coffee woke him up.

Four uniformed men came in, a sergeant and three constables.

They also took coffee and then, rather to Dow's surprise, came over and asked his permission to join him. He nodded, swallowed the mouthful he was chewing, and introduced himself. It turned out the men had been manning the roadblock all afternoon and were hoping he'd tell them what was going on.

Recalling Gobey's warning to keep the actual case secret, he was careful what he shared. "We're after some fugitives from the Jwaneng area."

"The diamond heist robbers?" one of the men asked.

Dow nodded. Obviously, they knew the basic story already, so he told them about the body that had been found on the road to Ramaka.

After a while, the sergeant spotted his camera and made appreciative noises. Dow was happy to show it to him, describing its features and flicking through the pictures.

The sergeant suddenly pointed at the camera. "Hey, please go back to that close-up, sir."

Dow scrolled back to the picture of the dead guard's face.

"That man was in an SUV we stopped. He was sitting in the back in the middle. I remember he had a logo of some sort on his shirt. And looked worried. But the driver's licence was in order, so I let them go. That was before we heard about the attack on the security company's vehicle."

Dow put down his fork, the food forgotten.

"Do you remember anything about the driver? Or the vehicle?"

The sergeant nodded. "I've got a good memory for detail. Let me think a minute." He paused. "It was a Toyota Land Cruiser. The J80 series. White. It had a Botswana B number plate, and the first two numbers were double eight. I remember thinking that it looked like 888. I'm not sure about the rest. The man who was driving had a Botswanan driver's licence. I think his second name was Poloko or Poloka. I don't remember his first name."

"How many people were in the car?"

"Five. Two up front and three in the back."

"Come on," Dow said, jumping to his feet. "We need to tell Inspector Pono about this. And your station commander. And the director of the CID. And we need to get out an APB on that SUV right away! This may be our first break in the case!"

Chapter 28

The guesthouse had three bedrooms, and Kubu was grateful to have a room to himself. He sometimes snored, and he was worried about disturbing the others. There was also a bathroom, a lounge with a TV, and a small kitchenette. Samkoa excused himself at once and headed to his room, but Mabaku collapsed onto the sofa. "I think I'll have a coffee and collect my thoughts," he said to Kubu. "Do you want to join me?"

It seemed more of an instruction than an invitation, but Kubu was happy to oblige. He wanted to know what Mabaku had deduced from the evening's interviews. He switched on the kettle, spooned instant coffee into two mugs, found milk in the fridge, and searched the cupboard for sugar. To his delight, he also found other provisions, including a packet of his favourite Romany Cream biscuits. When the coffee was ready, he put several on a plate and offered them to Mabaku. His boss took one, and so did Kubu.

"So what are your thoughts on all this?" Mabaku asked.

Kubu hesitated. His head was buzzing with ideas, but nothing was clear to him as yet.

"Well," he began tentatively, "one thing is the story about the three boxes. Tau said that no one could possibly know which box

contained the diamonds, but that's not really true. If this Peter
Tshane was working with one of the second group of guards, he
could have put the box containing the diamonds in a particular
position—facing the door, say. The guard who collected it would
then have known which box had the diamonds, and it would have
been easy to see which van picked up that particular box and tip
off the robbers."

Mabaku finished his biscuit and sipped his coffee before he
replied. "Yes, that's possible, but we know that the security van's
doors weren't forced open, which suggests one of the transit
company people was also in on it."

"Then the guard at the mine could have put the box in a particular position to be picked up."

"True, but it means there must've been two of the mine guards
working for the robbers. We certainly have to grill Tshane and the
guards who took the boxes for pickup. It also seems likely that if
the plan was leaked here at the mine, then it must have been by
someone senior or someone close to them. What did you make
of the three managers?"

Kubu was momentarily nonplussed. Was it possible that
Mabaku had already identified the guilty party? Had he missed
some important slip that had given the culprit away? He didn't
think so, but he realised he'd concentrated more on what they'd
said than on how they were saying it.

"I think Goodman was straight," he replied after a few moments
of thought. "He was concerned about the guards and their families
and had warned the others that the plan was risky." He felt on
pretty firm ground about the head of administration.

Mabaku shook his head. "That could be a clever strategy if you
wanted to deflect blame away from yourself. And we don't even
know if it's true. We need to check his claim with the others, and
to find out why they wouldn't delay."

Kubu hadn't thought about that possibility. He hesitated to
offer a further opinion, but Mabaku seemed to be waiting for him

to do so. "I didn't like Chamberlain," he said after a moment. "He seemed abrupt and quite casual about everything."

Mabaku nodded. "I didn't like him either. But there are lots of more or less honest people I don't like. We need more than that to make us suspect him of anything. What about Tau?"

"Tau? The head of security?"

"Ideal position to pull something like this off."

Kubu tried to go through the interview in his head. Tau had been helpful, and he couldn't think of anything he'd said that didn't seem reasonable.

Mabaku waited a few moments, then climbed off the sofa and stretched. "Well, I'm heading to bed. We'll pick it up in the morning. Turn off the lights when you're finished here." With that he headed towards the bathroom.

Kubu sat for a couple of minutes mulling it over. Somehow, he felt he'd disappointed Mabaku, but he couldn't see anything that he'd missed. He stood up and tried to estimate how many biscuits he could take without it being noticed. A few in hand, he headed for his bedroom.

What an incredible first day it's been, he thought. *Starting with the suitcases and now working with the assistant superintendent on the heist. I must go over everything in my mind before I go to sleep.*

But once he settled himself in the comfortable bed, it wasn't long before he was snoring.

TUESDAY
Chapter 29

The next morning, the three detectives found a café nearby where they could have breakfast. Kubu especially enjoyed his French toast and coffee since he didn't have to pay for it.

When they'd finished, Mabaku outlined the plans for the day.

"We have a lot to do. We need to get to the bottom of the explosion on that plane. Bengu, I want you to talk to the civil aviation people—they'll be at the airport. Fill them in about the robbery, and tell them about our concern that the fire may not have been accidental. Then visit the pilot and find out what his take on it is. Did he have any warning? Was he concerned about any aspects of the plane?"

He turned to Samkoa. "I want you to talk to everyone at the mine who might have seen something yesterday afternoon—anything unusual. The gate guards and so on. I'm going to talk to this Peter Tshane and the guards who brought the boxes to the pickup point. We'll meet up here at noon to compare notes."

Kubu had a question. "How will I get around? I don't know the town at all."

"We'll drop you at the airport. Get someone there to give you a lift to the hospital afterwards. It's only a few kilometres."

Kubu nodded, hoping he could persuade someone to do that.

At worst, he could walk the few kilometres, but it was already getting warm and it was only just after eight.

Mabaku settled the bill, and they dropped Kubu at the entrance gate to the airport. It was obvious from the activity there that an investigation was underway.

I seem to be specialising in airports, Kubu thought as he walked up to the entrance gate and displayed his badge.

The man who opened the gate for Kubu introduced himself as Phineas Nari.

"Let's go inside," Kubu said. "I have some questions for you."

When they were settled, Kubu pulled out his notebook. "Were you here when the plane caught fire yesterday morning?"

Nari nodded.

"Tell me what you saw."

For the next few minutes, Nari described what he'd seen, and Kubu wrote down the salient points.

"Did you see anyone on the airport grounds immediately before that?"

Nari shook his head. "No."

"Do planes burst into flames often?"

"I don't think so, but you'd better ask the civil aviation people. They're looking at the plane right now."

Kubu thanked Nari and walked slowly in the morning heat out to the plane. When he was about twenty metres away, a man in a white coat shouted at him.

"This is an accident scene. Please go back and leave the airport."

Kubu felt a little thrill as he took out his police badge. "Detective Sergeant Bengu from the Criminal Investigation Department, Botswana Police, sir. May I talk to you?"

The man scowled and walked over.

After the necessary introduction, Kubu explained that the CID was concerned that the plane had been purposefully torched rather than accidentally bursting into flames.

The man looked surprised. "Why do you think that?"

Kubu told him about the diamond robbery and their thinking that the airport had been purposefully put out of commission so the backup plan would be implemented.

The man stared at Kubu for a few long moments. "We're pretty sure it is a case of arson. Let's walk back and sit in the shade while I explain what we've found."

When they reached Nari's office, the civil-aviation investigator asked Nari to give them a few minutes alone. Then, while Kubu scribbled in his notebook as fast as he could, the man explained what he thought had happened.

"Aviation fuel, like petrol for your car, doesn't burn very well if a match is dropped into it. For a good fire, the petrol fumes have to mix with oxygen in the air. It's really the fumes that burn, not the liquid."

"So, if the tanks were full, the fuel wouldn't burn very well, even if something set it alight. Is that right?" Kubu asked.

The investigator nodded.

"How likely is it that the pilot would have taken off with tanks that were not full?"

"I can't say," the man responded. "But we can easily find out." He stood up, went to the door, and shouted for Nari to come over.

When Nari sat down, the investigator asked him whether he'd filled the tanks on the plane.

"Yes, sir. Mr. Roberts asked me to fill them yesterday. And he checked them this morning before he took off."

"Are you sure that the first flames came from the engine and not the fuel tank?"

"I was quite a long way away, but I think so."

"And the second fire?" Kubu asked.

"I'm pretty sure it was from the fuel tank."

After Nari left, the investigator told Kubu that what Nari had said corroborated what they'd found. "It looks to us that an incendiary device of some sort caused the fuel line in the engine to rupture, causing the fuel to catch fire. We think a second device was explosive and ruptured the right fuel tank, causing a big fire that consumed the right wing and the right undercarriage."

Kubu thought for a few moments. "How can you be so sure that what happened wasn't accidental?"

"Oh, it's very obvious to an experienced eye: the way the fuel line ruptured; the bent metal plates on the wing."

"How long would it take someone to put devices like that in the plane, and how would they activate them? Would they be on a timer of some sort?"

"The device in the fuel tank would take a few minutes—open the cap and either drop it in or fix it to the wall of the tank. The one in the engine would probably take longer if it was placed in a specific spot rather than just being pushed in. If it was specifically attached to the fuel line, for example, the engine casing would have to be removed, then replaced. It's not a difficult job but does take some time."

"Would it be obvious to someone like Nari?"

"Oh yes."

"Could it be done in the dark?"

"If whoever did it had a flashlight, it wouldn't be too difficult."

Kubu mulled over what he'd just heard.

The investigator interrupted his thoughts. "You asked about a timer."

Kubu nodded.

"It wouldn't make any sense to have one if the idea was to close the airport. The only way that could happen would be to have the fire occur while the plane was on the runway. There'd be no way to predict precisely when that would happen. The devices were probably triggered by radio."

"How close would the transmitter have to be?"

"Not close. All that would be necessary would be for the person to see when the plane was on the runway."

Kubu asked a few more questions but learnt nothing new.

He thanked the investigator for his time and asked for a business card in case he needed to ask anything else.

The investigator nodded, handed Kubu his card, and headed back to the plane.

Kubu immediately went to find Nari.

"Did you see anyone on or near the airport when the plane blew up?"

"No. I'm sure I was the only one around."

"And nobody during the night?"

Nari shook his head. "I come on duty at six in the morning. The night watchman didn't say that he'd seen anything and confirmed that later when I asked him again after the fire."

"Most night watchmen I see in Gaborone seem to sleep all night. Could he have missed someone coming into the airport?"

"I'm sure it's possible."

Kubu felt a pang of frustration. He wasn't making any headway.

"Is there anything out of the ordinary that you can remember that happened after the plane landed, whenever that was?"

"It came in the afternoon before. No problems."

"Anything else?"

"Not really. The only thing out of the ordinary was that a man stopped Mr. Roberts as he drove out of the airport. It looked as though he gave Mr. Roberts something."

Kubu perked up. "Did you recognise the man? Or see what he gave Roberts?"

"Unfortunately not."

"What did he look like?"

"Hard to say from a distance. But I'd say he was older and wore a jacket. Nothing else stuck out."

Again, Kubu felt frustration welling up. He'd established that the plane had been sabotaged but hadn't learnt anything about who was behind it or how they'd planted the devices.

"Can you give me a lift to the hospital, please? I need to speak to Roberts, but I don't have a car."

"Sure," Nari replied. "Follow me."

Chapter 30

While Kubu was at the airport, Mabaku used the office of someone at the mine who was on leave. The major's PA assisted him by contacting the guards he wanted to see.

He started by checking in with Director Gobey and learnt the bad news about the third security guard and the good news about their first lead to the robbers' vehicle. Just as he finished his call, there was a tentative knock on the door.

"Come in," he called out. The man who entered was big—perhaps two metres tall and broad with it. He walked up to the desk.

"Security Officer Tshane. They said you wanted to see me, sir." He stood stiffly, as if at attention.

Mabaku pointed to the chair in front of his desk, and Tshane lowered himself into it.

"I'm Assistant Superintendent Mabaku. I'm investigating the robbery yesterday. You are Peter Tshane? You were with Eddie Tau yesterday afternoon?"

Tshane nodded. "Yes, sir. I was with him. But I know nothing about the robbers. Nothing at all."

"How did you know he wanted you?"

Tshane looked confused and shook his head. He looked down at his hands.

"I mean, how did you know Tau wanted you to help him at the plant?"

"His secretary phoned and asked for me to come."

"So he asked for you?"

He nodded. "I usually help him with the diamond deliveries. Because I'm strong and carry the boxes. That's why. Otherwise, I have nothing to do with the diamonds."

"You met him at the plant?"

"Yes, we met outside and then went in through security together. Then he asked one of the men there to bring us the box for delivery to Gaborone."

"Go on."

"Well, then Rra Tau unlocked a side room, and we went in there with the diamonds. I was surprised."

"Is that unusual?"

"Yes. Normally, I just pick up the box, Rra Tau checks it and locks it, and then we take it out to the vehicle. That's what we always do."

"Rra Tau hadn't told you what you were going to do?"

"No, I thought it would be the same as always."

"What happened when you went into this room?"

"There were two more boxes there. I thought they were also full of diamonds, but Rra Tau opened them, and there was gravel inside. Just ordinary bits of rock. He told me to get a bag from the cupboard. It had more gravel in it, and we topped up the two boxes of stones until they weighed the same as the one with the diamonds."

"How did you know that?"

"There was a scale there."

"Did you do the weighing?"

Tshane shook his head. "Rra Tau did it."

"But you saw the weight?"

"No, I poured in the gravel while Rra Tau checked the scale."

So only Tau had known the weights. Mabaku made a note of that.

"And then?"

"Rra Tau checked the box with the diamonds—looked inside—and then locked all three boxes."

"Did you see inside the box?"

Tshane nodded but didn't meet Mabaku's eye. "Diamonds. Lots and lots of diamonds."

It all seemed reasonable, but Tshane's manner bothered Mabaku. He seemed to be telling the story truthfully, but there was also an undercurrent of nervousness.

"All right. What happened then?"

"Then Rra Tau asked me to take the three boxes and put them together for collection any way I liked."

"How did you put them?"

"Just next to each other."

"And which was the box with the diamonds?"

Tshane hesitated. "I think it was the one nearest the door."

"You don't know?"

"They all looked the same…" Again, he looked down at his hands as he answered.

"And then?"

"We left. Rra Tau locked the door, and he took me to the canteen, and we drank coffee together." He shook his head. "I didn't understand. Normally we take the box, and I carry it to the loading bay. Then I put it in the vehicle, and another guard and I climb in the back. Then the van is driven to the airport, and we load the box on the plane. We never just leave the box behind and drink coffee!"

"Did you ask Rra Tau about it?"

"He said other guards would move the boxes for us, but he didn't explain what it was all about. After about ten minutes, we went out to the loading bay, and the boxes were on the ground waiting to be loaded. Two other guards were waiting with them. Then Rra Tau told me I could go."

"Which was the box with the diamonds? Tell me the truth!"

Tshane swallowed. "I...I don't know. I suppose it was there. How could I know?"

Mabaku leant back in his chair. Everything Tshane had said agreed with what Tau had said. And there seemed to be nothing untoward about what he'd done. So what was upsetting the man then?

"Rra Tshane, is there anything else you want to tell me? Anything that may help with the inquiry into the robbery? We expect your full cooperation."

"I've told you everything! There's nothing else."

But why doesn't he look at me when he says it? Mabaku wondered.

"Thank you, Rra Tshane. I will probably have more questions later."

Tshane climbed to his feet and left without another word.

Chapter 31

Nari drove Kubu to the hospital where he'd taken the injured man the morning before. Kubu was a little embarrassed because it turned out to be less than a kilometre away. He told himself that he would have walked had he known how close it was.

He showed his badge to the receptionist and asked for Tony Roberts.

"He's in ward eleven—a private ward."

Kubu thought that she sounded disapproving that a person could have a private ward. He walked down the passage and found ward 11, knocked, and walked in. Roberts was sitting up in bed with his face bandaged.

"Mr. Roberts, my name is Detective Sergeant David Bengu of the Criminal Investigation Department, Botswana Police. Do you feel strong enough to answer a few questions?"

The man nodded.

"Thank you." Kubu pulled out his notebook. "I'll keep this as short as possible. First, Phineas Nari, the airport manager, says he filled the tanks of your plane the night before you took off. Did you check that they were full?"

"I did my normal pre-flight check, and they were full."

"Was there anything unusual about your pre-flight check?"

"Everything was fine."

"And what alerted you to a problem when you were taxiing to take off?"

"I heard an unusual sound from the right engine. When I leant across the passenger seat to see if I could see anything, I saw flames."

"What did you do then?"

"I shut down both engines, stopped fuel flow to the engine, and jumped out to see what was going on."

Kubu waited for Roberts to continue.

"As I walked around to the engine, there was a loud bang, and flames everywhere. As you can see, my face was burnt. And my hands." He waved his bandaged hands in the air.

"Do you have any idea what could have caused it?"

"I spent most of the night thinking about that. I was worried I'd screwed up and would be fired. I've only been flying for Debswana for nine months or so."

"And what was your conclusion?"

"I think I did everything correctly. It had to have been some extreme malfunction that caused sparking, probably of the electrical system."

"What's electrical in the fuel tank?"

Roberts shrugged. "I'm not sure—maybe the fuel pump."

Kubu made a note to ask the civil aviation inspector about that.

"One last thing, Mr. Roberts. Nari told me that he saw a man give you something as you drove out of the airport the day before the fire."

"A beggar. Gave me a small parcel wrapped in brown paper. I'm sure all he wanted was a handout."

"Can you remember what he looked like?"

"Hmm. He was old. Maybe in his fifties, maybe sixties. It's hard to tell how old blacks are. His face was very wrinkled, and he wore a dark jacket, which I thought was a bit odd. Made him look less deserving."

"Did you give him anything?"

Roberts shook his head.

"Then why did you take the packet?"

"It was easier to take it and drive off, than haggle with him."

"Did he say anything?"

"He muttered something I didn't understand. It sounded like hocus-pocus to me."

"What do you mean?"

"Whatever he said sounded like a song. It was strange."

"Do you still have the parcel?"

"I threw it in the back of the car. I was going to throw it out when I reached home but forgot. It must still be there."

"And your car is still at the airport?"

Roberts nodded. "Unless Phineas drove it back for me. I always leave the keys in the car."

Kubu thanked the injured man and walked back to reception. There was still an hour before he had to meet the assistant superintendent, so he decided he'd better return to the airport and check on Robert's car. However, he was unsuccessful in persuading anyone to give him a lift, so he set off on foot.

Chapter 32

The leader of the robbers and his men sat in the shade of a jack-alberry tree near the ramshackle house. Even there, they suffered from the heat. A breeze that should have cooled them lifted heat from the ground and enveloped them. They sweated profusely and grew grumpy.

The contrast of the adrenalin of the previous day and the nothingness of sitting around waiting eventually got to the leader. He wanted to get going, to get away from the danger of the Botswana police, who were searching everywhere for him and his men. He knew it was dangerous to cross the border into South Africa during the day. They'd seen helicopters flying low over the border fence. But the thought of doing nothing for the many hours until dark was more than he could handle.

He jumped up and looked at his men. "We've got to get going. The police will find us here. People will have seen us drive through the village."

He strode over to the house and banged on the door. "Ngaka, we must leave now," he shouted. "It's too dangerous to stay."

The door opened, and the doctor and his son walked out.

"Ngaka—" The leader addressed the older man, but Vusi interrupted.

"You will leave when I tell you!"

The leader took a step back, seeing raw anger in Vusi's eyes. "But…"

The doctor lifted his hands to the sky. "My friend, listen to my son. I see great danger if you leave now. You must wait until he says you can go."

The leader felt anger welling up. "It is our lives that are in danger, Ngaka. Not yours or your son's. We can see dangers better in daylight than at night. We're well armed and well prepared. We will go now. Your diamonds will be safer with us in South Africa than here."

"The spirits have told me that you will be safe if you leave tonight."

"Ngaka, the spirits don't have to face the police or maybe even the army."

"You will not reach the border if you leave now." The leader could barely hear what Vusi said, but he took another step back. "The diamonds are ours. The money is ours. You will do as I say. You will leave after supper, when I say. Not before. Not after. Tell your men to be patient, for their reward is great. Go."

With that Vusi turned and stalked back into the house.

The doctor turned also, then stopped at the door and spoke to the leader. "Do as my son says. He is wise and knows what is best for you."

The leader walked back to his men.

Maybe I've had this wrong, he pondered. *I thought the doctor was in charge, but maybe it's really his son.*

Chapter 33

"You look as though you've been rained on," Nari commented, looking at Kubu's drenched shirt as he opened the airport gate.

"Where's Roberts's car?" Kubu growled.

Nari pointed at a white Toyota Corolla parked near the office building. "The keys are probably on the sun visor."

Kubu walked over to the car and peered in the back seat. There he saw a package wrapped in brown paper.

"Do you have a bag of some sort?" he shouted to Nari, who was heading back to his air-conditioned office.

"I'll see if I can find one."

A few minutes later he came out and handed Kubu a plastic Pick n Pay bag. "What do you need that for?"

Kubu opened the back door and lifted the package using his handkerchief. He put it in the bag. "We just need to check what this is. Rra Roberts said the man who gave it to him was singing some sort of song."

"Fuck!"

Kubu was taken aback by the English expletive. "What do you mean?"

"I've heard stories over the past week of a powerful witch doctor being in Jwaneng."

"A witch doctor?"

Nari nodded.

"What do you think is in the package?"

"I don't want to know. Don't open it here, please. Take it away right now."

Kubu was puzzled by Nari's reaction. He'd always regarded the stories of witch doctors casting spells and people dying from them as folklore. His father was a traditional healer—a well-regarded one—but never cast spells on anyone.

"Please could I trouble you for a lift again? I need to meet my superior in town."

Nari shook his head. "No way I'm going anywhere with that parcel. Who knows what could happen to me and my family? Why don't you take Rra Roberts's car and drive yourself?"

Faced with the choice of another long walk in the sweltering heat or commandeering the injured pilot's car without permission, Kubu convinced himself that to reach the restaurant by noon he'd have to take the car. He was sure Assistant Superintendent Mabaku would approve his decision to borrow it—if he was on time.

Chapter 34

It was 12:15 p.m. before Mabaku and Samkoa arrived at the restaurant. Samkoa recounted his interviews with a variety of people at the mine. "No one I spoke to except the gate guards had any idea that the shipment was any different from normal. Of course, the guards saw three armoured trucks arrive and leave, instead of the one vehicle Jwaneng normally uses."

"Did they notice anything unusual near the gate?"

Samkoa shook his head. "The morning was a waste of time actually. I learnt nothing."

"Not true," Mabaku snapped. "You learnt a lot. You learnt nobody knew anything. That's important. How confident are you they were telling the truth?"

"I don't think any of them were lying."

"Good. And you, Bengu, what did you find out?"

Kubu recounted the information given to him by the civil-aviation investigator. "So we were right it was part of the heist," Mabaku interjected. "Go on."

When Kubu had finished his report on Roberts and the brown-paper parcel, Mabaku interjected again. "What did you make of that?"

"I think most of the witch doctor stuff is bogus," Kubu replied. "Old-fashioned ideas that have no place in today's world."

"Let me give you some advice, Bengu. First, never discount the power of the witch doctors. You may think they are bogus, but many people believe in their spells. And I can tell you from firsthand experience that I've seen things that can't be explained by logic—people falling sick in houses that a witch doctor has put a spell on; even people dying because of spells. It doesn't matter what you think; it's what other people believe that's important. So never reject something because you don't think it makes sense. Understood?"

"Yes, sir." Kubu felt disappointed that he hadn't impressed Mabaku.

"Second, you did a good job in getting the stories of what happened but a lousy job of asking the right questions."

Kubu didn't say anything, but he felt Mabaku wasn't being fair.

"Did you ask the civil aviation inspectors where the devices that were used to torch the plane could have been bought? Did you ask them if they'd seen any similar incidents? Or had they heard of similar incidents?"

Mabaku stared at Kubu.

"Did you?"

Kubu shook his head. "No, sir." Half an hour earlier he'd felt pleased with what he accomplished; now he felt he'd done nothing right.

"Did you ask that Nari bloke if he'd checked the perimeter fence to see if he could spot where the intruder or intruders had come onto the airport?"

Kubu shook his head again. Things were going from bad to worse.

"Where did Roberts work before? What's his background?"

"But, sir, Debswana would have vetted him before hiring him."

"How do you know that? Maybe he's somebody's friend. How

do you know that he's not part of the whole heist? Perhaps it was his job to close the runway."

"But his face was badly burnt…"

"What does that mean? It could have been an accident. Maybe his karma changed. You have no idea, have you?"

Kubu hung his head. He didn't want to look at Mabaku.

"And what's that Nari's background? Maybe he planted the bombs. He'd have plenty of opportunity. He doesn't earn much, I'd wager. A bribe to leave the gate open, or a payment for placing the bombs could make his life a lot easier. Or maybe they threatened to kill his children. Do you know if he has children?"

"I'm sorry sir," Kubu mumbled. "I'll do a better job next time."

"You'd better. After lunch go back and re-interview everyone. And this time dig deeper. Don't trust or believe what anyone says unless you can cross-check or corroborate it."

"Yes, sir." Kubu's stomach hurt, and he was so depressed he didn't even want to eat.

"I spoke to all the people on my list," Mabaku continued. "Basically, everyone involved in moving the diamonds from the mine to the armoured vehicles. I have to say the plan they'd thought out seems solid. As Chamberlain said, once the diamonds were in a box, two identical boxes were brought in and filled to the same weight with gravel. The guards who took them to the loading area didn't know which one contained the diamonds, and the people from the transit company didn't know which was which either. So the probability of the thieves picking the correct vehicle was one in three—not good odds for the size of the operation they needed."

The three men sat in silence for a few minutes, then Kubu ventured a comment. "As I mentioned last night, it could be done if two people at the mine were in on it. One would have to be either Tau or…hold on a second." Kubu flipped back in his notebook. "Or Peter Tshane. And the other would have to be one of the three guards who took the boxes to where they were going to be picked up. Tshane could put the box with diamonds in a particular position, say in the middle. The guard who was in on the plan would know which box to pick up, and he'd put it down in a predetermined position. The insider from the transit company would take it and put it in his vehicle."

"That's good, Bengu. I must say, Tshane seemed nervous when I spoke to him. What would you do next?"

Kubu thought for a moment, desperately wanting to get back in Mabaku's good graces. "I'd do thorough background checks on everyone involved, particularly Tau, Tshane, and the three guards. Maybe even Chamberlain and Goodman. Maybe they were in some sort of financial problem or had their family threatened. Something to make them cooperate if they weren't in the deal from the beginning."

"That's precisely what I'm going to do. Hopefully we'll have some preliminary information later today. What else?"

Kubu frowned. *What else?* he said to himself.

Mabaku waited patiently.

"I'd find out which guards carried the boxes and double check them. And find out if they had any relationship with Tau or Tshane."

"Right." Mabaku stood up. "So we've got plenty to do. Samkoa, you come with me. Bengu, you've a lot to follow up on. Meet here again at six."

"Assistant Superintendent Mabaku, sir," Kubu said tentatively. "I suppose you want a ride to the airport."

"No sir. I have a car."

Mabaku frowned but said nothing.

"I just want to promise that I won't disappoint you again."

Mabaku stared at him for a few moments, then burst out laughing. "You didn't disappoint me, Bengu. I just wanted to make sure you didn't think you'd done a good job."

Chapter 35

When he got back to the mine building, Mabaku went straight to Goodman's office.

"Do you have a list of all the personnel here at the mine?"

Goodman said he did and retrieved it from one of his filing cabinets. Mabaku found it dauntingly long, but it was organised by work area, which helped. He wasn't interested in the miners, who made up the large majority of the employees; he was interested in the people in the cleaning plant, the administration and management, and the guards. He marked those sections and asked to see their files.

"What, all of them?" Goodman asked. "Including mine and Eddie's?"

Mabaku nodded. "And Mr. Chamberlain's."

"I don't know...the files are confidential."

"Let's go and ask Mr. Chamberlain about that. I don't think he'll be happy about anything delaying the investigation."

Goodman hesitated, trying to choose between two undesirable courses of action. "I suppose it will be okay. I'll ask my secretary to go to the records section and find them for us. But as he's senior management, the major's will be at head office."

"Ask her to bring what she's got. And to be as quick as possible.

She can bring me the management ones first while she digs out the others."

———

Mabaku took his time over the two senior managers' files. He didn't know what he was looking for, but he hoped that his instincts would alert him to anything significant. He made several notes, but neither had anything unusual about their careers. They'd been successful in previous jobs, had performed well at Debswana, and had been promoted. The references he found in the files were all strong and complimentary. Finally, he set them aside and moved on to the guards, starting with Peter Tshane.

The man was from Gaborone. His first job had been with a bank, where he'd first been trained as a guard. After two years he'd moved to a jewellery store as one of two store guards. A year later he left, and his next job was at Jwaneng mine. Mabaku hesitated. There was a gap of almost six months between when he left Bright Star Jewellers and when he came to Jwaneng. What had he been doing during that time? There was a reference letter from the bank; they'd been happy with him. But nothing from the jeweller that might explain his departure.

Finally, there was a brief, typed note concerning the interview, which had been held by Tau, a security manager, and an HR person. And it had an explanation. In a brief paragraph, it was stated that Tshane had disagreed with the store manager on a variety of issues and had resigned. He'd spent time considering his future before deciding to apply to De Beers.

Did he need six months' consideration? Mabaku wondered. He went through the rest of the file but found nothing else odd. Tshane was a good employee. "Helpful, punctual, follows instructions." He was willing to do overtime when needed. In his latest assessment, his manager had suggested a promotion.

But Mabaku was worried by the unexplained six months.

He picked up the file and went across the corridor to Tau's office. The head of security's door was open, and he went straight in.

"I've been reviewing the personnel files," Mabaku told him. If Tau was surprised by that, he didn't show it. "Peter Tshane. There was gap from when he left his previous job at a jewellery store and when he joined you. And there's no reference letter from the store."

"Let me take a look," Tau said, and Mabaku handed him the file open to the summary of the interview.

"Oh, yes, I remember now. He said he didn't see eye to eye with the manager of the store. He was unhappy and decided to leave, even though he didn't have another job. He tried to find something in Gaborone for a while without success and then looked further afield. That's how he came to us." He added as an afterthought, "We've been very happy with him."

"Didn't you check his story with the store?"

Tau nodded. "We asked the HR person to phone the manager to confirm it." He paused. "Isn't that in the file?"

Mabaku shook his head.

"Well, easy enough to ask her." He glanced at the note again. "Oh, it was Jenny." He hesitated. "Goodman let her go. She was rather unreliable."

Mabaku asked if he could use the phone, and Tau slid it across the desk to him. After a quick call to directory enquiries, Mabaku dialled the number.

"Dumela. Bright Star Jewellers."

"This is Assistant Superintendent Mabaku of the CID. I need to speak to the manager."

There was a short pause, then a new voice came onto the line. "This is Abena Dibane. I'm the manager here. How can I help you?"

"Dumela, mma. I just need some information. Do you remember a man called Peter Tshane? He worked as a guard for your store a few years ago."

There was a pause, then, "Yes. I remember him."

"He said he left because the two of you didn't get on."

There was no response.

"Is that correct?"

"Assistant Superintendent, he left because I fired him. He stole a diamond ring."

That made Mabaku sit up. "Please tell me exactly what happened."

"The shop assistant was showing some rings to a customer. When the customer left, she took the most valuable ones to the safe, and when she returned, she realised one of the others was missing. Tshane was the only other person in the shop at that time.

"He denied it, of course. Said the customer must've palmed it, but my assistant was adamant that the ring had been on the counter when she left. I said we were locking the shop, and I was calling the police. No one was to leave, and we would all be searched. Suddenly he gave a cry and bent down and picked up the ring from behind a pot plant. He said it must have fallen down and slid behind the planter. He'd just suddenly seen a glint."

"What did you do then?"

"I didn't believe him, of course. Rings don't just roll onto the floor. They're laid out on velvet for display. He'd taken the ring but realised he couldn't get away with it. I said he could leave at once and not come back, or I was going to lay a charge with the police."

Mabaku nodded. He could see the woman's point. Even if Tshane hadn't taken the ring, she could never trust him in the future.

"Was this ring worth a lot?"

"Not really. About two thousand pula if I remember correctly."

That seemed like a lot of money to Mabaku, but he didn't pursue it.

"One last question. Did Debswana ever phone you and ask you for a reference for him?"

"Absolutely not. If they had, I would've told them the same thing."

Mabaku thanked her, ended the call, and turned back to Tau. "Your exemplary guard was fired on suspicion of theft of a diamond ring. And your HR person never bothered to follow up. I need another talk with Peter Tshane."

He left the head of security looking very upset.

Chapter 36

After Kubu returned to the airport and Nari had let him through the gate, the two went to Nari's office.

"Did you ever check to see where the bomber got into the airport?" Kubu asked.

Nari shrugged. "It wasn't worth it. The fence is quite high but isn't really a security fence. More one to keep cattle off the runway. They could have got in easily almost anywhere."

At first Kubu thought Nari's answer was reasonable, and then he realised it wasn't. He shook his head. "Please go now and try to find the place. And if you find it, be careful not to disturb it. There may be clues we can use to find the person who did it."

Nari grumbled but headed out, and Kubu walked over to the runway to speak to the investigator again. The man saw him approaching and came over.

"What can I do for you now, Sergeant?"

"I apologise for interrupting, but I have a couple more questions. First, where would someone get devices like the ones you suspect caused the fires? Both the devices and the radio receivers?"

"Anyone who can read can easily manufacture a simple bomb or incendiary device from commonly available chemicals and electronics."

"So, there's no source we could go to in the hopes of finding the bomber?"

"Unfortunately, that's right."

"Where would I go to buy the electronics to make a transmitter and receiver that could trigger the explosives?"

"It would be easiest to get the components in Joburg. There are lots of shops that sell stuff like that. Here in Botswana? Maybe a bit more difficult, but still easy. There are probably ten or so sources in the country."

Kubu was disappointed. He'd hoped for a pointer that would help the investigation. "One final thing. When the bomber placed the bombs, what parts of the plane would he have to touch? Maybe forensics can find fingerprints."

The investigator nodded. "Good thinking. He'd have to touch the filler cap to get into the fuel tank and maybe the wing around it. And the ladder he used to get there. To get into the engine, he'd have to touch the part he removed. We think the bomb was on the right side of the engine."

"Please can you be careful not to touch those parts anymore until forensics has a chance to process them?"

"Okay. We're going to move everything into the Debswana hangar so we can open the airport again. We'll set aside the filler cap and engine casing, but your forensics people will have to check the wing—we won't remove that from the fuselage unless we have to. At some stage, we'll probably send any pieces of interest to Pretoria for further investigation. They've better capabilities than we do."

Kubu shook the man's hand. "Once more, thank you for your help." Then he headed off to wait for Nari to return from his tour of the airport perimeter. He felt that this time his investigation would meet Mabaku's standards.

Chapter 37

Tshane looked even more nervous than he had the previous time Mabaku had interviewed him. He fiddled with his fingers while he watched the detective turn the pages of his file.

Mabaku made him wait for several minutes before he looked up and asked, "Why did you leave the employment of Bright Star Jewellers?"

Tshane went rigid. "The manager was very difficult. She—"

"You're lying to me!" Mabaku was almost shouting. "I want the truth!"

Tshane looked down. "She fired me. She said I stole a ring. It wasn't true! The assistant had knocked it onto the floor. She was a stupid, clumsy woman."

"But you didn't tell Rra Tau about this."

"No."

"Didn't you think they'd check?"

Tshane shrugged.

Mabaku slapped the desk. "I asked you a question."

"I had nothing to lose either way. I needed money. I'm good at my job. And her story wasn't true!"

Mabaku sat and looked at him for a long time. Then, in a

quieter voice, he said, "When did you first realise you could make a lot of money here at the mine?"

"What do you mean? I only have a guard's salary here."

"And that's not such a lot, is it?"

Again, Tshane shrugged. Then, seeing Mabaku's glare, he said, "It's okay. I get by."

"But when you were approached and offered a lot of money, you couldn't resist it, could you? Just for some information. Just for a little help."

Tshane shook his head. "I don't know what you're talking about."

"I'm talking about the people who asked about the diamond transport boxes and how security worked here at the mine. Maybe they bought you a few drinks. What harm could there be in telling them what everyone knew anyway?"

"No one asked me anything! We don't talk about mine security. Not even to our families. It's not allowed."

"Look, Tshane, I'm giving you a chance here. A chance to make things right. You didn't know what was going to happen. And you needed a bit of extra money. If you tell me now what you know, help us catch these murderers, recover the diamonds, I'll see what I can do. Maybe what you did wasn't that serious. Maybe all that happens is you lose your job. That's history anyway now that Rra Tau knows the real story about the jewellery store. Tell me right now what you know, and things can still work out for you. Otherwise I'll arrest you, and you'll spend the rest of your life in jail as an accessory to murder. The rest of your life!"

"No, no, I did nothing! I told no one anything. I know nothing about the robbery. If I could help you, I would. But I can't. Please. You can't arrest me. I've done nothing!"

Mabaku leant back in his chair and thought. He'd been sure that Tshane's nerves were because he was somehow involved in the robbery, but perhaps he was just scared of losing his job if the jewellery store story came out. He'd looked almost relieved when it did, as though the worst was over, instead of ahead.

"All right, Tshane. I'll give you some time to think it over. Maybe you'll remember something if you really think about it."

"There's…there's nothing to remember," Tshane stammered.

"This isn't the end of it, Tshane. I'll want to see you tomorrow. And the next day. Until you tell me the whole truth."

"I *have* told you the truth."

"Don't try to leave town. We'll be watching you. Now get out!"

Mabaku watched him leave, and then sighed. He'd keep pushing Tshane as hard as he could, but his gut feeling was that the guard actually was telling the truth. And most times, his gut was right.

Chapter 38

It didn't take long before Kubu was fidgeting. He didn't like waiting. He wanted to do something. Then he remembered the parcel
in the back of Roberts's car and went to fetch it, carefully carrying
it back in its Pick n Pay bag.

It wasn't heavy, and it rattled slightly when he shook it. When
he was back inside, he took it out of the bag, put it on the table,
and looked at it carefully. There was nothing unusual about it.
Whatever it was inside had been wrapped in brown paper and
bound with a long piece of brown twine. He nudged it around
with a pencil so he could see all sides. There was nothing suspicious other than the fact it had been given to Roberts by an
unknown man wearing a jacket in the sweltering heat.

Kubu wondered whether he should open it. There was a pair
of scissors on Nari's desk, so he could remove the twine without
damaging the paper and without any danger of leaving his own
fingerprints on the parcel. The one thing that bothered him was
the fact that it had been given to a white man, who probably
wouldn't be too fazed by whatever was inside. Why would a witch
doctor do that, if in fact the man *was* a witch doctor?

Unless...

Kubu pushed his chair back and moved to the door. What if

the parcel was yet another bomb—one designed to take out the pilot at some convenient point in case he discovered something about who had set the bombs on the plane?

If it were a bomb, Kubu reasoned, it too would have to be remotely set off if it were to be maximally effective. It wouldn't make any sense to kill the pilot before he took off.

He looked around and out the windows. The only person he could see was Nari, who was inspecting the fence several hundred metres away, abreast of one end of the runway.

It didn't take Kubu long to decide that discretion was the better part of valour. He picked up the phone on the desk and phoned through to CID headquarters.

"Elias, is that you?" he asked when the phone was answered.

"Yes. Who's that?"

"Elias, it's me, Kubu. I need your help, please. I have a parcel here that was given to the Debswana pilot the night before last— the night before the plane was bombed. I'm worried that it may be another bomb like the ones that caused the fire. A bomb that can be remotely triggered."

"I don't know anything about bombs."

"But do you know how I can get hold of the bomb squad— assuming there's such a thing?"

"Hold on and I'll get their number."

It wasn't long before he came back on the line and gave Kubu the number.

"One more thing, please," Kubu said. "Forensics is probably looking at the armoured car that was bombed. They also need to look at the plane because there's a chance that whoever placed the bombs may have left their fingerprints. Could you please let them know that they need to come to the airport as well? I've asked the civil-aviation inspectors to set aside the pieces that may have prints in case they're not here when forensics arrives."

"Anything else you'd like me to do?" Elias muttered.

"No, thank you. You've been a great help. I appreciate it," Kubu said cheerfully.

He immediately phoned the bomb squad and told them what he had in front of him.

"Don't touch it. Don't move it," the man on the line instructed. "It may be booby-trapped."

"It may just be a simple gift or maybe something from a witch doctor."

There was a silence on the line. "We can't take a chance. Leave it where it is, and we'll send someone out first thing tomorrow morning. Don't let anyone get close to it."

Kubu thanked the man, put down the phone, and hurried out of the office, hoping that he hadn't activated something when he moved the parcel.

———

Nari was not happy when Kubu told him he couldn't go back into his office.

"But my wallet and car keys are there. How am I going to get home?"

"I'll give you a lift."

Nari looked dubious. "What if there's a spell on the car?"

"There isn't," Kubu assured him. "The parcel is in your office, and I never opened it."

"I don't think so. I'll walk into town and get a taxi."

Kubu shrugged. "It's your choice, but I have to ask you some questions first."

"I've told you everything I know."

"I just need some background from you. Let's go and stand in the shade."

When they were standing out of the sun, Kubu continued. "Did you find anything? Anywhere they cut the fence or climbed over it?"

Nari shook his head. "Nothing. I think they came over the gate. It's about the same height as the fence. It wouldn't be too hard to climb over it if you had a ladder and were willing to jump."

"And getting out?"

"There's a button to open it on that wall over there." He pointed to a wall near the gate. "You've seen me open the gate for you."

"Who else knows about it?"

"Oh, everyone who's been to the airport. That's how they get out."

"Wouldn't the night watchman hear it?"

"Only if he was awake."

For the next ten minutes, Kubu grilled Nari about his previous jobs, his family, and his finances.

"What the fuck's going on here?" Nari asked as Kubu probed deeper and deeper. "I'm not a suspect."

Kubu pondered that for a moment. How would the assistant superintendent proceed now? He decided he'd be forceful and call Nari's bluff. "Of course you are! You had perfect access to place the bombs. You've admitted you're terrified of the witch doctor. He probably told you that he'd put a spell on your house or family if you didn't do it. Or maybe he just offered you money. You could always do with extra money, couldn't you? Maybe buy a new car? Or your wife a present? You're not only a suspect— you're the prime one."

"No!" Nari shouted. "You're wrong. I never did anything. I'd never do anything like that."

"It was so easy, wasn't it? Open the filler cap, drop in the bomb. And when no one was here, put the second one in the engine. Easy." Kubu paused. "How much did he pay you?"

Nari looked as though he was going to hit Kubu. "No," he screamed. "It's not true."

Chapter 39

As he drove back to the hospital, Kubu was quite pleased with how he'd questioned Nari. He'd have to check what Nari had told him, but he was confident that the man didn't have anything to do with the bombs.

He was just approaching the parking area of the hospital when the car pulled to the left, and he heard a flapping sound coming from the front of the car. Although he'd never been in a car that had a puncture before, he realised what had happened. He pulled over onto the dirt shoulder and stopped.

"What do I do now?" he wondered as he looked at the flat tyre. Changing a wheel was not something one learnt growing up in a home without a car. His parents never could afford one and walked or used a bus when they needed to travel.

Kubu shrugged, locked the car, and headed towards the hospital.

Assistant Superintendent Mabaku is going to enjoy this one, he thought ruefully.

———

Kubu went straight to the private ward and sat down. "Mr. Roberts, I apologise for intruding again, but I have some more questions."

The bandaged head nodded.

"Where were you employed before you came here?"

The man took a deep breath. "I flew for a company called Heavenly Charters out of Lanseria, in Johannesburg."

"And why—"

"Why did I leave?" Roberts interrupted. "I was fired."

Kubu sat up a bit straighter.

"It was last March. I'd just returned from a long day's flying, dodging massive thunderheads, with complaining passengers. I was exhausted. My boss told me he needed me to fly an important client down to Durban. There were nasty thunderstorms all through the highveld, and it would be a night flight. I told him it would be dangerous for me to fly under the circumstances. He told me I had to go. I refused. I've read enough accident reports to know that fatigue is a big killer. He said if I didn't go, he'd fire me. I told him to go ahead, and he did. On the spot."

"And when were you employed by Debswana?"

"About three months later. Pilots' jobs are hard to get these days. Specially if you want to earn a living wage."

"And Debswana wasn't worried about you being fired?"

Roberts laughed. "It was ironic. They hired me because I had refused to fly. They said that they wanted cautious pilots who wouldn't put any of their management at risk. And you know what?"

Kubu shook his head.

"I'm earning much more now. With benefits and retirement. More than my arsehole boss at Heavenly Charters." He laughed again.

Kubu asked a few more questions and then took his leave, confident that Roberts was not involved in the heist. However, he remembered what Mabaku had said the evening before and resolved to dig further, just in case.

There was no way he was going to walk the kilometre or so to the restaurant to meet with the others, so he asked the receptionist to call for a taxi.

As he waited for it to arrive, he used the receptionist's phone to call Elias at headquarters.

"Elias, this is Kubu. I need your help again, please."

"For God's sake, I'm not your lackey," Elias grumbled.

"Well, the assistant superintendent wants us to move as quickly as possible, and I don't have the resources to find out what I need."

"And what's that?"

"Phineas Nari is the manager at Jwaneng Airport. He works for Debswana. Please could you check with them to see if he's ever been in any trouble with them?"

"His records will be at the mine," Elias interrupted, "not at Debswana headquarters. You can check them yourself."

Kubu hesitated a moment. "I'll do that. But in the meantime, please contact the mine's HR department and find out which bank his salary is deposited to. Then contact the bank to check for any unusual activity, particularly deposits. Also, the name of the Debswana pilot who was burnt is Tony Roberts—presumably Anthony Roberts. Check with Debswana about him too, and phone a company called Heavenly Charters at Lanseria. Roberts claims he was fired because he refused to fly what he considered a dangerous trip. See what the company has to say."

"Is that all? Surely you can find more for me to do."

"No, that's it for now." Kubu smiled. "Thanks very much. Now please could you put me through to Detective Sergeant Neo?"

There were a few clicks and a short delay. "Detective Sergeant Neo."

"Mathew, it's Kubu. Have you had any more thoughts about the suitcases? I've been so busy, I haven't had a chance to think about our case."

"I keep telling you that you're wasting your time. And mine. The bags were stolen at their destination. End of story."

Kubu rolled his eyes. "Okay, Mathew. Let's assume you're right. If so, it's unlikely that this is the first time it's happened.

Please contact British Airways and Air France baggage sections in London and Paris and ask if something like this has ever happened before—that a large number of bags have been reported missing even though they were scanned all the way through."

There was silence on the line.

"Mathew, are you there?"

"Yes, I'm here. The others are right. You're a real pain in the arse."

"Will you do what I asked, Mathew?"

There was another pause. "I suppose so."

"Thank you, Mathew. I'll call you back when I have the time."

As he put down the phone, a man walked up to reception. "You called a taxi?"

"That's for me," Kubu replied and headed for the door.

Chapter 40

"I don't feel I've made much progress," Mabaku said as the three detectives enjoyed a drink at the restaurant. "My instinct is that the Tshane guard guy isn't involved, although he was fired from his last job, allegedly for stealing a diamond ring. He and Tau, the head of security, were the only ones present when the three boxes were closed. They knew at that time which box contained the diamonds."

"How do we know that for certain?" Kubu asked.

Mabaku looked at Kubu. "What do you mean?"

"Well, what if the person or people who originally packed the box marked the box in some way that only someone who knew what to look for would notice?"

"How would they do that?"

"I don't know." Kubu shrugged. "Maybe invisible paint visible to someone with special glasses? Or a very small mark on the lid?"

"That's possible, but they'd have to know about the backup plan before they packed the diamonds."

"Which would point to an inside job again," Samkoa chipped in.

"And they would have to be told that the backup plan was going to be used."

"We should check whether any information about the fire at the airport reached the packers at the mine," Kubu suggested.

"Okay. That's your job in the morning. One other thing: the guards where the armoured vehicles picked up the boxes noticed that one of the security company men inspected the locks on the boxes before being authorized to do so. And that's who was found dead last night." He turned to Kubu. "Did you find anything useful this afternoon?"

Kubu shook his head. "I don't think either the manager or the pilot were involved." He hesitated. "But I've asked Elias at headquarters to check into their finances and so on."

"And he said he'd do it?"

"He said he would, but I don't know whether he will."

"Amazing!" Mabaku muttered.

Samkoa looked glum. "I didn't find anything useful either."

Mabaku sat quietly for a few moments. "Well, I'm not sure we've made any real progress. But...in my experience, when that is the case, the culprit is usually an unlikely one, often an insider. We're going to have to look at people who don't want to be looked at. I'm going to get authority to tap the home phones of Goodman, Tau, and Chamberlain. We'll probably get nothing, but I can't think of anything better to do right now."

The three men digested the implications of that for a few minutes. Then Kubu spoke quietly. "I have one more question."

"What is it?" Mabaku asked as he stood up.

"Well, it's a little embarrassing."

"Get on with it, Bengu, I've things to do."

"I borrowed the pilot's car, and it's got a puncture. After dinner, could one of you show me how to change a wheel?"

Chapter 41

That night, the leader and his men ate dikgobe prepared by the woman who served the doctor and the man he called his son. They rolled the cracked maize into balls with their fingers and used it to mop up sauce. And there was Shake Shake sorghum beer again to wash down the dryness.

At eight thirty, the doctor rose from the table and addressed the leader of the robbers. "You need to go. It is the right time now."

This time no one questioned his decision. He went into the back of his house and returned with Vusi carrying the Debswana transport box. It was now wrapped in sacking, and a strange, pungent aroma came from it. Two of the men jumped up and moved back. The doctor looked at them and nodded.

"There is powerful muti here. It will keep you safe. You need fear nothing. But you must not open the covering. If you do, it will turn on you. It will…" He shook his head. "Do not open it. I have warned you. I will not speak of it again." He turned to the leader. "Hide it under the animal skins you will find at your vehicle. If you are stopped, say you are bringing the hides to sell. Now you will follow my son from this place to the border."

He turned and walked away without a word of farewell.

The leader shrugged. He didn't like the doctor or whatever

nastiness he'd added to the box of diamonds, but they'd been paid. He was happy to leave Botswana.

Vusi carried the box to their SUV and shoved it against the back seat. Then he waited until the leader's men had loaded the goat skins and wild-animal skins, filling the back section of the vehicle almost to the roof. Their tannic smell covered up the unpleasant one coming from the box. Once all was ready, he walked over to a rusty bakkie and climbed into the cab. It coughed a few times before it started, and then they headed back towards the main road in convoy.

The moon was in the last quarter and wouldn't be up until later. All the leader could see in their headlights was the dust of the bakkie in front of them. Should they be stopped for smuggling the hides across the border, a healthy bribe should see them on their way, but he kept their weapons available in case. He wasn't sure how much faith he had in the doctor's powerful medicine, but he knew none of them would touch the box until they delivered it in Johannesburg.

The roads became farm tracks servicing the fields, and then bush tracks through the acacia scrub. Fortunately, it hadn't rained much that summer or the track would be impassable, even for a four-by-four. After a while, they came to the border fence. There was a service track running along it on the Botswana side, and the vegetation had been cleared for about five metres from the fence on both sides. For the first time, the leader felt exposed, recalling the patrolling helicopters they'd heard from the witch doctor's house during the day. But there was no sound of them now, nor any searching lights.

They followed the border track for some way. Suddenly, the bakkie ahead of them pulled over and swung round to pick up the fence in its headlights. Leaving the lights on, Vusi climbed out and walked up to one of the sections.

From a distance, this section of the fence looked the same as all the others—about two metres high with coiled barbed wire at the top—but close-up one could see that at one point there were two fence posts instead of just one. He unlinked them, and then pulled one section back, opening a gap through the fence below the barbed-wire coil. He signalled to the leader to drive up.

He pointed to tyre tracks heading into the bush. "Go through there. You'll find a track just beyond those bushes. Turn right and head south for about a kilometre. Watch for a track on your left. After that, keep heading east. It will take you to the Lobatla road."

"If there is a fork?" No bush tracks were direct.

"It doesn't matter. They all go to the main road eventually."

The leader nodded. They would probably take a few wrong turns, but they had plenty of time. At least they would be across the border, out of Botswana. He doubted the South African police would be as excited by Debswana's problems as the Botswana police were. He thanked the man, and they drove through the gap in the fence. The doctor's son carefully replaced the loose fence section behind them.

Chapter 42

When Kubu and Samkoa returned to their accommodation an hour after they'd finished dinner, Samkoa's hands were filthy, and Kubu now knew how to change a wheel.

Kubu immediately headed to his bedroom, exhausted from a long day full of new experiences. He collapsed into bed, looking forward to a good night's sleep.

However, his active mind had other ideas, and he tossed and turned with images of armoured vehicles burning and masked people shooting at him. He saw piles of shining diamonds and suitcases falling out of airplanes. At one stage he saw the manager at Sir Seretse Khama airport telling him not to worry because the baggage tags would survive the impact with the ground.

Then he saw the bags hitting the sand in the middle of the Sahara Desert, creating a sandstorm. When the storm settled, all that remained were the tags. The suitcases themselves had been destroyed. And a camel arrived at the scene, and the manager jumped off and picked up the tags. "I'll make sure they get to their destinations," she shouted as she jumped back on the camel and headed back the way she'd come.

Kubu woke with a start.

"I know how they did it," he said out loud. "Very clever indeed."

He picked up the phone and dialled CID headquarters. When the call was answered, he interrupted the very sleepy greeting.

"This is Detective Sergeant Bengu. Please put me through to Detective Sergeant Neo's voice mail."

There was a grunt, and a few clicks later, Kubu was able to leave his message.

"Neo, it's me. Kubu. I know how the suitcases were stolen, but I need one more piece of information to be sure. Please can you contact British Airways and Air France in Joburg and ask them if their records show that some bags didn't make it on the flights in question? That's right—didn't make it. And if so, did any passengers report those bags missing? I'll call you when I have the chance."

After that, he drifted off again, and this time his sleep was undisturbed.

Chapter 43

The robbers moved at a snail's pace following the tracks of another vehicle that had crossed the border illegally for reasons of its own. As the witch doctor's son had promised, very soon they came to a track.

Although he had no reason to be, the leader was uncomfortable. Everything had gone smoothly, exactly as they'd planned. Except what they were doing now. Creeping back into South Africa with the diamonds had not been part of the plan.

He told the driver to stop, and the vehicle came to a halt. The leader climbed out and stood alone, listening. The only sounds were those of the nightjars and the cicadas. He felt there should be something else but couldn't put his finger on it. Something wasn't right, but he didn't know what. He waited a couple of minutes, feeling foolish, then shrugged. He got back into the vehicle and told the driver to go on. But the discomfort remained.

After half a kilometre, they came to a drift across a dry river course. It was quite deep, and the driver had to ease down into it in low-range gear.

Suddenly, they saw flashes and heard the crackling of automatic rifle fire. Two bright lights pinned them from ahead. The windscreen shattered, and the engine cut out. With a yell, the leader ducked down and grabbed an AK-47.

His mind was in turmoil. Who could be shooting at them and why?

The men in the seat behind were firing back at the flashes in the darkness. One managed to take out one of the spotlights.

"Fuck! Get us out of here!" he screamed at the driver. There was no response. The man was slumped over the steering wheel.

"Fuck!" He leant across and opened the driver door. Pushing the man out of the vehicle, he clambered over and tried to restart the engine, keeping his head down. It turned over but wouldn't catch. Something was broken. Another burst of gunfire—behind them this time.

"Fuck, we're surrounded! We've got to get out of here!" He tried the engine again with the same result.

One of his men tried to escape into the bush where at least he'd be less visible. He fired a long burst, then flung open his door, rolled out onto the ground clutching his rifle, and tried to scramble behind some acacia shrubs. Then the spotlight found him, followed by a volley of bullets.

He screamed, and the leader watched his body jerk and contort.

Another burst of gunfire came from behind, and the man behind him screamed.

The leader realised he was on his own. The others were dead. There was no hope of escape. But he still had the money, carefully hidden in the seat padding.

Maybe I can use that to negotiate, he thought.

More bursts of gunfire raked the vehicle from both sides as he cowered.

"All right!" he shouted into the night. "I give up."

He threw out one of the guns so that it landed in the beam of light. The firing stopped.

"Police! Come out with your hands up!" a voice shouted in Setswana.

"All right, brother, I'm coming. Don't shoot. Don't shoot."

Carefully he opened the door and eased himself out, keeping his hands in the air.

The spotlight picked him out. There was a burst of gunfire, and he slumped into the dust of the track.

———

Vusi waited at the fence border crossing and smoked. When he heard the sound of automatic fire in the distance and then, after a few minutes, the silence return, he flicked his cigarette into the sand and climbed back into the driver's seat. With the engine still warm, the bakkie started at once. He made a U-turn and headed back into the bush.

WEDNESDAY
Chapter 44

Director Gobey's request had presented the deputy commissioner with something of a problem. It was a reasonable and, in fact, necessary request to interview Debswana's senior management. They needed to find out if there was any possibility that the backup plan had leaked out of Debswana's head office in Gaborone. However, the matter was sensitive. There could be no suggestion that any of the men who captained Debswana were suspects. The situation needed to be handled carefully and tactfully. The deputy commissioner had addressed the dilemma by passing it on to his superior, the commissioner of police.

That had led to all three of them—Gobey, the deputy commissioner, and the commissioner—meeting at 9:45 the next morning outside Debswana's corporate headquarters. There was no question of demanding that the directors present themselves at the CID; the policemen needed to go to them.

They were welcomed at reception by an attractive, smartly dressed young woman, who showed them into the boardroom. The commissioner's eyebrows lifted when he recognised the man sitting at the head of the table.

"I didn't expect him to be here," he muttered.

The chairman waved them to three vacant seats next to each

other and introduced himself. He was a large white man with a salt-and-pepper beard and penetrating grey eyes.

"Thank you for coming, gentlemen. I'm the chairman of the De Beers group of companies, which, as I'm sure you know, is a fifty percent owner with your government of the Debswana company."

He turned to the commissioner. "Commissioner, I know you, of course. Perhaps you'd introduce the other two."

The commissioner did so, and then the chairman spent a minute or so introducing the men around the table. "Now, perhaps you will fill us in on just where you are with the case, and how close you are to making arrests and recovering our property."

The commissioner cleared his throat. "We can certainly do that. I just want to clarify that the purpose of this meeting is to help us trace who is behind the operation and—"

"You're not suggesting it was one of us?" one of the directors interrupted.

"No, certainly not. I'm suggesting that you may be able to help us, if you're willing to do so."

The chairman raised a hand. "Of course, we'll help in any way we can. I have some suggestions about that. But first, the update."

The commissioner looked put out. "Very well." He nodded to the deputy commissioner, who went through what they'd discovered, deliberately emphasising the importance of the leaking of the backup plan. He hoped they could move on to the questions quickly. This was not the normal way the CID made inquiries.

At the end, the chairman leant back in his seat and stroked his beard. "In summary, Deputy Commissioner, you have deduced the rather obvious fact that this was planned and set up in advance. That somebody who knew about Jwaneng's backup plan engineered a situation that could be used to exploit it. But you have no idea who that could be, nor how the box containing the diamonds was identified, nor where the stones are now. Not a lot of progress, is it?"

"Sir, it has been only two days." It was Gobey who responded. "I think we've discovered a lot in that short time. I realise you're concerned about the loss of the diamonds, but—"

"No, Director Gobey, you are quite wrong," interrupted the chairman. "The retail value of diamonds is around fifteen thousand dollars per carat, so a hundred thousand carats would be worth one and a half billion dollars." Gobey sat back, stunned by the number. "But that's retail for high-quality cut-and-polished stones. We're talking raw stones here. Jwaneng is a rich mine, and seventy percent of its stones are gem quality, but they need sorting, polishing, cutting, and then to be sold by our central selling organisation. That's a lot of value-add." The chairman shrugged. "I wouldn't value the raw carats at more than, say, a hundred dollars a carat."

That was ten million dollars and still sounded like a lot of money to Gobey, but the chairman hadn't finished. "So, from a financial point of view, this theft isn't very significant to us at all. There will be a hiccup in our production this month, but we'll use stockpiled diamonds to make up the difference. After a few months, it will all have smoothed out. There'll be no significant impact on our bottom line." He paused. "But that's not the point. If these men get away with this, Botswana—"

"They won't get away with it," the commissioner interjected. "We will bring them all to swift justice."

The chairman held up his hand, clearly unimpressed. "Please hear me out. I said 'if.' This is a reputational risk for us, Commissioner. Others will try the same thing. Botswana's reputation as a safe country will suffer." He was now addressing his comments to the commissioner with an unwavering stare. "*Your* reputation will suffer. Do I make myself quite clear?"

The deputy commissioner had had enough. "Gentlemen, we all want the same thing. I assure you that catching the culprits is the top priority of the Botswana police. But we need your full cooperation. I trust we can rely on that?"

No one around the table spoke. They were all looking at the chairman. "Of course," he said after a moment.

"Good. Then I'll ask Director Gobey to proceed."

Gobey leant forward. "The key to this plot is the backup plan. We need to find out who knew about it and whether that knowledge could have escaped from this room."

"Wouldn't it be better to ask the people at the mine? Or the security company?" one of the directors chipped in. "Instead of wasting our time?"

Gobey nodded. "We have. We're following up every possibility. I'm sure you agree that we need to do that." He glanced at his notes and turned to the man who'd interrupted him.

"Mr. Delaney, were you aware of the Jwaneng backup plan?"

Delaney nodded.

"The details of it?"

"Yes. I'm a member of Debswana Exco, and it was discussed there."

"Were there any documents about it in your possession before or after the meeting?"

The man shook his head. "Debswana is very strict on security. Minutes are not distributed. There are central records that can be consulted by the directors if they need to."

Gobey hesitated. "Is it possible that you mentioned it to someone? Your secretary, perhaps? Or your wife?"

"Are you suggesting I leaked strictly confidential company information? That's outrageous!"

This time there was no hesitation on Gobey's part. "I'm not suggesting anything. I'm doing my job, and right now, my job is investigating a triple murder."

The deputy commissioner gave a small smile. He was glad that these men were being reminded that there was more at stake here than their batch of raw diamonds, which they didn't even care much about. Lives had been lost.

"Please just answer the director's question, John," the chairman chided. "Time is moving on."

For the next half hour, Gobey asked each of the directors whether they'd known about the plan and its details, and whether there was any possible way that information could have leaked from them to anyone else. After the initial exchange, the men around the table answered without argument.

At last, Gobey had worked his way around the table. He turned to the chairman.

"Yes, Director Gobey," he said before Gobey asked, "I knew about the plan. I wasn't convinced it was a good one, but I like our people to make their own decisions. And no, I told no one about it, nor did I discuss it with colleagues other than the ones in this room." He paused. "Well, I hope that was useful to you."

His tone made it clear that he thought the exercise had been a waste of time. The deputy commissioner tended to agree. They'd learnt nothing, and if anyone present did know something or had leaked the plan, he'd lied about it.

There was a knock on the door, and the young lady from reception walked in and addressed the chairman. "Excuse me, sir, the deputy commissioner's office phoned. They want him to contact them. They said it was very urgent."

Chapter 45

Neo puzzled over Kubu's voice message. *Kubu really is strange,* he thought. *But he's not stupid.* He'd been right about the airlines suspecting foul play because of the number of pieces of luggage that had gone missing from a single starting airport—in this case, Seretse Khama airport in Gaborone.

But now it seemed Kubu wanted to know about suitcases that had *not* gone missing. Neo shook his head. But unable to think of any reason not to do as Kubu requested, he phoned British Airways and was soon talking to the agent he'd spoken to before. The man was clearly getting a little tired of the issue.

"So now you want to know if any suitcases missed the flight but then actually didn't miss the flight?"

"Umm, yes. At least the computer would say they missed the flight, but the passengers didn't report them missing."

"Detective, is this supposed to be a joke? Our computers are one hundred percent reliable. All bags are scanned going onto the aircraft. It's imperative for security. And I've never heard of a passenger forgetting to report that he'd lost his bag!"

Neo squirmed, but then had an idea. "But what if a passenger picked up the wrong bag and took it home? And it was his bag that had actually gone missing? Then the wrong bag would be reported lost, wouldn't it?" He held his breath.

"Wait."

The minutes ticked by, and Neo wondered if he'd been cut off. Perhaps the man had lost patience altogether. But then at last the agent came back on the line, and his tone had changed.

"I checked the flight record. There were seven bags that missed that flight from Johannesburg according to the computer record. But they were never reported lost, and no one's said they took the wrong bag. But of course, seven bags were reported lost although they *had* apparently made the flight. How did you know about this?"

"Oh, we've been thinking it through and making connections. That's what detectives do, you know." Before the man could ask any more questions, Neo thanked him and hung up.

He was feeling much more confident as he phoned Air France. But he still had no idea what Kubu was driving at.

Chapter 46

When the deputy commissioner returned to the Debswana meeting, he looked around the table.

"I have news. I've received important information you should all hear. The South African police contacted us half an hour ago. Last night, they attempted to stop an SUV crossing illegally into South Africa through the border fence. The men in the vehicle opened fire on them with automatic weapons, and the shooting continued until all the occupants of the vehicle were dead.

"The SA police then discovered that the back of the vehicle was packed with animal hides. They remembered our alert and realised that the vehicle matched the description we'd supplied. Also, its number plate was consistent with what one of our men remembered. So, they pulled the skins out and found a box underneath. They believe it's the raw diamonds, but the box was still locked so they didn't try to open it. We'll go over there to investigate right away. But it looks promising that the robbers have paid for their crimes and that your property has been recovered."

The chairman's face broke into a smile. "That's absolutely excellent news, Deputy Commissioner! I'm delighted."

The deputy commissioner held up a hand. "Of course, even if this is correct, we still need to find out how they got the information about the backup plan and so on. We must get to the bottom of this. No one must slip through the cracks."

The chairman nodded.

The commissioner rose to his feet. "Gentlemen, please excuse us. We need to get to work on all this right away. Thank you for your time." He took a moment to shake hands with the chairman, and then he left the meeting room, followed by the other two.

As they walked, Gobey commented, "Pity all the robbers were killed. I'd have liked to get my hands on them."

The deputy commissioner sympathised, but he was already thinking ahead. "We'll head straight out there with an armoured car, complete the formalities, and bring the box back to Debswana. They can open it and check the diamonds, and then the pressure is off. We can take our time to track down exactly what happened, and who was behind this." The commissioner nodded, smiling.

The deputy commissioner was smiling too. All three of them would come out of this well, even if it had been the South Africans who'd killed the robbers. Promotions might well be a possibility. He knew the commissioner was eying a job in the government. And that would leave his job available.

He headed back to his office in high spirits.

Chapter 47

It fell to Director Gobey to lead the team to bring back the diamonds from South Africa. While he arranged the vehicles and uniformed police to escort himself and Sergeant Neo, the deputy commissioner smoothed out the legal niceties with Pretoria.

Gobey planned to leave as soon as everything was in place and head south to Zeerust, about an hour and a half away. It was police from Motswedi, a small rural town well off the beaten track and not far from the border, who had stopped the SUV and killed the robbers. However, the diamonds and the SUV had been taken from there to the much larger and more secure facility in Zeerust.

It took quite a while to complete the formalities and to receive the necessary faxed authorisations. Gobey used the time to leave instructions for Mabaku and Dow to continue their investigations through the afternoon, then to return to Gaborone that evening. He expected everyone to attend a meeting at eight the following morning. Recovering the diamonds and the death of the robbers was good, but there was still much more to be done.

Finally, the deputy commissioner sent the required authorisations to the CID, and they could get underway. Sergeant Neo drove one of the police cars with Gobey in front and two constables in the back. A driver with two more constables followed in an armoured personnel carrier borrowed from the defence force.

After negotiating the traffic in Tlokwane, delays at the border, and the unfenced roads through the villages of northwestern South Africa, they arrived at the Zeerust police station at three in the afternoon. Gobey looked at the rather ordinary building—a typical small-town police station—and wondered what Motswedi was like if this was the larger and more secure facility.

Gobey and Neo were taken to Colonel Piet Venter, an Afrikaner policeman who had built a career in the ultraconservative rural towns of the old Transvaal.

"Good afternoon, my friends. Sit, sit," he said in heavily accented English. "Can I get you a coffee, perhaps, or a tea?"

"Thank you, Colonel," Gobey replied. "But we need to get back as soon as possible. We've brought all the paperwork." He passed the file across to Venter.

Venter nodded, opened the file, and started reading the faxed documents carefully.

"Ja, this is just for the box, Director Gobey. We think these skelms are all South African, and it turns out the SUV was stolen in Johannesburg a few weeks ago. So, we'll keep the bodies and the SUV—what's left of it—but you will be informed of everything we find, and we'll get you fingerprints and so on as soon as possible. That okay?"

Gobey nodded. "But the SUV has Botswana number plates."

Venter laughed. "Ja, but they're fake. Dead easy to buy them."

He started to read again, but then suddenly lifted his head. "It's a bit of a strange story, you know. Of course, we alerted all the police stations around here when we got your APB. But that wasn't why the Motswedi guys were out on patrol last night. They said they were looking for smugglers. Smuggling what, hey?" He shook his head. "You sure you won't have that coffee? It's Nescafé."

Gobey was intrigued. He wondered where the colonel's story was heading. He changed his mind and accepted the coffee.

Venter stood up and went to the door. "Paulina!" he shouted. "Koffee vir die mense asseblief. Maar gou-gou!"

When he returned, Gobey had a question. "I thought they were smuggling animal skins?"

Venter nodded. "Ja, but what for? We have lots of animal skins this side. Why take the risk?"

"But it was just a cover."

"Ja, I know that, my friend. But why were our guys looking for smugglers in the first place, hey?"

"Did you ask them?"

Venter shrugged. "They said there were rumours. Where did those come from?"

Gobey had no answer for that. In due course, Paulina brought their cups of coffee, which he and Neo sipped while Venter continued to plough through the documents.

At last Venter closed the file and climbed to his feet. "Well, it's all in order. Let's get it done then, hey?"

With a sigh of relief, Gobey gulped down the rest of his coffee and stood up. Neo followed his example.

"Please follow me."

The colonel led them back to reception and into a side corridor. At the end was a heavy, steel strong-room door. He fiddled with a bunch of keys until he found the right one and pulled the door open. They were accosted by an unpleasant smell as they went in, and Gobey wondered what was causing it.

They found themselves in a small room with weapons in racks around the walls and a large table in the middle containing an assortment of presumably valuable or sensitive items. Among them was a metal box that Gobey immediately realised was the Debswana diamond transport box.

"It was wrapped up in sacking when it got here," Venter informed them. "Jislaaik, but my men got a fright when they unwrapped it." He gave a snort of laughter. "Come, take a look." He led the two men around to the other side of the box and pointed.

Gobey stepped back so suddenly that he bumped into Neo and nearly fell. Neo immediately headed for the door but managed to stop himself when he got there. Venter watched their reactions with a sardonic smile.

He steadied Gobey by his arm. "Careful, my friend. You'll fall over something."

Chapter 48

Across the front of the box between the two locks was what looked like the mummy of a small animal. The skull was exposed, and rodent teeth were bared outwards. Perhaps it had once been a bat, because where one might expect paws or legs, there were what appeared to be papery wings wrapped around the body. A separate skeletal claw grasped each padlock. It was obvious what it was: a fetish, something placed as a warning—or worse—by a witch doctor.

Gobey pulled himself together. "Neo, take it out to the armoured vehicle."

Neo didn't respond. It was clear that he wasn't coming any closer.

Venter grabbed one end of the box. "Here, I'll give you a hand. You take the other end." He started to lift the box. "Don't worry. We fingerprinted it, but it was wiped as clean as a pure conscience. Not that you find many of those around here." He chuckled, then added, "Not even a partial."

"They won't take it," Neo murmured. "The men. They won't go in the vehicle with it if they see that."

Gobey realised he was right. "Do you still have the sacking, Colonel?"

Venter looked doubtful. "I'll see what I can find."

He went out, leaving Neo just inside the door and Gobey trying to stare down his fear. When Venter returned, it was with a worn blanket. He carefully wrapped the box and then again invited Gobey to carry it with him.

They lifted it together, but it wasn't particularly heavy. However, when they got outside the station, one look at the constables was enough to tell Gobey that they'd heard all about the box—probably they'd been talking to some of the local policemen. They backed away, and Gobey feared he might have a mutiny on his hands.

He turned to Neo. "Open the boot of our vehicle. We'll take it."

Neo didn't look happy but did as instructed. They lowered the box into the boot, and Gobey slammed it shut.

Venter passed Gobey a clipboard with more forms. "I need you to sign these." Gobey signed in several places and turned to go, but Venter hadn't finished. "Come take a look at the SUV before you go."

Gobey hesitated, keen to get going.

"It's just over there. It won't take a minute."

Gobey walked with him across the yard to a fenced enclosure. It was obvious which vehicle was the robbers' SUV. It looked as though it'd been in a war. Bullet holes peppered the body, and the tyres were down to the rims. All the windows were shattered. He looked through the empty windscreen. There was dried blood on the steering wheel and all over the back seat. The front seats were shredded.

He pointed at the seat. "What did that?"

The colonel smiled. "Interesting, hey? That's not bullets. Someone used a knife, I'll bet."

"Looking for something in the seats…"

"Maybe finding something, hey? They didn't tear up the back seats."

Gobey nodded. "Thank you, Colonel."

"It's my pleasure, my friend. Let's get back to your vehicles before all your men run away."

Gobey smiled weakly, and they shook hands.

A few minutes later, Neo and Gobey set off, with the armoured vehicle following close behind.

Gobey hoped that they wouldn't be stopped at the border and made to unwrap the box. He couldn't imagine what the customs officials would do. He took a deep breath. He couldn't wait to get the box, the diamonds, and most of all the fetish, off his hands.

Chapter 49

In the end, the trip was uneventful, and they reached the Debswana sorting plant just after 5:00 p.m. The deputy commissioner met them in the secure loading bay, and he introduced the head of the plant.

"I've explained that the box and the diamonds are evidence, part of our case against the robbers and whoever was working with them. However, we've agreed that they can keep the gemstones here for the moment. Probably safer anyway. But we keep the box and everything else."

"The witch doctor put something on the locks. It's...very unpleasant," Gobey informed him.

"Really? Bring it inside, Neo. Let's take a look."

Neo swallowed hard and walked up to the boot but didn't touch the box.

The deputy commissioner looked surprised, and then frowned.

"I'll do it," Gobey said and lifted it out. Then they followed the head of the plant into the building.

He dumped the box on a table and unwrapped the blanket.

None of the men said anything for a few moments. Then the deputy commissioner told Neo to fetch the evidence kit.

When Neo returned, the deputy commissioner used forceps

to detach each claw and drop them into evidence bags. Finally, he dislodged the fetish itself and bagged it. The others watched him in silence as he sealed the bags.

He handed the Debswana man a pair of latex gloves. "Touch the locks and the front of the box as little as possible. I doubt our South African friends tested for fingerprints there. You can unlock the box now. Try to hold the padlocks only by the sharp corners."

The man took out the envelope with the six keys and started trying them in the locks. He tried five keys before he found the right one for the first lock. He gave a sigh of relief when it sprang open. The deputy commissioner used the forceps to lift it and drop it in a bag.

The man was lucky with the remaining lock. The second key he tried fitted, and the lock sprang open. The deputy commissioner bagged that one too.

Then he took hold of the two hasps by their edges and lifted the lid.

"Oh my God," the Debswana man said.

The detectives looked into the box, dumbfounded.

"It doesn't make any sense," Gobey muttered.

The box was filled with the same worthless gravel as the others.

THURSDAY
Chapter 50

It was a sombre group that assembled the following morning in the conference room at CID headquarters. The news that the diamonds had not been recovered after all had spread like a bushfire on the Savuti plains, leaving everyone without any sense of accomplishment. If anything, however, the bad news made everyone all the more determined to crack the case, and they were all eager to find out what others had discovered. By the time Gobey walked in, every chair was occupied, and a couple of men were standing at the back.

Gobey settled himself at the head of the table and looked around the room. "Good morning, gentlemen. We've been scattered all over the place, so it's time for all of us to be on the same page. You may have heard that those responsible for the theft of the diamonds attempted to shoot their way out of a South African police stakeout the night before last. All were killed, and the diamonds were apparently recovered. Unfortunately, when we returned the box of diamonds to Debswana yesterday afternoon, we discovered that the box contained only gravel, just like the other two boxes."

A murmur rippled around the room.

"Not only that, but there was a fetish of some sort clinging to the locks. That caused consternation among everyone who saw it. Even some of our own men were reluctant to touch the box, so I ended up having to carry it." He glared at Neo. "It goes without saying that Debswana management is very upset by what has happened, and the commissioner is blaming us for losing the diamonds." He shook his head but added no additional comment. Then he poured a glass of water from the jug in front of him and took a long drink.

He's trying hard not to say something rude about the commissioner, Kubu thought. He glanced at Mabaku, who was looking studiously at a sheet of paper in front of him.

Gobey drained the glass and put it back on the table.

"Given all that we've seen and heard," he continued, "I think it's reasonable to make some assumptions. One, someone on the inside, who knew of the backup, gave its details to the robbers. Two, the plan to steal the diamonds must have taken considerable time and coordination to pull together. And three, the burning of the plane on the Jwaneng airport was the first step of the plan. As of yesterday morning, I thought there was a fourth assumption, namely that the sale or transfer of the diamonds was going to be handled in South Africa, probably Johannesburg. However, since there were no diamonds in the box we recovered yesterday, that assumption probably no longer holds."

Mabaku raised his hand. "Actually, Director, I think there was a fifth assumption we made, which has also fallen away. And that is that the box in the hijacked van had the diamonds."

Another murmur went around the room.

"What do you mean? The other two boxes had no diamonds. The diamonds had to have been in the one we recovered in South Africa."

Mabaku shook his head. "I think that's likely, but it's not definite. We'll have to look into the teams in the other two vehicles to be confident they didn't switch the diamonds for rocks en route to Gabs."

Or determine whether the diamonds ever left the mine, Kubu thought.

Gobey took a deep breath and looked around at the men, all listening closely.

"I'm going to ask each group to bring the rest of us up to speed on its progress. I'll start."

For the next few minutes, Gobey outlined what he'd learnt at the Gaborone Cash in Transit facility. "At this point, my position is that it's unlikely that knowledge of the backup plan came from there, even though it is likely that one of the guards in the hijacked van was part of the plot. That was a man called Kenosi, who was found at the side of a road on the evening of the robbery. He'd been shot three times. The head of the company—a Rra Henkel—was confident that the other two guards were not involved. They were both executed at short range with gunshots to the face. One was a woman."

"What about Henkel himself?" someone asked.

"We will be looking into his finances and spending habits, as well as his phone calls and people he associated with. I'd be surprised if he was involved, but, of course, I may be wrong."

He turned to Mabaku. "You went to Jwaneng, Assistant Superintendent. Tell us what you found."

Mabaku cleared his throat. "Three people at the mine knew of the backup plan. The head of the mine, Chamberlain, conceived the plan in the first place and had it approved by the Debswana board. The head of security, Eddie Tau, and head of operations, Elijah Goodman, also knew of it. We'll be looking closely at their backgrounds and lifestyles and so on. If one of them did tip off the robbers, the most likely is Tau, because he was one of two men present when the diamonds were locked into their container and the two decoys prepared. He could have marked the box with the diamonds in some way, so Kenosi would know which it was. One of the guards where the boxes were loaded told us that Kenosi checked the locks on all three boxes before being authorised to touch them. He could have been looking for a hidden mark, but so far we haven't been able to find it."

Inspector Dow raised his hand. "I think we know how he did it."

Gobey nodded for him to continue.

"When forensics examined Kenosi's body, they found what appeared to be a small electronic device of some sort in his shirt pocket. One of the electronics fundis in forensics is looking at it right now, but he told me that he thought it was for a transponder."

"What does that mean?" Mabaku asked.

"Apparently, a transponder responds to a signal by emitting one back. It means that someone could have hidden a small transponder among the diamonds, and Kenosi's device would have guided him to the correct box."

"I didn't know they had batteries that small."

"The guy in forensics said that transponders often don't have a battery. He said they can be energised by the signal they receive." Dow scratched his head. "I've no idea what that means, except that transponders can be very small."

Mabaku nodded as he caught on. "So, one would be virtually impossible to notice in a box of diamonds."

"That's correct."

"That means we need to examine the contents of all three boxes to see if we can find this transponder thing. Just what we need right now."

Chapter 51

Gobey wanted to keep the meeting moving on. "You can examine the boxes later. Now, what about the other guard who helped Tau?"

"Peter Tshane. At first, I thought he could be involved, but after pushing him hard, I changed my mind. But we'll continue to dig into his background."

"Anyone else?"

"It could also be someone in the packing area, like the person who initially filled the box with diamonds. He could have marked the box in a way Kenosi could identify it, such as putting a transponder among the diamonds. We don't think it is one of them, but we need to dig there too."

Gobey continued the meeting by having the other groups report. There was a great deal of interesting information, but little was useful in pointing to who had been behind the robbery.

"We'll have to wait for details from the SA police—fingerprints, IDs, and so on. They said they'd expedite them."

"What about people inside Debswana?" one of the detectives asked.

Gobey glared at him. "I can assure you that no one who knew the plan inside Debswana was involved. I met with them yesterday, and they confirmed that."

That isn't very convincing, Kubu thought.

"There's one other thing I need to mention," Gobey continued. "When I spoke to a Colonel Venter in Zeerust, he hinted that the behaviour of the police who took the robbers out was strange. They're from a small town called Motswedi. He said he could find no reason why they would have set up a stakeout for the four-by-four. They said people in the four-by-four opened fire when ordered to stop. The police retaliated and sprayed it with automatic weapons. I saw the vehicle, or what remains of it. Nobody could have survived such an assault."

The men in the room digested the implications of what Gobey had said.

"Does Venter think that they knew about the diamonds and then stole them?" one of the detectives asked.

"He didn't say, but questioned why they were so heavily armed for what appeared to be a small-time operation bringing hides into South Africa."

Another detective put up his hand. "Maybe they were tipped off about the diamonds."

"Debswana tells me that the locks are the best in the world. They are sure that the Motswedi police couldn't have picked them at all, let alone in the brief time between the shoot-out and when they reported the incident—a mere twenty minutes later."

The men sat in silence, trying to put together the pieces of the puzzle.

"There is one other thing," Gobey said. "The front seats of the four-by-four were slashed open with what Venter thinks was a knife. I saw the seats and agree with him. But the back seats hadn't been touched."

"Sounds to me they had something hidden there," Dow commented. "Maybe the robbers had opened the box somehow and hidden the diamonds in the front seats, hoping if there was any trouble, people would focus on the box. A sort of misdirection."

"Gentlemen, gentlemen," Gobey interrupted. "Our difficult

case became much more difficult yesterday when the third box was full of rocks. We have to solve this case. We must find the diamonds." He looked around. "Anyone got anything else to say?"

Kubu put up his hand. "Sir, we found a package in the back of the pilot's car at Jwaneng airport. It was given to him by an unknown man as he left the airport the night before the plane was sabotaged. I alerted the bomb squad and heard from them early this morning. The package wasn't a bomb as I feared, but a fetish of some sort. So was the one on the box, so perhaps there's a link there. My guess is that the man at the gate was either a witch doctor or working for one. Probably the former because most people here don't want to get close to a witch doctor."

Mabaku laughed. "I would have liked to see their faces when they opened it."

Then Inspector Dow had something to say, and he wasn't laughing. "When we were going over the scene where we found the armoured car, some herd boys came round with their cows. I chatted to them to see if they'd seen or heard anything the day before. They said they hadn't, but they did tell me a man had come to them and told them they had to keep their cows on the road the following afternoon. That was the afternoon of the hijack. They laughed at him and asked what the cows would eat on the road. But he said he was a witch doctor, and it would be very bad luck to let them wander in the veld. He gave them ten pula and said a man would give them more money the next day, and after that they must keep the cattle on the road. They thought he was a man with much power since he had so much money, so they went to a lot of trouble the next day with the cows. Clearly, it was designed to block the road after the robbery. At the time, I thought the man was just pretending to be a witch doctor to scare the boys, but after Detective Sergeant Bengu's story, I think it may have been the same man who went on to Jwaneng and gave the pilot that package. So far, we haven't been able to trace him."

Gobey frowned, and no one said anything. Wherever they looked, a witch doctor seemed to be involved, and no one liked that.

Chapter 52

When the CID meeting eventually adjourned an hour or so later, everyone had a long list of tasks to take care of. It was obvious to Kubu that despite a plethora of facts, they actually had little or no idea of who was responsible for the theft of the diamonds, or if in fact they had actually been stolen on the way to Gaborone.

As the detectives walked out of the conference room, Kubu asked Mabaku if he had time for a short meeting.

Mabaku frowned but told Kubu to come to his office in fifteen minutes.

Kubu decided there was time to catch up on the suitcase mystery with Neo. He stuck his head into Neo's office and asked if he could chat for a few minutes. Neo waved him in.

"I've only got a few minutes before I have to see the assistant superintendent. Have you found out anything about the suitcases?"

Neo opened a file and pulled out a sheet of paper. "Both airlines said this was the first time they'd had an incident like this. A few suitcases here and there, yes, but nothing like this. I also asked about your second question. By the way, what were you doing up at three in the morning?"

"I couldn't sleep. My mind was going hell for leather."

"I didn't understand what you wanted at first. It made no sense to be asking about suitcases that didn't get on the planes, but I asked anyway. The two airlines said that the tag scans in Joburg indicated that a total of fifteen suitcases had missed their flights. But they didn't do anything at the time because they were confident that the bags would show up sometime, either in Joburg or at their destinations. And that's what happened. Nobody reported them missing."

"We've solved the puzzle, Mathew. All we need is one more piece of evidence."

Neo scratched his head, trying to understand what Kubu was alluding to. "I still don't understand. Explain it to me."

"I will as soon as we're certain. We need some more help from the two airlines though. They know you by now, so could you do that?"

"I suppose so."

"Please ask them to contact the passengers whose bags the airlines thought had missed the flights in Joburg. Ask each passenger to check their baggage tags. If the tags are still on their suitcases, have them give the airline the baggage tag numbers."

Neo frowned. "I understand what you're asking me to do, but I've no idea why."

"Don't worry. I'll tell you later. Right now I have to go to my meeting with the assistant superintendent."

———

Kubu knocked on Mabaku's door and went in when he shouted for him to enter.

"Sir ..."

"What is it, Bengu? I hope it's important."

"Sir, I had two thoughts during the meeting, but I didn't feel comfortable saying them in front of everyone."

"Why not?"

"Sir, I'd like to tell you, but please don't shout at me."

"Sit down!"

"Sir, you raised the possibility that one of the other vans had the diamonds and that the security team in the van somehow managed to switch them."

Mabaku nodded, brow furrowed.

"Sir, what if the diamonds never left the mine? What if they weren't in the box when it left the packing plant? What if Tau and Tshane switched the diamonds for gravel before the boxes were taken outside to wait for the vans?"

Mabaku thought for a few moments, then wrote something on a piece of paper. "True, but unlikely. They'd still have to get the diamonds through security. The second thought?"

"Sir, when Director Gobey went through the list of people who knew of the backup plan, he left off one name."

Mabaku put down the paper he was holding but said nothing.

"Sir, I don't want to appear insubordinate, but Director Gobey also knew of the plan."

Mabaku stared at Kubu, who expected one of Mabaku's famous explosions. But Mabaku didn't say anything for what seemed to Kubu to be a very long time.

He's going to fire me, Kubu thought. *Or shout at me. He's just building up steam.*

Eventually Mabaku stood up. "For now, we have to keep this between ourselves, Detective Sergeant. Don't you dare mention it to anyone else." He waved at the door, and Kubu stood up and left.

As he walked back to his office, Kubu realised he was shaking. He didn't know whether Mabaku was pleased or furious.

But I'm sure I'll know in short order, he thought.

Chapter 53

At about the same time, the commissioner of police was having his day spoilt for the second time. The first time had been a disgruntled call from the chairman of Debswana, who'd made it clear that he was very dissatisfied by the outcome of what he referred to as "the so-called diamond recovery." The second was a much more fractious call from Major Chamberlain.

"Commissioner, this whole matter has been shockingly mishandled from beginning to end. I have no confidence whatsoever left in the Botswana CID. How come the South African police were in position to nab the robbers and your people didn't even know it was happening? Then Director Gobey heads off to South Africa and returns to Debswana with great fanfare. And an empty box!"

The commissioner parried. "It wasn't empty. It'd been filled with gravel just like the other boxes." Then he counter-attacked. "And that opens the possibility that the diamonds never even left your mine."

The major broke off his tirade for a moment. "I wasn't told that. Is it the same type of gravel?" He didn't wait for a reply. "I'll ask one of our geologists in Gaborone to check it. Anyway, it changes nothing. Either the South African police stole the gems, or the robbers removed them from the box before they went over the border. The question is, what are you doing to find out?"

"We've only just discovered the diamonds weren't in the box," the commissioner protested.

"It was yesterday evening! Do you mean to say you've done nothing since then?"

"I know Director Gobey's on top of this. He'll get to the bottom of it."

The major paused. "I wouldn't put my money on Gobey, if I were you. Has it occurred to you that *he* had custody of the diamonds between Zeerust and Gaborone?"

"Are you suggesting Director Gobey stole the diamonds? That's outrageous!"

"I'm suggesting it's something *I* would check if I was commissioner of police. But you haven't. And while we're talking about Gobey, there's something else you should know. He was on the committee that approved the backup plan, but he changed what we proposed. Our directors wanted a police escort as well as the security company transport. Gobey vetoed it. Said it was too expensive and that as a private company, we had no right to call on the police for our own security needs. At the time, I thought he was just hostile to us, but now it occurs to me that if we *had* had a police escort, the heist would never have succeeded. He opened the way for this whole mess! Maybe he had his own reasons for doing that."

"Major, you're completely out of line here! You're impugning a senior, respected officer with an impeccable record. Let us do our job, and you stick to yours."

"So you'll ignore what I've told you? I'll certainly raise this with our chairman."

"I didn't say I'd ignore it. Now, I have a police force to run. Good day."

The commissioner hung up and sat fuming. Chamberlain was an officious pain in the neck, and the commissioner would like nothing better than to kick him out of Botswana. But the major's wife was related in some way to the chairman of Debswana, and Debswana was too powerful to be treated that way.

As he cooled down, he realised that the major did have a couple of valid points, even if he'd distorted them. He picked up the phone and asked his PA to reach the deputy commissioner.

Chapter 54

Kubu had hardly made himself comfortable back in his small office when Mabaku strode in. Kubu braced himself.

Mabaku glanced around. "You settled in?" He didn't wait for an answer. "Come on, I want you with me when I interview Mma Kenosi. You can take notes. Keep your ears open." He turned and headed out towards the parking lot. Kubu hastily grabbed his notebook and followed.

As they drove to the woman's house, Mabaku looked worried. "This isn't going to be easy. We have to explore with her whether her husband was in on the robbery. Obviously, she's going to deny it."

Kubu nodded. "He had the transponder thing. And he was the one who called in the false coordinates. He used the code word alert the second time, but not the first."

Mabaku nodded. "Maybe the wife was in on it too, or maybe she noticed something suspicious. At least she may be able to throw some light on his state of mind."

Kubu felt very uncomfortable. The woman had only been told about her husband's death a couple of days before, and now they were going to grill her about his activities. It seemed tasteless, even nasty.

"He's gone, but she has to go on living," Kubu said, suddenly realising what that might be like.

Mabaku glanced at him. He didn't comment, but his slow nod told Kubu that this was something his boss had known for a long time.

They pulled up outside a small house in a good but not expensive area of Gaborone. He sat in the car for a few moments examining the surroundings before he climbed out and motioned Kubu to join him.

"Let me do the talking," he said tersely and headed up the paved walkway to the house with Kubu tagging along behind him. Kubu thought how much he'd love to own a house like this one day, maybe with a small family. He looked at the sand that surrounded it and decided he'd have to plant a succulent garden. Nothing else would grow. But judging by how much of his salary his secondhand car was absorbing, he doubted whether home ownership was in his future.

An elderly lady answered the door and introduced herself as Mma Kenosi's mother. Mabaku explained the purpose of their visit. The woman was not impressed.

"My daughter is not well. Can't this wait at least another day?"

Mabaku made it clear that it could not, and after a moment she shrugged and led them into the lounge.

A woman dressed in black was sitting on a sofa with a half-full cup of tea next to her. Her eyes were red from crying, and she looked as though tears were still very close. Her mother explained who the men were, and the woman nodded and waved them to the armchairs opposite her.

The mother glanced at her cup and picked it up. "I'll make you fresh tea." Turning to the detectives, she asked if they would like anything, her Motswana instinct for hospitality overcoming her annoyance at the intrusion. Mabaku thanked her but declined. Kubu would have liked a cup of tea, with perhaps a biscuit on the side, but didn't say so.

"Mma," Mabaku began, "first we must tell you how sorry we are about your husband's death. It must be very hard for you. I apologise that we must worry you now so soon, but we won't rest until we bring his killers to justice. And for that we need your help."

Mma Kenosi nodded. "I'll help you if I can." Her voice sounded hoarse. *From crying,* Kubu thought.

"Thank you. When was the last time you saw your husband?"

"The day before yesterday. In the morning. We had breakfast, and he left early. He likes the early shifts. But he told me he might be later than usual because they were expecting a busy day."

"Did he say why it was particularly busy?"

"No, just that they were expecting a full day."

Kubu made a note that they must check with the manager if there was any reason for Kenosi to think he would work late before the Jwaneng issue came up.

"Did he tell you he might be very late?"

She shook her head. "I got a message in the afternoon from his work. They were short of men and needed him to go out of Gaborone. They said he wouldn't be home until around seven that evening, but I mustn't worry." She bit her lip. "I heard about the heist on the radio about six, I think, and right after that Rra Henkel phoned. He told me that my husband was on that mission to Jwaneng, but that he wasn't one of the guards who died. He hoped he would be found alive very soon. That's what he said. He hoped. But in my heart, I knew…"

She didn't sob, but tears squeezed out of her eyes and wet her cheeks. She brushed them away with irritation.

At that point the mother bustled in and gave her daughter the new tea. She glared at the detectives. "Go outside for a few minutes and let her recover." She headed to the front door and waited until Mabaku and Kubu had left.

"Shouldn't we come back some other time?" Kubu asked.

Mabaku kicked the dirt. "She'll be fine. Waste of time coming back."

Chapter 55

It was nearly ten minutes before Mma Kenosi's mother summoned them back.

She glared at Mabaku. "Be quick!"

The two policemen returned to the lounge and sat down.

Mabaku cleared his throat. "Mma Kenosi, was there anything unusual about the way your husband behaved at breakfast the day of the heist? Did he seem worried or distracted?"

She took a long time about her answer, looking at her hands rather than Mabaku. When she eventually responded, she didn't look up. "You think he knew what was going to happen."

Mabaku said nothing and waited.

"You think he was involved with the robbers!"

"No, mma. We're trying to establish what happened. We don't think one thing or another. But we need to explore every possibility."

She cleared her throat and looked him in the eye. "No! You think he was involved, don't you?"

"Do *you* think he was involved, mma?"

Kubu expected her to react strongly and vehemently deny it, but he was surprised. She took her time in answering, "No, I don't." Again Mabaku waited, and after a few moments, she added so quietly that they could hardly hear her, "But maybe he knew something. I don't know…"

"Why do you think that? Did he say anything?"

She didn't reply.

"Mma Kenosi, these people murdered your husband," Mabaku said sharply. "They shot him in cold blood in the chest three times. Are these the people you want to protect?"

Kubu flinched.

She started to cry and blew her nose a couple of times, but after a few moments she recovered enough to say, "I think it was something to do with that witch doctor. Why don't you ask him?"

"Witch doctor!" Kubu burst out. "What witch doctor?"

Mabaku frowned but let the question stand.

Mma Kenosi's anger faded. "Someone he knew. I think he was a witch doctor."

Kubu was amazed. Another witch doctor? Or could it be the same one?

The woman looked at the expression on Kubu's face. "You didn't know my husband. He was so ambitious, so keen to get ahead. He wanted to be successful, to be someone people looked up to." She shook her head sadly. "He didn't seem to realise that he already was. He had a family. *We* looked up to him. The kids adored him, and he was so good with them. That's why he liked the early shifts, so he could be home early enough to kick a soccer ball around with them. I truly loved him." For a few moments she choked up and couldn't continue.

"But it wasn't enough for him. He wanted a bigger house, to become a manager and be paid more money, to be respected at work. Recently, he spent extra time there helping with scheduling. He even worked with the maintenance people the last two weeks. He said he needed to understand every aspect of the business. He worked so hard, but…" Again, her voice broke, and she sipped her tea.

Kubu made a note. If Kenosi had been helping the maintenance staff and had access to the schedule, he could have arranged to disable the vehicle's security system as well as make sure that particular vehicle was on standby when they called for additional vehicles for Jwaneng.

"But he wasn't a patient man," Mma Kenosi continued. "A few months ago, he said he'd seen a man who could help him succeed. Make things go his way. He didn't say it was a witch doctor, but who else can do that? I said he must tell the priest, that things like that are nonsense and wrong. He said if it was nonsense I didn't need to worry myself about it. I was angry, but he didn't listen to me. And I know he saw that man again, although he didn't tell me.

"The night before the robbery, he said he needed to see some-one urgently. I was sure it was the witch doctor again and said he shouldn't go. But he ignored me. He said he wouldn't be late. And he wasn't. But when he came home, he looked shocked, like he'd seen a ghost. And he wouldn't talk about it at all." She paused for another sip of tea. "But the next morning he seemed to be okay. Just very quiet over breakfast as we got the kids ready for school."

"You never met this man you think was a witch doctor?"

"Never."

"Do you know anything about him that might help us to trace him?"

"Nothing. I have nothing to do with people like that."

Mabaku climbed to his feet. "Thank you, mma. You've been very helpful. I know it's been hard for you to tell us these things, but it will help us."

"Find the ones who killed my husband, Assistant Superintendent. Just find them and hang them until they're dead." Then she closed her eyes, as if trying to shut them out of her mind.

Chapter 56

As they drove back to CID headquarters, Kubu and Mabaku discussed Kenosi's mysterious contact.

"Another witch doctor!" Kubu was incredulous. "Or could it be the same one who was at Jwaneng? How can anyone take these people seriously?"

Mabaku glanced at him. "Be careful, Bengu. You're letting your prejudice cloud your judgement. It's not important what you or I think about witch doctors. What's important is what Kenosi thought. Don't forget the issue of your bomb at the airport." He gave a wry smile. "The bomb squad was probably much more concerned with the fetish than they would have been about a bomb!"

A car cut in front of him and he hooted, commenting that no one seemed able to drive properly in Gabs anymore.

"And you're missing something else. Mma Kenosi deduced that the man was a witch doctor, but Kenosi didn't tell her that. It could have been someone who promised him a lot of money—maybe said they could go into business together. Give him a start up the ladder, in exchange for some inside work at Gaborone Cash in Transit. It sounds as though Kenosi would have jumped at that, and maybe that's how it started. Maybe by the time it got out of hand, Kenosi was in too deep to get out. Maybe there never was a witch doctor."

Kubu thought about it and then nodded. He'd missed that altogether. He realised that he still had a great deal to learn.

Mabaku glanced at him again. "Well, whoever or whatever he is, it's going to be your job to find him. So, you'd better start thinking about how you're going to do that."

Mabaku's tone was gruff, but he was giving the new detective a very important assignment. Kubu knew he'd better not fail.

Chapter 57

Kubu was beginning to feel overwhelmed. He'd been given the task of following up on several of the people involved in the case—Nari, the airport manager, and Roberts, the pilot, all the guards on the hijacked armoured van, as well as Tshane, and the personnel who had initially packed the diamonds. Not to mention the case of the missing suitcases! Now Mabaku had added the witch doctor, if indeed he existed.

He was thankful that Elias had gathered some of the financial stuff. He wouldn't have known how to go about that or who to speak to. So far nothing suspicious had turned up.

Kubu doodled in his notebook for a few minutes, trying to decide how to proceed. Eventually, he listed the names of the people he was looking into and tore the page out. He was first going to check whether they had any criminal records. He doubted they would have, but he needed to be thorough. However, he didn't know where to find the records.

He stood up and walked down the passage to reception. Elias looked up and scowled.

Kubu smiled back. "Good afternoon, Elias. How are you doing?"

"I'm not doing anything else for you. It took me hours to get the information you asked for."

"And I thank you for that. It was very useful. Now, I just want to know where to find the records department. I need to check up on some things on my to-do list."

"Are you sure you don't want me to do them for you?"

"Quite sure, thank you."

"Go out the front door. It's the second building on the right."

Kubu thanked him and headed out into the heat. He decided to keep a steady pace over the fifty or so metres. If he sped up, he would generate more heat internally. Slowing down would give the sun more time to scorch him. He was sure, though, that whatever he did, he'd arrived soaked.

He found the records department easily enough and tapped on the little bell on the desk inside. A few moments later, a young woman emerged from a back room. Kubu blinked. She was gorgeous.

"How can I help you?" Her smile was warm.

"Um. Er." Kubu was struggling to get his mind back to the task at hand.

"I'm Joy Serome. Pleased to meet you." She stuck out her hand. Kubu hesitated, then shook hands. "I'm...uh."

"Oh, I know who you are." Joy had a twinkle in her eye. "You are Kubu, the new man."

"How did you..."

"Everyone's heard of you. New man. Never been on the beat. Mabaku's hippo. The only person ever to get Elias to do something."

Kubu blushed, speechless.

Joy laughed. Kubu felt his heart constrict.

"What can I do for you?"

Kubu took a deep breath, trying to find his composure.

"Two things, please. Here are some names. Would it be possible to check if they've ever been in trouble?" He pulled the piece of paper, now crumpled, from a pocket and handed it to her. "Also, could you check if there've been any major diamond robberies in Botswana in the past five years? And also in South Africa."

"And I suppose you want it yesterday?"

"As soon as you can, please. We need all the help we can get."

"For the Debswana robbery?"

He nodded.

"I'll see what I can do. Come back in an hour."

"Thank you," he stammered and left.

He didn't notice the heat as he walked back towards the CID building. All he wanted to do was to turn and go back. To see her again. He stopped.

She was probably just making fun of me. If I go back, she'll have a story for all her friends. "That Kubu guy is so fat," *she'd say.* "And he thought I was interested in him!" *And they'd all laugh.*

Kubu continued towards the CID.

"But there *was* a connection," he said out loud. "I didn't dream that up."

He stopped again and glanced back at the records building. It was as though he were attached to a piece of elastic—the farther he moved from records, the stronger the pull back.

Don't be a fool. Wait an hour.

Eventually, he started walking again, and this time he made it back to his office without stopping.

———

It's amazing how long an hour can be, Kubu thought as he waited to head back to records. He tried thinking about the case and about the various people on the list he'd given Joy. He didn't think anything of interest was going to turn up.

He went and made himself a cup of coffee, but the communal biscuit tin was empty.

Probably a sign. She's probably married. Or has a boyfriend.

He admonished himself for not checking to see whether she wore any rings.

I'll check when I go back.

He looked at the clock for about the twentieth time. Still ten minutes to go. He didn't want to arrive early, in case she thought he was being too pushy. But he also didn't want to be late, because she may think he wasn't interested in her.

Then his rational side kicked in. She probably only saw him as another customer. No more. No less. He immediately felt depressed.

He spent the last few minutes before he went back trying to work out what to say. Everything he thought of sounded either weak or pretentious. *Maybe just doing my job is the best thing,* he thought. *Don't show any interest, but work out how to go back soon.*

With two minutes to go before the hour was up, Kubu stood up, took a deep breath, and headed out to the records building.

Chapter 58

Ting! He tapped the little bell on the desk. There was no response. He waited some more, wrestling with his emotions. Maybe she'd forgotten what he'd asked and had gone home. Or she was probably having a good laugh with her friends. Either way, it meant she wasn't interested in him.

He'd never felt this way. His stomach was beginning to ache, and his heart was pounding. And a blanket of despondency was descending over him.

"I'll count to ten," he said to himself. "Then I'll go back to the office."

One! He took a few deep breaths.

And two. He stretched out the pause.

Three. He peered through the window into the area where she worked.

Four. Still nothing.

Five. He took a long time to say it.

And six.

And seven.

And eight.

Nine.

Counting to ten is unrealistic, he thought. *I better start over again. Go to twenty this time.*

One.

Two.

He was beginning to despair.

Three.

Four.

And five.

"Hello, Kubu. Sorry I didn't come when you rang the bell. I was just finishing getting what you wanted."

Kubu's heart nearly stopped.

"I...uh...um...I thought you'd gone home."

She smiled at him. His knees nearly gave in.

What's happening to me? I'm behaving like an idiot.

He took a deep breath.

"Have you had a chance to look..." he stammered.

"Oh, yes. I have it here. Very little, actually. Just one of the people is on our records. Interestingly, for an inside job at a jewellery shop. But he was never charged."

She handed him a folder.

"There have also been a few diamond robberies here and in South Africa, but nothing of the size of this one. You'll have to sign for the folder, then bring it back tomorrow if you're finished with it. If you still need it, phone me, and I'll take care of it here."

Kubu didn't know what to say. He just stood there.

"Are you all right?" Joy asked.

He nodded.

"Please sign here," she said, pointing at a ledger.

He picked up a pen and scribbled his name.

"Thank you," he blurted out and hurried out.

Damn! I forgot to check if she was wearing a wedding band.

———

He made it back to his office without stopping. He was too embarrassed. He was also worried that someone would see him gazing back and know why. Then he'd become the laughingstock of the department.

He shut the door and collapsed in his chair.

What's going on? Some sort of demon has crawled inside me. I'm not myself.

He breathed deeply a few times.

I've got to get to work. Otherwise Mabaku will tear me apart.

He opened the folder. The only information in it was a report from Bright Star Jewellers that an employee, a Mr. P. Tshane, had stolen a diamond ring, but had then returned it. He'd been fired. No charge had been laid and no action taken.

His mind wandered.

I wonder where she lives. I could drive to work tomorrow and offer her a lift home.

He shook his head, trying to refocus on the case. None of the potential suspects had ever run foul of the police, and from what Elias had been able to find out, there were no indications of unusual money transactions by any of them. It wasn't looking promising.

Kubu gazed out of the window.

She's so beautiful. She must be married!

He leant back in his chair. He couldn't believe how he was behaving. He'd always sworn that he wouldn't be swayed by how a woman looked. If he was to be attracted to one, it had to be because of who she was, not what she looked like.

He smiled. He was sure Shakespeare would have something to say about his condition, but he couldn't think of an appropriate quote.

At that moment, Mabaku opened the door and marched in. "What are you smiling about? Is it a smile of satisfaction? That you've solved the case?"

Kubu blushed. "N... no, sir. Just some private thoughts."

"We don't pay you for private thoughts. What have you found?"

"Nothing, sir. Other than a mention of Tshane's brush with the jeweller, no one has any record, not even parking tickets."

"And the witch doctor?"

"I haven't had a chance to follow up on that. It's next on my list."

"Take it seriously. Don't fall into the trap of thinking they're charlatans."

"Yes, sir."

Mabaku turned and marched out.

If I find the witch doctor, maybe he can give me a little help!

Kubu immediately admonished himself. He didn't believe in witch doctors or their stupid spells. It was all traditional rubbish.

He picked up the phone and called the Jwaneng airport, hoping that Nari had plucked up enough courage to return to his office.

"Jwaneng Airport," Kubu heard from the other end.

"Rra Nari?"

"Yes. Who's that?"

"This is Detective Sergeant Bengu. I'm pleased you're back in your office."

"You've no idea how many problems I've had. When the bomb squad arrived, a guy in a space suit went in. About five minutes later, he came out holding the parcel in a huge pair of tongs. They took it out towards the runway. Then they put it on the ground and opened it."

Kubu could imagine Nari shuddering.

"Apparently, there was nothing dangerous in it, because they picked it up and brought it back to the terminal building. I was just about to ask them what was in it, when the spaceman handed it to me. I looked down and nearly died. There was a dead crow in the box. Without a head. I threw the parcel away as far as I could."

"That must have been very frightening. Where's the parcel now?"

"It is still on the apron. I'm too scared to pick it up and get rid of it."

"Okay. Leave it there. I'll ask the Jwaneng police to come and take it to check for fingerprints. Make sure no one else touches it."

"Nobody is that crazy."

"Okay." Kubu got to the point. "Please tell me again what the witch doctor looked like."

"I didn't see him well, but I think he was quite old—maybe fifty or sixty. About my height. That's a metre seventy. He stood up straight."

What was he wearing?"

"A dark suit and a dark hat."

"What did he do when Roberts drove off?"

"He walked in the direction of town."

Kubu thanked Nari and put down the phone. He hadn't learnt anything new.

He leant back in his chair and again his mind wandered.

I wonder if she likes wine.

Chapter 59

When Kubu managed to get his mind off Joy Serome, he thought hard about his assignment to investigate the mysterious witch doctor. The more he thought about how to do that, the more worried he became. His parents were strict Christians, and that was how Kubu had been raised. Anything to do with witchcraft or witch doctors was quite outside his experience. He didn't know where to begin.

However, Wilmon, Kubu's father, was a traditional healer and had come across quite different kinds of healers. Much to his disapproval, many of those men and women went much further than the tools of herbs and prayer. A few even used human body parts in their muti.

Kubu decided his father would be a good place to start with the investigation. There were other benefits too: it would be nice to spend the evening with his parents, and it would be good to take his Land Rover for a drive. His parents hadn't seen it yet, and he was keen to show it off to them.

However, a visit posed a dilemma. Kubu realised he'd have to take something to eat. His parents wouldn't be expecting him, and there was no way to let them know he was coming since they didn't have a telephone. Once he was there, Amantle, his mother, would insist that they had plenty of food for dinner and would share it with him. His mother was frugal and would have made exactly the amount she and her husband required. If Kubu shared with them, they'd all go hungry. Yet if he bought a takeaway for himself, his mother would be hurt, imagining that he was rejecting her cooking.

Eventually he hit on a solution. His parents loved fried fish and chips, which they occasionally enjoyed as a special treat. He would buy two servings and take them with him to share.

———

For most of the trip from Gaborone to Mochudi, Kubu sang lustily. He loved opera and had memorized a number of Mozart and Verdi arias, although he wasn't quite sure he was pronouncing the words correctly. Nor was he certain what they all meant.

As he entered the small town, he stopped singing to concentrate. He'd never driven to his parents' home before and couldn't use the usual shortcuts between houses and through the gardens of his friends' parents that he used when walking from the bus terminus.

As he negotiated the dirt roads, Kubu reflected on how fortunate he was to have Wilmon and Amantle as parents. They were the salt of the earth. Christians in an African way, simultaneously believing in the body and blood of Christ and respecting the ancestors. They were honest and hard-working and demanded the same of their only child. Most important, they were loving, both of each other, as well as of him.

As he pulled up in front of their home, Kubu looked at the small, rectangular house with walls made from a combination of mud and brick, capped with a roof of ubiquitous corrugated iron.

I grew up here, Kubu thought, *in a house that now seems too small to happily accommodate three people, but then was a mansion filled with delights.*

He remembered how proud his parents had been when they were able to install a tap that brought cold water into their kitchen. It was only when he first went to school in Gaborone that he learnt that most people had indoor toilets and electricity.

As Kubu heaved himself out of the Land Rover, he saw his father walk out the front door with a puzzled look on his face. Kubu walked up to him.

"Dumela, rra." He extended his right arm with the left crossed over it as a mark of respect.

Wilmon responded solemnly, "Dumela, David. How are you, my son?"

"I'm well, Father. How are you and Mother?"

"We are also fine, my son." Wilmon's voice was strong but quiet. It was the same proud greeting Kubu heard every time he visited.

Wilmon frowned, and he pointed at the Land Rover. "What's that?"

"It's my new car."

"How can you afford such a thing? It costs a fortune to keep and to run. I am told that petrol is very dear."

"Father, have you forgotten that I'm now a policeman and earn a salary?"

"I know that, but it is more important to save money than to spend it on luxuries. And you know that walking is good for you."

At that moment, Amantle came out of the house. "David. I thought I heard your voice."

"Dumela. How are you?"

"I am well, thank you. Come inside."

Kubu produced the fish and chips and invited his parents to join him for some supper. Amantle eyed the fish, but immediately exclaimed, "Oh, we have plenty of goat stew, do we not, Wilmon? You can share that, David. Keep the fish for your supper tomorrow."

Kubu's mouth watered. "Goat stew! I love that! But we must

have the fish or it will spoil, and I'll have wasted my money." He frowned, then smiled. "I have an idea. Let's have both. We'll have two courses tonight like the fancy restaurants. First the fish, then the stew. It'll be a feast!"

Amantle hesitated, clearly tempted. Wilmon stood by with a small smile. If Amantle didn't see through Kubu's ruse, he certainly did. After a moment, Amantle accepted the fish and took it to warm in a pan over her wood stove, where the stew was already simmering, spreading tempting aromas.

Kubu needed something to take his mind off how hungry it made him. He turned back to his father. "And how are your herbs coming on, Father?"

"Let me show you." Wilmon was visibly pleased to be asked, as Kubu knew he would be.

"Supper will be ready in five minutes," Amantle called after them as the two men walked outside.

They walked to the back of the house, where Wilmon grew a variety of plants and herbs that he used to make potions and salves for various ailments. What had started purely as a hobby had expanded to a small enterprise because of Wilmon's reputation for providing inexpensive but effective treatments. Wilmon pointed out one that alleviated fevers.

"The doctors would give you an expensive medicine instead." He shook his head. "The problem with doctors is that they know nothing about the traditional remedies that our people have used for hundreds of years. I could teach them a thing or two."

Kubu nodded. "You certainly could, Father. And they'd be better doctors for it."

Wilmon gave an approving nod. "Let's go in. We mustn't let your mother's food get cold."

Chapter 60

They settled around the table, and Wilmon said grace, giving special thanks for having their son with them. When he was finished, Amantle dished up the fish, and they tucked in. Kubu would have liked a glass of dry white wine to cut the rather greasy batter, but drinking alcohol at the dinner table would have scandalized his parents, so they drank water as usual.

When the last chip had disappeared from the plate, Amantle asked if the men had had enough to eat and if the goat should be saved for the next day. Kubu assured her that he wasn't full and was soon enjoying the meat, tasty, if tough, in its thick gravy.

Kubu was bursting to tell them about his new life, and he started between mouthfuls. "I can't believe I've only been at the CID for four days. So much has happened! Of course, the big case is the Debswana diamond heist, but I've been working on all sorts of things already. It's all so interesting. It's hard to believe that the government is paying me to do this."

Amantle looked worried. "I hope you will keep away from the tsotsis."

"Mother, I will investigate whatever crime my boss assigns to me. I can't choose."

"But you must be careful. There are some very dangerous people in Botswana these days."

Wilmon shook his head. "I am told that they are from South Africa."

"One strange thing," Kubu continued, "is how the other detectives behave. I don't think they like me because I became a detective straight from university. A few have tried to make it difficult for me, but I ignore that. And some don't seem to like it that I want to work hard."

"Typical government workers!" Wilmon grumbled. "Pay them a fortune, and they do nothing."

Kubu decided not to engage because he knew his father's position would only harden if he did.

To change the subject, and rather to his surprise, he started to tell them about Joy. "I also met a very pleasant young woman. She's not a policeman, of course. She works in the records department. But she was so helpful and got me the information I needed right away…" His voice trailed off, and he looked down at his plate.

Amantle pounced. "You like her? What is her name?"

"Joy Serome."

Amantle thought for a moment. "Serome is not a very common name. There is an old lady of that name who lives near here, but I do not think she has family around here."

Kubu concentrated on chewing a particularly tough chunk of goat.

"But I will ask her. Maybe she has a daughter in Gaborone. It is good to find out about a person's family."

Kubu cringed. What had he done, he wondered. Now Amantle would be asking questions all over Mochudi, and rumours would spread like wildfire. And if she did come across one of Joy's relatives, Joy might find out, and it would be terribly embarrassing.

"No, no, don't worry. She's just someone I met. I don't even know her."

Amantle gave a knowing smile but didn't push the subject. "I will clear up. You can talk to your father. You did come to ask him something, did you not? Or was it just this Serome woman who brought you out here?"

Kubu realised she'd seen right through him, and from his father's quiet smile, he guessed Wilmon had too. He laughed.

"You're right as usual, Mother. But please don't ask about the Seromes. At least not until..." He broke off, unsure of until what.

Amantle just nodded and collected the plates. "I will see if there is some bush tea and make it for you." Wilmon said nothing. He was busy picking goat sinew out of his teeth with a sharpened twig.

Kubu took a deep breath and turned to the subject of witch doctors.

"Father, as you know, the CID is investigating the huge diamond robbery from Debswana's Jwaneng mine."

Wilmon nodded. "I have heard about it on the radio." He was proud of his small transistor radio, which he used sparingly, mainly just for the news, to save the batteries.

"We have reason to believe that a witch doctor is involved, but we're not sure how or why. Assistant Superintendent Mabaku wants me to look into it." He digressed for a few minutes to tell his father about Mabaku and how much he admired him. Wilmon just nodded until Kubu finished.

Then he said, "Why do you think a witch doctor is involved in the diamond robbery?"

"Three things have come up, Father, that make us think that. The first was a gift to a pilot who was going to fly from Jwaneng. An old but well-dressed man gave him a package when he left the airport. It turned out to contain a crow with its head chopped off. The next morning the plane caught fire on the runway, but we're pretty sure it was the result of sabotage. The second thing concerned one of the guards in the armoured vehicle that was transporting the diamonds—a man called Kenosi. His wife said he'd had some contact with a man who promised to help him succeed. Kenosi's wife was convinced the man was a witch doctor, although she never met him. The third thing was when the box that was supposed to contain the diamonds was recovered in South Africa. It was sealed with some sort of fetish."

Wilmon thought for a few moments before he spoke. "And what was the reaction to all this?"

Kubu laughed. "Everyone was terrified! It's hard to believe. The airport manager wouldn't go into his office while the parcel for the pilot was in it. The guard, Kenosi, was probably persuaded to help hijack the vehicle. And the police who recovered the box with the diamonds—the one with the fetish—were too scared to even have it in their vehicle. It's amazing."

Wilmon nodded but didn't smile. "Please tell me exactly what happened."

Kubu did so, and his father listened attentively. At one point, Amantle came in with their tea but left quickly when she caught the drift of Kubu's story.

When Kubu reached the point at which the Debswana staff discovered that the box recovered from South Africa was full of gravel, he stopped and sipped his tea. Wilmon did the same, and Kubu wondered if he was going to comment at all. At last his father put down his cup and sighed.

"My son, you need to understand how these spells actually work." Kubu opened his mouth to interrupt, but his father held up his hand. "You think it is all nonsense, and so it is, but that does not mean that it is harmless or that it does not work. These men claim to produce miracles, but only God can do that. What the devil can do is to make men believe, and if they believe, then the witchcraft has power.

"Think about your pilot on the plane. He was a white man, and he did not believe. It did not occur to him that the fetish had caused the fire. He assumed it was some sort of electrical problem. But those who believed were scared to even touch this material, even though it had nothing to do with them. Similarly, your security guard. He believed that these spells and potions could make him rich and successful, so he was willing to do anything to achieve that. And the fetish that sealed the box? What better way of preventing anyone from opening it? They would believe an awful curse would descend on them. No lock is as safe as that."

Kubu stared at his father. As far he could remember, it was one of the longest speeches Wilmon had ever made. He was not a man of many words, but those he uttered usually were carefully chosen.

"So, you think this witch doctor was using his power to somehow control the robbers?"

Wilmon nodded. "But not the way you are thinking. He was using his reputation and their fear and belief. That is psychology, not magic."

Kubu shook his head. He was beginning to get confused. "So, he has no real power at all?"

"My son, you are not listening to my words. He has great power—because people believe. But that is the limit of his power. Your white pilot had no interest or concern for his spells. He realised that sabotage was the cause of his accident."

"So why would the witch doctor even give him the package? What did it achieve? That's been worrying me."

Wilmon rubbed his chin and didn't respond for what seemed like a long time. "I do not know the answer to that. Perhaps this man truly believes he can control the natural world, that he is the devil's creature. Or maybe he does not really understand..."

Kubu thought about it all for a few seconds. "Father, you've helped me a great deal. But how can I find out more? I need to trace this man. Who might know where to find him?"

Wilmon shrugged. "If he has the power of fear, few will talk about him. The risk is great, even if it exists only in their own minds."

"But surely someone..."

Wilmon rose, consulted a small notebook, and jotted down a name and a number for Kubu. "This man is in Gaborone. He will talk to you if you tell him you are my son. Whether or not he can help you, I do not know."

Shortly after that, Kubu thanked his father for his advice, took his leave of his mother, and started the trip back to the city. Fortunately, at that time of the evening on a weekday, the road was not busy, and he could drive and think at the same time. He felt he had a stronger understanding of what he was up against but still no clear way to take the investigation forward. He was beginning to think that this witch doctor might be a much more difficult adversary than he had supposed.

FRIDAY
Chapter 61

When Mabaku arrived at his desk on Friday morning, he phoned Kubu. "I need to speak to you. Please come to my office."

Kubu was there in about thirty seconds flat.

"Yes, sir?" he asked, concerned that Mabaku was going to reprimand him for not having made progress with finding the witch doctor.

"Sit down. Any progress on finding the witch doctor?"

"No, sir. But one of the few facts we have doesn't make sense. And that is, why the witch doctor would give the pilot a fetish. Most whites aren't bothered by such things. The witch doctor would certainly know that. So why do it?"

"Well, one possibility would be…"

At that moment the phone rang.

"Assistant Superintendent Mabaku." And a few seconds later, "Yes, Director. Of course, I can take the call, sir."

Kubu stood up to leave, but Mabaku waved him back to his chair.

"Colonel Venter, Director Gobey says you have some information for us about what happened in South Africa. May I put you on speakerphone? One of my colleagues, Detective Sergeant Bengu, is with me. He's also working on the case."

After receiving Venter's consent, he pressed the button on his phone. "Go ahead, Colonel."

"Director Gobey probably told you," the heavily accented voice boomed out of the phone, "that I was puzzled why the Motswedi police were out looking for smugglers. And why were they so heavily armed, hey? For gunrunners, maybe, but for okes smuggling animal hides? Nee! It didn't make sense, hey. So, I decided to shake the bushes to see what fell out."

Mabaku indicated to Kubu that he should take notes.

"And you know what fell out, Assistant Superintendent? Vrot fruit! There were some bad apples in the tree, my friend. Very bad apples."

Venter stopped, and Kubu and Mabaku looked at each other, wondering if Venter was expecting a reaction.

But Venter continued. "I went to Motswedi and threatened to take out my sjambok and whip them if they didn't tell me why they went out that night. Have you ever seen someone's back after a sjambokking, Assistant Superintendent? It's not lekker, hey. Anyway, eventually, one of the men told me they'd received a tip. That a Land Cruiser filled with guns and things was coming through a hole in the border fence. And the men were very dangerous and would shoot if the police tried to stop them. And there was money hidden in the front seats. Lots of money. So, when they saw the Cruiser, they tried to stop it, but the okes inside started shooting. At least that's their story. Anyway, then the police opened fire, and the okes in the Cruiser had no chance. The police took the money and brought the box and the guns back to the station. Then they phoned Zeerust and reported what happened. At least, sort of what happened."

Mabaku started to ask a question, but Venter interrupted him. "I'll fax you my report. It has all the information. Then, you can phone with any questions. Okay?"

Mabaku thanked the colonel and promised the Botswana

Police Service would follow up on their side of the border and keep Venter informed. Then he hung up.

"Well, well. This could be a breakthrough. And you've got yourself another job, Detective Sergeant. After we get the report, go down to where they went through the fence and scout around. See if you can pick up anything useful."

"Sir, does Colonel Venter really whip his men to get information?" Kubu asked, appalled that a policeman could act that way.

Mabaku shrugged.

Kubu hesitated, none the wiser. "Sir, there is a problem about going to the fence."

Mabaku frowned. "Yes?"

"Sir, if I have to stay overnight, I don't have enough money to pay for it. I haven't received my first month's pay yet."

"Tell the hotel to send the bill to the CID. We're good for the money. If they won't let you stay, tell them we'll look into all their licences and tax returns and everything else."

"Yes, sir." Kubu stood up and returned to his office.

What a wonderful job I have, he thought as he settled back in his chair. *Always something interesting going on.*

Chapter 62

While he waited for the fax from Colonel Venter, Kubu thought about how to carry out Mabaku's instructions. Several issues that Colonel Venter had mentioned niggled at him. He wasn't sure where Motswedi was, nor whether that was where the robbers had come through from Botswana. The colonel had referred to a hole in the border fence but hadn't told them where it was. Presumably more detail would be in the report. Then there was the issue of the person who'd tipped off the Motswedi police. If he knew the robbers were going to cross the border into South Africa, he might know a lot more about them and their movements.

He needed that report.

In the meantime, he needed to find out where Motswedi actually was, and for that he needed a map of the area of South Africa bordering Botswana. He didn't know where to find one but could guess who would. He almost jumped out of his chair.

However, halfway to the records building, his pace slowed as he started to have second thoughts. Perhaps Joy would think he was an idiot because everyone else knew where to look for maps. Alternatively, she might think the whole thing was just a ploy to see her again, which, of course, he knew it was. He stopped. He should rather ask Elias. Then Elias might suggest the records office, and then he would have a reason to go there.

Get a grip on yourself. You have a reasonable question. At worst, she'll just say she doesn't know. Then you can go back to Elias.

He started walking again and was soon in Joy's office. Tentatively, he rang the bell. After a moment, Joy appeared from the back room, holding a half-eaten muffin.

"Sorry, Detective Sergeant." She held up the muffin. "Breakfast! I got a bit delayed this morning."

Kubu's heart sank—she was being so formal. "Oh, I'm sorry. Shall I…um…shall I come back…er…later?"

Joy shook her head and smiled. "No, no, it's fine. Did you have more questions about those files you took?"

Kubu realised he should have brought them with him to return. "No, thank you, I'm still studying them."

He couldn't think what else to say. Joy waited.

After what seemed forever, he remembered the map. "Actually, I want to ask your advice. I need to see a map—a really good one—of the area of South Africa next to southeastern Botswana." He felt pleased with himself for getting it out sensibly, but Joy looked pensive, and his heart sank.

She's going to ask why I came here instead of—

"I think I may have something," she said and disappeared into the back room. After a couple of minutes, she was back, without the muffin, but carrying a rolled-up map, which she spread on the desk. As soon as she unrolled it, it coiled up again, so the two of them had to hold the corners down. It was a detailed topographic map of southeastern Botswana, but it also included the bordering region of South Africa.

"There it is." Kubu pointed out Motswedi. The free corner of the map immediately rolled up, and Joy laughed.

"You hang onto it, and I'll get some books to hold the corners down."

A few minutes later, Kubu was studying the layout. The road

the robbers had probably taken from the Sejelo roadblock led to Otse, and from there it wasn't far to the border. Motswedi was nearby on the South African side. It all made sense.

"Can I borrow this?"

"I'm not supposed to…but I'm sure it will be safe with you, Detective Sergeant."

"Oh, call me Kubu. Everyone does," Kubu blurted. He was simply so used to telling everyone that, he didn't think twice. He expected her to laugh at him, but she just smiled.

"Okay, Kubu. Please bring it back as soon as you're finished with it."

Kubu thanked her and beat a hasty retreat, clutching the map.

Chapter 63

On the way back to his office, he looked in on Miriam and discovered that the fax had arrived.

She'd used a guillotine to cut the glossy roll into separate pages that she'd stapled together. It was quite a thick wad.

She handed him the document. "I tried to call a couple of times. The director said I should give it to Assistant Superintendent Mabaku. He said I should give it to you, but you're to leave it with me as soon as you've finished reading it."

Kubu nodded, thanked her for her trouble, and moved towards the door.

"Oh, Kubu," she called him back. "Assistant Superintendent Mabaku left this for you also. He said you'd probably need it." She held out a sealed envelope.

Kubu thanked her again and made his way back to his office. He was keen to get into the report, so he set the envelope aside and turned to the fax.

The first part concerned what the South African police had found out about the dead robbers. They were all South Africans who had been members of uMkhonto weSizwe, the armed wing of the African National Congress. Venter noted that there were several cases of jobless freedom fighters turning to crime. "Won the war but lost themselves," as he put it. Two of the men already had records, one for assault and one for burglary, but nothing really serious.

Kubu was more interested in what Venter had discovered at Motswedi. One could criticise his methods, but Venter had recovered a lot of money in South African rands and a couple of automatic weapons that hadn't been turned in after the ambush. He also gave detailed directions to the spot in the border fence where the robbers had crossed. Apparently it was a hidden makeshift gate in the fence where smugglers could come and go. The colonel had secured it again but pointed out that anyone with a pair of wire cutters could get through almost anywhere.

Kubu worked out roughly where the gate had been, using his map. Again, it seemed to fit with a direct route from Sejelo into South Africa.

There's one thing that doesn't quite fit, he thought. *The robbers went through the border the night after the robbery. Probably they'd spent the night of the robbery somewhere around Otse, then crossed the next night. And I'll bet that was when they emptied the box of its cargo of diamonds.*

Suddenly he felt excited. Mabaku had handed him a plum assignment. If he could pull it off, he might even break the case. As soon as he'd finished a careful study of the report, he asked the switchboard to connect him to the number given at the top of the fax, and soon he had Colonel Venter on the line. He explained who he was, and Venter repeated that he was happy to answer any questions. Kubu asked about a few unclear points in the report, and then came to the issue that most concerned him.

"Colonel, you mention that the Motswedi police acted on a tip from a reliable source. Could you tell me who that was and how to contact him? I think he may know some key facts about the robbers."

"Nee, jong," Venter responded. "It's not so easy. The Motswedi lot trust this man, and he's given them some good tips before, but all he'd say to me was that it came from one of your people, a man in Botswana. I said I wanted to know who that was, but he was shit-scared. I told him the sjambok would get it out of him fast, but no dice, hey. Man, he was more scared of this Botswana kêrel than he was of me." From the tone of his voice, he took that as a personal insult. "And now the fokker has disappeared altogether."

Kubu's heart sank. He'd been sure that the informant would be the link to the diamonds.

"Do you think it might be the local chief or some powerful person in Otse? He might be scared of someone like that."

Venter thought for a moment. "He'd be more scared of me than someone like that! But remember that thing tied on the diamond box? My guess is it's the witch doctor thing. That's what he's so piss-scared of."

They talked for a short while longer, but Kubu realised Venter was almost certainly right. He thanked the colonel and then disconnected. He'd come full circle back to the witch doctor. With a sigh, he reached for Mabaku's envelope and opened it. Inside was a set of photographs. Several were of the contents of the package that had been given to the pilot, and several more were of the fetish from the diamond transport box.

———

After he'd returned Venter's report to Miriam and digested his conversation with the SAPS colonel, Kubu realised that he needed to know more about witch doctors, and that reminded him of the name his father had given him the night before. He dug out the slip of paper. There was a single name, Katlego, so he assumed it was a surname. Below it was a telephone number. He called it, and when it was answered, he went into his official routine. "Rra Katlego? This is Detective Sergeant David Bengu." As usual, he enjoyed the ring of that statement. "I'm making enquiries about a certain witch doctor, and—" He broke off, realising that the line was dead. The person on the other end had hung up.

After a moment's thought, he decided that his approach had been too officious. He redialled the number and tried again.

"Rra Katlego, this is David Bengu again. I'm Wilmon Bengu's son. He gave me your number and said you might be willing to help me with a problem. It is a police matter, but I'm really asking personally for your help and advice if you'd be kind enough to spare me a little time."

There was a long silence, but at least the line remained open. Finally, he heard a deep voice. "I am Katlego. Meet me in an hour at Africa Mall." There was a click, and the line went dead.

Kubu put down the phone. *Katlego* meant success, and Kubu wondered if it was the man's real name or one chosen to give his clients confidence. And how were they to meet at Africa Mall? Africa Mall was a sprawl of shops in the centre of Gaborone. How would he find the right man?

"Well," he said aloud, "maybe I must just hope that he has the power to find me." He meant it flippantly, but the idea gave him a most uncomfortable feeling.

Chapter 64

An hour later, he arrived at Africa Mall. With no address to go to, he stood in the main walking street surrounded by small stalls selling colourful tourist mementoes or brightly patterned fabric. There were hawkers galore, pushing their faces into those of potential buyers. "Best price in town. Good quality! Buy three, get one free."

Kubu growled at anyone who came too close and waited for something to happen. After a few minutes, a tall, smartly dressed man approached him and looked him over.

"So, you're Wilmon Bengu's son. Okay, you can buy me a coffee. That café over there will do."

Is this a witch doctor? Kubu wondered. Somehow, he'd expected an old man dressed in animal skins, not a fit-looking businessman. From the look of the man's clothes, Kubu realised he was getting off cheaply if all he had to pay for was a coffee—assuming the man's advice was any good.

They settled themselves at an outdoor table. Kubu would have preferred somewhere more private, both to ask his questions and because he wondered what people who knew him would think if they saw him talking to a witch doctor. Suppose Joy came past, for example? However, it was midmorning, and his colleagues would be at work. He relaxed a bit, and Katlego smiled as though he knew the reason for Kubu's discomfort.

"Your father is well?" Katlego asked, after he'd ordered his coffee.

Kubu nodded. "Very well, thank you, rra. He sends his regards."

"And your mother?"

"She is also well."

"Good. Now what is this about?"

Kubu explained the situation with the witch doctor and his fetishes, at least to the extent he felt was appropriate. Katlego asked no questions until Kubu had finished.

"Show me the pictures."

Kubu gave a start, recalling that he had indeed brought Mabaku's envelope with him. He slid out the photographs and passed them to Katlego. He studied them carefully for a few minutes while he drank his coffee, sometimes flipping back to a previous one.

Eventually, he finished his coffee and passed the photographs back to Kubu.

"These are Zulu fetishes. The first one is some sort of threat spirit. The second is a guardian. That makes sense with the box it was protecting." He paused. "Avoid touching either of them." It was said as a matter of fact, and Kubu felt a chill.

"Did you say they were Zulu? How do you know? Why a Zulu fetish here in Botswana?"

"Yes, I said so, and I do know. As for why Zulu fetishes here, I can't say." He shrugged. "Maybe your witch doctor needs others to help him with his spells."

"Would that be usual? To get help?"

Katlego shook his head. "Of course not. That's a silly question. How can a spell be potent if the person who weaves it does not cast it?"

Kubu leant forward, interested. "Would people know the difference? I mean other than experts such as yourself."

"Probably not."

"So maybe this man isn't a real witch doctor at all. Maybe he just uses this as a…a sort of disguise."

Katlego looked at him for several moments. "I see you aren't stupid. Good. But let me tell you this. A disguise is clothes, or a false beard, stuff like that." He waved at the envelope. "If you hide behind this sort of stuff, you will pay for it in the end and not with money."

He rose to his feet.

"Good luck to you, David Bengu. If you want help again, it will cost you much more than a coffee. Give my regards to your father when you see him next." He turned and walked off down the street.

Kubu paid for the coffee and headed in the opposite direction back to the CID. He needed to look at the faxed report again. He wanted to check the tribal origins of the dead robbers.

———

When he returned to the CID, Kubu felt an idea playing around the edge of his mind, but he couldn't quite pin it down. He spread the pictures of the fetishes on his desk and looked at them for a few moments, but it didn't help. The idea wouldn't crystallise.

Eventually he grabbed his phone. "Mathew? Have you got a few minutes? I need your help."

"Now? I've got work to do. I'm following up the backgrounds of the Gaborone Cash in Transit guards."

"It won't take long."

Neo sighed. "Okay. What I'm doing isn't going anywhere anyway."

A few minutes later he walked in but stopped when he saw the pictures. Kubu waved him to a seat and explained what he'd discovered. Neo listened but looked more and more puzzled.

"You're saying these aren't from a Tswana witch doctor?"

Kubu nodded. "And maybe he doesn't know much about the witch doctor business at all. Why did he give this to the pilot?" He indicated the picture of the decapitated crow.

Neo suppressed a shudder. "So, maybe this man is from South Africa and maybe he's not a witch doctor at all. So what?"

Kubu said nothing for a few moments. "So maybe we're looking for the wrong person. We're looking for a witch doctor involved with the robbery. Maybe we should be looking for a robber playing the role of a witch doctor. A South African witch doctor. Maybe..."

He climbed to his feet. "I need to ask Elias something. Thanks, Mathew. You've been a big help!"

Neo shook his head and went back to his office, muttering that the longer he knew Kubu, the stranger he became.

Kubu walked to reception and asked Elias for the file of old APBs. He flipped through them until he came to the one for Vusi Tuelo. He read it again carefully and stared at the pinched face that looked up at him from the sheet.

The idea he couldn't pin down suddenly came into focus.

Chapter 65

The drive south to Otse was hot, and Kubu was uncomfortable. He had all the windows open—the police Land Rover didn't run to air-conditioning—and he often took gulps from a bottle of water he'd brought with him. But his mind wasn't on the heat.

In the first place, it was hard to keep his mind off Joy. If he was to get to know her, he'd have to ask her on a date. The thought terrified him. He was sure she would turn him down, but suppose she accepted? That was almost worse. He'd never been on a date and had no idea how to handle such a thing. Perhaps they could go to a movie, he thought. Then they wouldn't need to talk much, and he wouldn't make an idiot of himself. But if they didn't talk, how would they get to know one another? Anyway, how would he know what movie to choose? He didn't know what sort of thing she liked. No, he would ask her out to dinner. But then another problem arose. He didn't want to take her for a hamburger at Wimpy, but rather somewhere classy like the Gaborone Sun. However, that was out of the question until he received his first pay cheque.

With relief, he deferred the whole issue until the end of the month and focussed on the witch doctor instead. Colonel Venter had had no idea of the tribal connections of the robbers and had been uninterested in the background of the fetishes, believing it was all nonsense. Kubu thought so too, but the discussion with his father and his meeting with Katlego had changed his view of its significance.

The best strategy seemed to be to start with the local police in Otse and see whether they had any suggestions. He also needed to find the spot where the robbers had crossed the border. Perhaps he'd pick up clues there.

His stomach reminded him it was lunchtime, and as he reached the outskirts of Otse, he spotted a cheap-looking guesthouse with a few Formica tables lining the side of the road.

He left half an hour later after an acceptable lunch, with a reservation to stay overnight. Fortunately, he'd managed to persuade the owner to put it all on account and to send the bill to the CID. Also, he'd learnt that the local police station consisted of a one-room office with a single policeman—a Constable Murewa from Ramotswa police station, but based in Otse.

Kubu followed the owner's directions to a small house in the town and introduced himself to the constable. He explained why the CID was interested in a witch doctor and why he suspected the man might be somewhere around Otse.

The constable hesitated. "There are a couple of witch doctors in town, but they've been here for a long time. People respect them, and they don't seem to do any harm. I steer clear of them myself." He paused. "There is one other thing…"

"What's that?"

"Probably nothing. There was a woman who came in here with a story of a witch doctor in a house out by Manyelanong Hill. She said her goats stopped giving milk, and she was sure it was this man's fault."

"Did you investigate?"

The constable shook his head. "Sometimes people make up these stories to get even with someone they don't like. It was hot and dry. Sometimes goats don't give milk." He shrugged.

Kubu fetched his map and spread it out on a table.

"Can you show me where this witch doctor was supposed to be?"

The constable had a reasonable idea of where the woman lived, and thus where the man the woman had complained about would likely be. Before Kubu could stop him, he marked it clearly on the map. Kubu wondered how he would explain that to Joy. It gave him a sinking feeling. The constable also had a couple of tips for getting to the border road, but Kubu wasn't concentrating.

"You know the local pubs and guesthouses," he interrupted. "Will you please check with them if they hosted four men on Monday evening, probably foreign and driving a white Toyota Land Cruiser?"

"Sure," the constable replied. "I can do that."

———

Back in the Land Rover, Kubu headed out of the town in the direction of South Africa. The road rapidly deteriorated into little more than a cart track with the grass growing between the wheel ruts scraping the undercarriage of his Land Rover.

Stopping from time to time to check the map, he eventually came to the road along the fence with South Africa. He followed it to the southwest, driving slowly in second gear so he could carefully examine the fence. Eventually he spotted a section where he could see that the wires weren't tight and an extra post had been added.

He was dripping with sweat, and it was a relief to pull over and get out of the vehicle, although it was even hotter in the afternoon sun. He examined the fence carefully. It was clear that the gateway had been there for a long time. Probably the locals knew all about it, he thought. Perhaps the robbers had entered Botswana that way also.

His idea of finding clues there now seemed unlikely to him. Nevertheless, he scanned the tyre tracks on his side of the border, trying to make sense of them. It seemed a vehicle had pulled off the road and then turned back the way it had come. Perhaps it was lost, Kubu thought. But it was a strange coincidence to turn exactly at the illegal crossing point.

Then he spotted a cigarette butt. That was even more odd. It was as though someone had driven to the crossing, relaxed and smoked a cigarette, and then headed back. Kubu was sure there was more to it than that. He went back to his vehicle, collected an evidence bag, and carefully bagged the stub.

Having checked the fence, it was time to see if he could track down the mysterious man who lived near Manyelanong Hill. He unrolled his map and planned the route to the point the constable had marked. Then he set off.

It looked straightforward, provided the roads followed the map. But that wasn't the case. One road didn't exist anymore; another forked where it wasn't supposed to. A couple of times he had to retrace his route, but he did seem to be getting closer.

Eventually, he came upon a small kraal—a group of three huts with a rudimentary fence holding a few goats, and a cooking fire in the clearing in front. An elderly woman was tending a three-legged pot straddling the fire.

Kubu stopped, clambered out of his vehicle, and walked over to her.

"Dumela, mma," he began. "I'm so sorry to worry you, but I'm looking for a house near here, opposite Manyelanong Hill. Perhaps you know it?"

For a few moments, she said nothing. Then she pointed. "Yes, I know it. It is that way. You will see the house on a rise, but do not go up to it." She shook her head.

"Why not, mma?"

She shook her head again. "A witch doctor stays there. A bad man. A very bad man."

"Do you know this man, mma?" he asked, feeling his excitement build.

She shrugged.

"You say he's a bad man. Why is that?"

"That is what I think. What business is it of yours, rra?"

"I'm just curious, mma. Has he been there a long time?"

"Sometimes he is there. Sometimes not. They do that. Come and go. Sometimes as other creatures." She made the sign of the cross.

Kubu waited, but she went back to stirring her pot. After a moment she said, "Was there something else, rra?"

He shook his head, thanked her, and headed for his vehicle.

This could be a breakthrough! he thought as he climbed in. *If this is the witch doctor from the robbery, he may be the key to the case.*

As he drove, he realised he was jumping to conclusions. It was possible that the man wasn't the one he was looking for—maybe he wasn't a witch doctor at all. Nevertheless, he couldn't wait to reach the house and investigate.

Chapter 66

Assistant Superintendent Mabaku didn't manage to see the deputy commissioner until late in the afternoon. He sat outside his office, wondering whether he'd leave it in one piece. Or still with a job. He certainly didn't feel his normally confident self.

"The deputy commissioner will see you now."

Mabaku stood up and nodded at the very attractive PA. "Thank you, Godsend. Wish me good luck!"

She looked at him quizzically, wondering what a lowly assistant superintendent was seeing her boss about and why he needed good luck with it.

Mabaku walked into the office, closed the door behind him, and stood in front of the imposing desk. "Good afternoon, Deputy Commissioner."

"Please sit down."

Mabaku sat down on the edge of one of the chairs.

"I hope you have something important to tell me, Assistant Superintendent. I've a dinner with a delegation from the Organisation of African Unity this evening."

Mabaku took a deep breath. "Sir, I have a very sensitive matter to raise." He stopped to see if there was any reaction.

The deputy commissioner's face was impassive. "Go on."

"Sir, as you know, we're investigating the Debswana diamond robbery. We know that you want it resolved urgently." There was no response.

"Sir, one line of investigation is to dig into the backgrounds of everyone who knew about the backup plan—to see if there is anything that may indicate an involvement."

The deputy commissioner nodded.

"Obviously some of the people who knew about the plan may be very upset if they find out what we're doing."

"You needn't worry, Assistant Superintendent. I've told all the Debswana directors what we'll be doing. They weren't happy, but they've agreed."

"Thank you, sir. That's a relief. But that's not why I'm here."

The deputy commission frowned but didn't say anything.

"Sir, I believe we have to check into the affairs of the director of the CID, Director Gobey." Mabaku took another deep breath and continued, his words falling over each other. "It's not that we suspect him of anything, of course, but if we're to leave no stone unturned, as you said, we have to look under every rock. We have to be thorough, and the director was one of those who knew the details of the backup plan."

There was a prolonged silence. Mabaku could feel his heart beating.

"If we do this investigation, Assistant Superintendent, what would you propose we do?"

"Sir, three things. I'd look into his finances—in strict confidence, of course. Second, I'd speak to his wife to see if she's noticed anything out of the ordinary. And third, if necessary, I'd talk to some of his friends—but that would only happen if the first two raised a flag."

Another silence.

"Of course, sir, I don't expect anything to come of this, but I feel we have to be thorough even if it means stepping on a few toes."

"I understand, Assistant Superintendent. I need to give this some thought. Go for a walk and come back in half an hour."

Mabaku stood up. "Yes, sir. Thank you, sir." He turned and walked out, gently closing the door behind him.

"I crossed my fingers." Godsend smiled. "Did it work?"

"Thank you. I don't know yet. But please keep them crossed."

Chapter 67

Kubu followed the woman's instructions and soon came to the point where a track, even rougher than the one he was following, led to a small house up a slope to the right. He turned onto it and bumped up the hill.

He came to a gate, but it was hanging open, so he continued up to the house. As he reached it, he suddenly realised what a big risk he was taking. What if this was the man he'd been looking for? How would he react to a policeman at his door?

His heart beat faster as he pulled up outside the house.

He knew he should report where he was and what he was doing, so he tried to call in on the police radio. He was rewarded by a burst of static. Clearly, he was out of range.

He hesitated, unsure of what to do, afraid of an unfriendly welcome. Still, there was no need to tell the man who he really was. He could simply say he was lost and ask for directions back to Otse.

He looked around, but there was no sign of a vehicle.

Maybe no one's here, he thought.

He walked to the front door and knocked, but there was no response. He waited a moment and then hammered on it more loudly. Still nothing. He tried the door and it opened.

Kubu stepped back, unsure what to do next. He suspected that the house was empty, but he had no right to go in, and the owner could be back at any moment. Maybe he didn't bother to lock his doors—after all, who would dare break into a witch doctor's house? Kubu knew that the prudent course of action was to head back to town and call the CID, but he pushed the door open and stepped into the house.

He was immediately aware of the nasty smell of rotting meat and wondered if the place had been empty for longer than a few days. He found himself in a living room with a kitchen at one end and doors leading off it. One was on the far side of the lounge and closed; the two closer ones were open, and a cursory inspection revealed a bedroom and a bathroom.

The kitchen was a mess, with dishes piled in the sink. There was an ashtray with several cigarette butts on the counter, and Kubu immediately thought of the one he'd collected at the fence. Perhaps forensics could match them. Next to the back door, he spotted a sack. It was open, and he glanced into it. It was half full of what looked like gravel. Kubu pulled out a handful and let the pieces run through his fingers.

Gravel chips! he thought. *Maybe the same as the ones in the Debswana boxes.*

He felt an adrenaline rush. He dropped several of the chips into his pocket, and involuntarily turned around to check that he wasn't being watched. Then he walked over and tried the closed door. It was locked, but the key was in the lock. He turned it, opened the door, and stepped into the room. Now the smell was overpowering, fetid, and sour, and he gagged, trying not to throw up. There was an angry buzz of disturbed flies.

A man was lying on the floor, unseeing eyes staring upwards, his head haloed in a pool of congealed blood. Kubu gasped and bent over for a closer look, but he didn't need to. It was obvious that the man's throat had been cut from one side of his neck to the other.

Chapter 68

As soon as Mabaku had stepped out of the office, the deputy commissioner phoned his boss.

"Commissioner, Assistant Superintendent Mabaku of the CID just approached me for permission to take a look at Gobey—a routine investigation because Gobey was aware of the backup plan. Mabaku doesn't think he'll turn up anything but feels it's necessary to be thorough."

He listened to the response. "Thank you, Commissioner. I'll let you know what I find, if anything. Also, Mabaku suggests we speak to Gobey's wife to see if she's noticed anything. I don't think that's a good idea. I suggest we revisit the idea if I find something unusual."

———

When Mabaku returned half an hour later, Godsend held up both hands with fingers crossed. "Please go straight in. He's waiting for you."

Those were very ominous words, Mabaku thought as he went into the office.

"Please sit down."

Again, Mabaku sat on the very edge of the chair.

"I've spoken to the commissioner about your request. We both have the highest regard for Director Gobey and cannot imagine he'd be involved in any way. However, we agree with you that we need to be thorough. Unfortunately, there are times when people who should know better do something stupid. So, I will look at his financial situation and will do it in such a way not even the bankers will know we're interested in him. If there's anything there, I'll let you know. In the meantime, you're to do nothing and say nothing to anyone. Understood?"

"Yes, sir."

Mabaku felt relief wash over him. He'd done his duty, and the last thing he wanted to do was to investigate his boss.

"What is your plan now?"

Mabaku rubbed his chin. "It seems to me that there are two avenues to explore." He filled in the deputy commissioner on what they'd discovered from Colonel Venter. "I think I should go to South Africa and follow up with him. We can't ignore the possibility that the Motswedi police have the diamonds hidden somewhere." He paused. "The other thing that I suggest is a little deception or misdirection. Stir things up a bit. Perhaps you could phone Chamberlain at Jwaneng and tell him that the police have a breakthrough, and you expect to pick up and question a suspect in the morning. Then do the same with Tau, the security manager, and the operations guy, Goodman. Hopefully, if any of them is involved, he'll make a mistake of some sort."

"Thank you, Assistant Superintendent. Go and speak to Venter, and I'll take care of the rest."

"Sir, what about Director Gobey?"

"What about him, Assistant Superintendent?"

"Do I tell him about going to South Africa?"

"Of course you do. He's your superior officer. Just tell him you're following up on what Venter told you."

"Yes, sir. Thank you, sir. Enjoy your dinner." He stood up and headed for the door. As he walked past Godsend, he gave her a thumbs up. He'd emerged from his interactions with the deputy commissioner unscathed. He still had a job and knew what to do next.

The deputy commissioner was also pleased with his interactions with Assistant Superintendent Mabaku.

I like him, he thought. *He's willing to put himself on the line for what he thinks is right. Maybe I've found the next director of the CID.*

Chapter 69

Kubu drove straight to Constable Murewa's office in Otse. The constable was locking up for the day as Kubu burst in.

"I found the witch doctor!" Kubu told him. "But he's dead. Murdered. We need to contact the CID at once."

"What? Someone's been murdered? I have to contact Ramotswa."

Kubu shook his head. "I need CID headquarters in Gaborone."

The constable nodded and indicated the phone on his desk. Kubu dropped into the desk chair and a few moments later was talking to the director's secretary because Mabaku wasn't available.

"Hello Miriam, it's Kubu. Assistant Superintendent Mabaku is out. Is Director Gobey there? I'm in Otse, and I need help. It's urgent."

"Hold on. I'll put you through to the director."

There was a pause, and then Gobey came on the line. "What's going on, Detective Sergeant?"

Kubu took a deep breath and told the director the whole story. Gobey asked a few questions and then said, "I'll send out Inspector Dow and the forensics people. Tell the local police to secure the scene until they get there. No one should go into the house before that." He paused. "Why on earth did you go in? You thought a dangerous criminal may be there. Why didn't you call in first? Didn't you learn anything at that university you went to?"

"I...I did try, sir," Kubu stuttered, "but I was out of range of the radio."

"Suppose the man hadn't been dead? He might have killed you!" The director's voice rose. "At best you would be lying knocked out on the floor, and he would be long gone, you idiot!"

"Yes, sir. You're quite right. I didn't think it through—"

"You didn't think at all!" He paused. "And what makes you think the dead man is the witch doctor anyway?"

Kubu realised he had no answer for that. Maybe the man was the witch doctor's victim. Maybe the witch doctor was still very much alive.

"Well?"

Again, Kubu took a deep breath. "Actually, maybe he isn't. I just thought—"

"You should do less thinking and more detective work. Now get the local police out there to secure the scene and wait for the inspector where you are. Where are you anyway?"

Kubu said that the best place to meet the inspector would be at the guesthouse where he was staying and described where it was. Gobey noted that and hung up.

Kubu was then faced with convincing Constable Murewa to secure the scene. The constable was anything but enthusiastic about going out alone to the witch doctor's house. However, after checking with his superior at Ramotswa, he accepted it and headed out.

———

It was a long evening for Kubu, who was still shaken up by discovering the murdered man. Dow came with a couple of constables, a forensics unit, and a van to remove the body. Kubu led them all out to the house on the hill, and the constable was relieved to be able to go home for the night. Dow took lots of photographs, and the forensics people started their work.

Dow searched the body but found nothing to identify the man, but Kubu realised that he definitely wasn't Vusi Tuelo, the man on the APB sheet. He was much older and looked nothing like the South African police picture. Kubu recalled Nari's description of the man who'd given the pilot the package. That could fit. Perhaps this man was the witch doctor after all.

They also searched for the murder weapon, but there was no sign of it. Eventually, the body was loaded into the van to be taken back to Gaborone for autopsy, together with a variety of forensic evidence.

At that point Dow called it a day.

Chapter 70

The deputy commissioner sat and thought for a few minutes about Mabaku's idea of stirring the pot. That was never a bad thing—people who were worried about something often did stupid things when pressure was applied.

He used his Rolodex to find the phone number of Jwaneng mine, and when the switchboard answered, he asked to be put through to Major Chamberlain.

"I hope you've made some progress," the major said as soon as the deputy commissioner identified himself.

"As a matter of fact, we have, Major. I thought you'd like to know."

"Of course, I'd like to know. What have you found?"

"I can't give you any details, because we're at a critical point in the investigation. Just let me say, we've made a breakthrough."

"Dammit, it was my diamonds that were stolen. I've a right to know everything you know."

"I'm afraid I can't risk the progress we've made. If our suspect got wind of this—"

"What suspect, Deputy Commissioner? I demand to know."

"Major, you have to realise—"

"If you don't tell me right now, I'll call the chairman of De

Beers, who will call the commissioner, or even maybe President Mogae. And you may find yourself out of a job."

The deputy commissioner smiled. He was enjoying stirring this pot.

"Okay, Major. I can't tell you all we know, but I'll give you one piece of information. But you have to promise that you will tell no one. I repeat no one. Do you agree?"

There was a silence on the line.

"All right, Deputy Commissioner. I agree, but I'm not happy about it."

"Major, tomorrow morning, we're going to arrest someone we're sure was involved in the robbery."

"Who?"

"I can't tell you that, Major. All I can tell you is that it's someone at Jwaneng—someone *senior* at Jwaneng."

"If it's one of my people, you have to tell me, Deputy Commissioner. I have a right to know!"

The deputy commissioner moved the phone away from his ear.

"Calm down, Major. You'll find out soon enough. I have to go now. Don't forget your promise. You can't tell anyone." He put down the phone.

If he's involved, he thought, *he's not going to spend the night twiddling his thumbs.*

Then he phoned the head of administration at the mine, Elijah Goodman.

"Good afternoon, Rra Goodman. I'm phoning to give you some information about the robbery."

"Have you caught who did it?"

"No, but we'll be making an arrest in Jwaneng tomorrow morning."

"Can you tell me who it is?"

"Unfortunately not," the deputy commissioner replied. "And I have to ask you to keep this information to yourself for the time being."

"Of course, and I look forward to tomorrow. Thank you."

After he hung up, the deputy commissioner sat thinking for a few minutes. He decided that he'd be surprised if Goodman was involved in the robbery.

Finally, he called Eddie Tau, the head of security, and told him about the arrest he was going to make the next day.

"Who is it? I need to know."

"I can't tell you at the moment, and you have to promise not to say a word about this call to anyone. Not Major Chamberlain. Not Goodman. Nor anyone else."

"Deputy Commissioner, you know you can trust me. As head of security, I really do have to know now. People may be at risk, or maybe even another robbery."

"Rra Tau, you'll know in the morning. Thank you."

The deputy commissioner hung up for the last time and leant back, wondering what each would do if connected to the robbery. He thought there were three possibilities: one, they'd say nothing; two, they'd talk to any others involved to come up with a plan; and, three, they'd offer to collaborate with the police in return for a reduced sentence.

He knew what he would do—never get involved in the first place.

He stood up and started thinking about excuses for leaving the evening's dinner early. He really hated all the bullshit that bubbled up at such meetings.

He locked the door to his office and walked down the passage. Then he stopped. He knew what his excuse would be—he was going to arrest a suspect in the diamond heist case.

I wish, he thought.

Chapter 71

The major's daughter was visiting from Johannesburg, and as he was very fond of her, his wife expected he'd be in a good mood. However, that evening he seemed distracted and hardly contributed to the conversation over drinks.

"Something worrying you, David?" she asked.

"It's just the mine. It's been really tough since the robbery. Let's talk about something else."

They lapsed into silence but were saved by the phone ringing.

"I'll get it." The major climbed to his feet and walked to the study to take the call.

"Yes, hello, Major Chamberlain speaking."

"Major, it's Eddie. I need to speak to you right away."

"Eddie? Well, you are speaking to me."

"Not over the phone. And I need to speak to you alone."

"We're about to have our dinner."

"It won't take long. It's really important and really urgent. It's about the robbery."

"Can't it wait a couple of hours?"

"That may be too late."

The major hesitated. He decided that if Tau had something

to say about the robbery, he'd better listen. "I'll meet you at the office. Give me fifteen minutes."

"Not at the office. Please come round to my house. My wife's at her mother's, so we'll be alone."

"This better be worth it, Eddie. All right. Ten minutes."

———

Tau let the major in and led him to the lounge. There was a bottle of whisky on the coffee table, with a glass already poured.

"Take a seat. You want a drink?"

The major shook his head as he sat down. "What is it, Eddie? What's so urgent it couldn't wait till after dinner?"

Tau took a sip of his drink. "It was me, Major. I leaked the backup plan. But—"

"*You what?*" the major roared.

"I had no idea how it would all turn out! Those men killed and the woman. You have to believe me…"

"What did you think would happen? That they'd calmly hand over the box of diamonds and shake hands like gentlemen?" He glared at Tau. "Why did you do it? Don't I pay you enough?"

Tau took his time before he replied. "You won't believe this, but it was a witch doctor. He told me he'd had a vision, and he'd sought me out to tell me. He didn't ask me for a thebe. I know you'll say it's all nonsense, but he already knew all sorts of things no one outside the mine could know. In fact, he already knew about the backup plan, but not the details. He told me all sorts of things…" He shook his head. "He said the ancestors had told it all to him in the vision and promised me great wealth. I believed him, God help me."

"How could you be so stupid?" The major paused. "I'd better have that drink."

Eddie poured him a double.

"But that wasn't all you did, was it? You did something that let them know which box had the diamonds, didn't you? Don't lie to me, Eddie."

Tau said nothing. Then he shook his head again.

The major let the silence drag for a few seconds. "Listen, Eddie. Once you admit the contact with the witch doctor to the police, it's all over. That Mabaku is a nasty piece of work. He'll get the whole story out of you one way or another. If I see through you, he will too. Now tell me the truth. All of it. Afterwards you must go to the police. I'll try to do my best for you, but I have to know everything."

Tau looked at him with surprise. He'd expected the major's anger, but not any suggestion of support. He took a deep breath.

"Last week the witch doctor came to see me again. He said some people needed my help—just a very small thing—and they'd pay me very well. Just as he'd foreseen."

"And you *believed* him?"

Tau shook his head. "I was suspicious and asked what he wanted me to do. He said he'd had another vision. Something was burning and the backup plan would be implemented. He wanted me to put something in the box with the diamonds when I fetched them. Something very small that no one would ever find."

The major started to say something, but Tau hadn't finished. "I told him no way. I wasn't doing anything like that. I told him I didn't believe in his visions, and I wouldn't be seeing him again. I got up to leave. Then he said, 'Half a million pula.' My God. Half a million pula!"

"You fell for it?"

"I said I'd think about it. He said I had to decide right away. And if I didn't agree, he'd make sure you found out everything that had passed between us—particularly about the backup plan."

"So, you did it."

"I had to! You would've fired me!"

"You got that right!" The major took a sip of his drink. "Eddie, can you identify this witch doctor? Can you help the police to trace him? If so, we can negotiate with them. Work out a plea bargain. I can vouch for you. But they have to catch him." He held out his glass for refill. After Tau had obliged, he continued. "Now tell me everything you did or discovered, step by step from the beginning. All the details. Don't leave anything out."

Tau poured himself another whisky. "Okay, I'd better start with the first meeting with the witch doctor."

———

When he'd finished and answered the major's questions, Tau said, "I'll go to the police in the morning."

The major shook his head. "We go right now."

Tau poured himself another whisky. "Please, Major. I need a little time to think it through... A few hours... please. And I need to try to explain all this to my wife."

"So, what made you tell me now?"

"I had a call from the deputy commissioner this evening. They're planning to make an arrest tomorrow. One of us. Obviously, it must be me."

"He called you too? That's interesting..." The major paused. "You have to preempt the arrest and turn yourself in right now."

"I can't go now. I've had too many of these." He held up his glass. "I'll go first thing in the morning and make a full confession. I promise."

The major emptied his glass. "Very well. But if you don't, I'll call the deputy commissioner and repeat everything you've told me. That's a promise."

He glanced around the room. "Do you have a phone? I need to let my wife know I'm on my way home for supper."

"It's in the study."

After a few minutes the major returned.

"Don't worry, I'll see myself out. Just remember, I'll be in contact with the police first thing in the morning."

Tau let him go. He poured himself another shot and downed it.

SATURDAY
Chapter 72

The deputy commissioner was ruing that he hadn't done what he'd planned at the dinner the previous evening. It wasn't the conversation that had kept him from going home early but rather the fine wines, generously provided by the French Embassy, not to mention the cognac that was offered after the meal. He'd have to remember to be a little more abstemious at the next meeting.

He reluctantly opened a folder. Budgeting was one of his least enjoyable responsibilities. Certainly, much of it was pro forma, but grappling with the unknown was what caused his headaches. How was the police service going to cope with the rapidly growing incidence of domestic violence? How many protests were there going to be, requiring huge numbers of overtime hours? How many visiting heads of state, with their sometimes ridiculous security requirements? He remembered with dismay what the Americans had demanded when President Clinton visited earlier in the year.

He took a deep breath and started jotting down notes.

Then his phone rang.

"Major Chamberlain on the phone, sir," his PA said. "He doesn't sound happy."

"Please put him through."

There were a few clicks, and then he was connected.

"Major Chamber—" he started to say.

"It's Tau! He's dead!"

"Calm down, Major. You say Tau's dead?"

"Yes. He committed suicide last night. It was him!"

"What do you mean it was him? Don't you know it's him?"

"No. I mean it was Tau who took the diamonds."

"Major, please slow down. I'm not following you."

"Dammit, listen to what I'm saying. Last night before dinner, Tau phoned me at home and asked to see me urgently. In private. We arranged to meet at his house. He confessed his involvement in the robbery. Your phone call must have made him realise he'd been found out. He wanted to know what he should do. I told him to go to the police immediately. He said he wanted to tell his wife first, then he'd turn himself in."

"What exactly did he say?"

"He said he'd been contacted some time ago by a witch doctor who persuaded him to talk about the backup plan. Later, the man told him that the plan would soon be put into use and asked him to put a small device in the diamond box."

"Why would he agree to that?"

"He said the man offered him a lot of money—half a million pula. For one minute's work. He couldn't resist. After your call, he thought if he confessed before being arrested, he'd get a lighter sentence."

"And what did you do?"

"I went home, told my wife, and tried to phone your office. No one answered. That's why I'm calling you now."

It took another five minutes for the deputy commissioner to extract the rest of the story. The major had received a panicked phone call from Tau's wife around eight that morning. Apparently, after she'd returned home quite late the previous evening, he'd received a call and told her he needed to go out for a quick meeting. She waited a while for him to return, and when he didn't, she'd gone to bed. When she woke up, she saw he'd never come to bed and wasn't elsewhere in the house. She'd run outside to see if his car was there. It wasn't. She was worried he may have had an accident and called the police. Apparently, it took them a while to find the car. He was in it. He'd killed himself. That's when she'd called the major.

"Major, what time was that?"

"Just before eight. I was about to go to work. I drove to where Tau's car was. The police asked me if I could identify the body, and I told them it was Tau. Good thing I've seen bodies before. Then I went right over to her house to comfort her."

"And why do you think it was a suicide?"

"The police told me they'd found a gun on the floor. If he'd been murdered, the murderer would have taken it with him."

"That's probably right. And where are you right now?"

"In my office."

"And where is she?"

"In the mine's infirmary, seeing one of our doctors."

"All right, this is what you must do. You must stay at the mine until the police tell you that you can leave. And Mma Tau must stay in the infirmary until the police tell her that she can leave. Understood?"

There was silence on the line.

"Major, I asked you if you understood my instructions."

Another silence, then, "Okay, but I warn you, I'm going to have all your heads for this. You know I have connections to the chairman. All of you are totally incompetent."

The deputy commissioner put down the phone, used his Rolodex to find two numbers, and then picked it up again. The first call was to the station commander at the Jwaneng police station. "I've just received a phone call from Major Chamberlain at the mine. He says his security man, Tau, committed suicide last night. What can you tell me about that?"

The station commander confirmed that Tau's wife had phoned the station at 7:03 a.m. to report her husband missing.

"What did you do?"

"There was only the receptionist at the station. A cow had wandered onto the A2, and a car swerved to avoid it. Right into an oncoming lorry. We think there are three people dead. All available personnel were trying to sort that out. It took us a while to pull some back into town to look for the car."

"How long did it take you to find it?

"Not long. It was in the Pick n Pay parking area just off Teemane Avenue.

"And what did you find?"

"Tau was in the car, shot in the head. Blood all over the place. He was dead."

"Do you think he was murdered?"

"No. It was suicide. Definitely. We found a revolver on the floor. Only one round fired."

The deputy commissioner thought he was probably right but wondered if they'd done the follow-up. "Forensics can try to match the bullet with the gun. And I assume you're having the gun and the car fingerprinted?"

There was a pause. "I'll get that done right away."

The deputy commissioner rolled his eyes. Maybe the major was right about the police incompetence. "Thank you, Station Commander. I'll coordinate with Director Gobey to send one of the detectives from headquarters to support yours. Probably Assistant Superintendent Mabaku."

"Thank you, sir."

The deputy commissioner then phoned Gobey to apprise him of the situation and to suggest that Mabaku be sent to Jwaneng as soon as possible.

"I'll take care of that, Deputy Commissioner," Gobey said. "I'm meeting with him in a few minutes. I don't see any problems."

"Have him call me before he leaves. I'll tell him what I know."

Finally, the deputy commissioner walked down the passage

and filled in the commissioner with the latest information from Jwaneng mine.

The world's going mad, he thought as he sat down at his desk again. He shuffled through the papers in front of him, found the one he wanted, and scribbled a note on it.

Money for four more detectives for the CID?

Chapter 73

A few minutes after the director had spoken to the deputy commissioner, Mabaku arrived at the director's office. He'd survived his encounter with the deputy commissioner the day before, but this was his first opportunity to see the director since then. He prayed that Gobey had no inkling of his visit to the deputy commissioner.

Miriam checked with the director and then waved him in. Gobey glanced up from his paperwork and indicated the seat in front of his desk.

"I was just about to send for you, Mabaku. What do you want?" It wasn't a promising start.

"Sir, Colonel Venter discovered what happened at Motswedi, but now we must consider the possibility that the South African police either took the diamonds or know more about the robbery than they've told us. I'd like your permission to travel to South Africa to look into it."

Gobey nodded. "Normally, I'd say go ahead, but something else has come up that I need you to attend to."

Mabaku frowned but said nothing.

Gobey then told him about Tau's apparent suicide. "Get the details from the deputy commissioner. Then I want you to go to

Jwaneng immediately. I've cleared the way for your involvement with the police there, but I have a feeling they won't be happy. They don't like us interfering."

"Of course, Director. I think this may be our first big break in the case."

"I hope so." Gobey paused. "That's all."

"Yes, sir." Mabaku breathed a sigh of relief as he left the office.

Chapter 74

Kubu and Dow were up early to start their investigation of the Otse murder. They visited the kraal where Kubu had stopped for directions, and they found out that a woman sometimes worked at the house and where she lived. That was good news.

As Kubu drove, he wondered about the motive for the murder. He was sure it was connected with the robbery, and most likely the dead man knew something about it. Kenosi and the other security guards and the team that had carried out the robbery had all been killed and now, perhaps, the witch doctor himself. He felt a chill. Whoever was behind the robbery was eliminating every connection to himself.

Kubu followed the directions carefully and found the woman's home with no wrong turns. It was another small kraal, with goats and chickens, and several young children playing barefoot outside. A boy ran up to the Land Rover, and Kubu asked him if this was where the woman who worked at the house up the hill lived. The boy said yes, she was his mother, and he would take them to her. Kubu was relieved. He'd been worried that whoever was behind all the murders might have eliminated her too.

The boy took them to a field where the woman was working

with a hoe. She straightened up as she saw them coming and waited for them to approach.

"Dumela, mma," Dow greeted her. "We're from the CID in Gaborone." They showed her their identification. "We need to ask you some questions. Can we stand over there?" He pointed towards a large tree nearby that would give some shade. The morning was already hot.

The woman nodded and walked over to the tree with them. Then she asked, "What do you want to know, rra?"

"Mma, a man has been murdered. We don't know who he is, and we think you may be able to help us."

"Why would I be able to help? I know nothing about a dead man."

"Let me show you a picture of him. I have it here on my camera. You may recognise him." He flicked to the image he wanted and showed it to her.

"Aii! It's the ngaka—the doctor! Who did this horrible thing? Aii!" She started to sob.

"That's what we want to find out. Please tell us everything you know about him."

For a few moments she was unable to answer, and then she pulled herself together. "Until just last week, I worked for the man in the house up the hill. This is his father."

"Who was this man you worked for?"

"He told me to call him Rra Vusi."

Immediately Kubu jumped in, excited. "Vusi is his first name? Do you know what his last name is?"

The woman shook her head.

"This man, Rra Vusi, that you worked for. Can you describe him?"

The woman tried, but all they learnt was that he was middle-aged and of medium height. "Oh, yes. There is one other thing. His face reminded me of a jackal." She grimaced. "His eyes were cold and never smiled."

Kubu remembered thinking Tuelo's face looked pinched. *Perhaps it could remind one of a jackal*, he thought.

"And the dead man is his father?" Dow prompted. "Do you know his name?"

She shook her head. "I don't know his name. I just called him Ngaka."

Doctor, Kubu thought. "This doctor," he asked. "Was he a real doctor or maybe a witch doctor?"

She took a few moments to answer. "Some say he was a witch doctor, but I never saw him do anything that made me think that. I never felt scared of him."

"When did you stop working for them?"

"Four days ago. Tuesday was my last day. RraVusi said he didn't need me anymore, but he paid me for the rest of the month."

"Did he say why?"

She shook her head. "Sometimes he comes and sometimes he goes. I don't ask what his business is."

"Did Rra Vusi and the ngaka have a car?"

"A bakkie."

"Do you know the licence-plate number?"

She shook her head.

"Do you know what make and model it is? And its colour?"

She shook her head again. "It was old. Sort of white."

That wasn't much help. Botswana was full of old, white bakkies.

Dow changed tack. "Was there anyone else in the house?"

"It was me and Rra Vusi and the ngaka. That's all."

"Did anyone else come while you were there?"

She nodded. "There were four men who came in a big car. They stayed the night and left the next night."

"When was this?"

"It was the day before he told me to go. So last Monday."

Dow started fiddling with his camera again, so Kubu asked, "What did their car look like?"

"It was white. Big, and the back opened."

Dow had found what he wanted—pictures he'd taken of the photographs of the robbers that had been sent to the CID by the South African police. He showed them to the woman.

"They're dead too! Aii! Who has killed all these people?"

"Are these the men who visited?"

She nodded.

The detectives paused, wondering if they'd missed anything. Then Kubu asked, "These men who visited, were they Batswana?"

She shook her head.

"And the ngaka and Vusi?"

She shook her head again. "None of them. They're from South Africa, I think. Or maybe Zimbabwe. They don't speak much Setswana."

Kubu gave a small smile. That was consistent with the robbers being from South Africa and could explain why the witch doctor used Zulu fetishes. It all seemed to fit.

Chapter 75

Mabaku had left the CID building as soon as he could and had negotiated the long and boring road from Gaborone to Jwaneng. Since the traffic had been light, the most important things he'd had to do were to look out for cows on the highway and prevent sweat dripping into his eyes. For the most part, that afforded him plenty of time to think about the case.

He was quite sure that Eddie Tau's death was no coincidence, coming as it did so soon after the deputy commissioner had stirred things up. The robbery could never have taken place without insider knowledge, and now it seemed that the culprit was Tau.

He hoped the official finding would in fact be suicide. That would neatly tidy up one part of the investigation. On the other hand, if the finding of the forensic pathologist was the only other alternative, namely murder... Mabaku grimaced as he contemplated the fallout. What a mess it would be.

———

Mabaku wasn't in a good mood when he pulled up in front of the Jwaneng police station. Even though the trip was just over two hours, sitting doing nothing for such a long time wasn't what he liked to do. He was a man of action.

He walked into the station, announced himself to the receptionist, and was immediately sent through to the station commander's office, who met him with a broad smile. "Good morning, Assistant Superintendent. You didn't have to make the trip, you know. It's an open-and-shut case."

Mabaku frowned. "Are you sure?"

The station commander nodded. "Definitely! Death by suicide. The gun was on the floor of the car. There are no suspects, and from what Major Chamberlain says, he had a strong motive to take his own life. Here, take a look at these pictures from the scene." He shoved a folder across his desk to Mabaku. "You see? Everything properly documented," he added smugly. "The body has been sent to Gabs for autopsy."

Mabaku sat down and opened the file. It contained a number of gruesome pictures of Tau, slumped in the car with a hole in his right temple and blood everywhere from a gaping wound on the other side of his head. He passed the folder back.

"Have you checked that it was Tau's gun?"

The station commander hesitated for a few moments. "Not yet."

"And fingerprints?"

"They're being done now."

"I noticed he had his watch on his right arm, and he shot himself on the right side of the head. Do you know if he was right-handed or left-handed?"

"Why would that matter?"

Mabaku took a deep breath. "Do you know?"

The station commander shook his head.

Mabaku took out his notebook. "Okay, tell me the whole story."

The station commander related how the police had been called early in the morning—7:03, to be precise—by a hysterical Mma

Tau. Her husband hadn't come home the night before, and she was worried he'd had an accident. They'd started looking and quickly found his car in the Pick n Pay parking area. He was in it, dead from a head shot. His gun was on the floor of the car. Obviously, it was suicide.

"Did you get statements from Mma Tau and Chamberlain?"

The station commander shook his head. "Only from Chamberlain. We thought she needed some time to recover."

Mabaku sighed. "Please get me a copy of Chamberlain's right away. I need to see what's in it before I speak to him."

"I can tell you what he told me." Mabaku could tell the man wanted to relate the story, but he didn't have the time to listen. Reading the statement would be much quicker.

He shook his head. "That's okay. Unless there's something I need to know that's not in the report."

"It's all there." He pulled several sheets of paper from a folder and handed them to Mabaku. Then he leant back with a satisfied smile. "You see, Assistant Superintendent, we don't always need help from the experts in Gabs."

Mabaku thought it was a good thing the station commander couldn't read his thoughts. "But I will need to conduct my own investigation, by order of the deputy commissioner. I'm sure what I find will corroborate everything you've said, but I don't have a choice."

The station commander scowled. "You guys never think we in the field can do anything properly. Well, you're going to find out this time." He stood up. "Let me know what you need, and I'll arrange it."

Mabaku thanked him and left. *So many assumptions and probably second-rate forensics,* he thought. *I just hope the car has been declared a crime scene.*

Chapter 76

As they drove back to Otse after talking to the old woman who'd worked for the doctor, Kubu shared his idea with Dow.

"Sir, I have a theory about this man. Actually, it's just a guess, but a man called Vusi Tuelo is wanted by the South African police for murder and armed robbery. I saw an APB about him last Monday, and I checked yesterday. He's still at large, and they think he may be hiding out here or in Zimbabwe. If it's him, maybe he's here for a purpose, not just to hide out."

Dow hesitated. "Vusi is quite a common name."

"Yes, sir, but according to the woman, this man is from South Africa. And Tuelo is an expert safecracker. He wouldn't have any trouble with the locks on the Debswana diamond transport box. He would have the contacts to recruit the robbers too."

"Good thinking, Kubu. It's certainly a possibility. We need to get that information out. Did the APB have a picture?"

Kubu nodded, and Dow smiled.

As soon as they reached the constable's office. Dow phoned the director while Kubu and the constable strolled outside to allow him to speak in private. When he was finished, he called them back.

"I have some important news. The security manager at Jwaneng took his own life last night. The assistant superintendent is already on his way there."

Kubu gasped. "That's it then. He's the inside leak. I'd never have guessed it. I wonder how he's connected to Tuelo and the witch doctor."

"I hope it's that simple, although it never is. Anyway, I filled the director in on what we've discovered. He'll have an alert sent out about Tuelo. I don't think there's much more we can do here, and the director agrees. Forensics will check the fingerprints and so on that they collected last night, and the pathologist will do the autopsy this afternoon."

He turned to the constable. "You know where to pick up local rumours. Please ask around to see if anyone knows anything about this man Vusi, particularly when he left and where he went. It's worth trying, but I doubt you'll find anything."

Kubu thought he was correct about that. Tuelo, if it was Tuelo, had slipped away in the night, probably after killing the witch doctor, who almost certainly wasn't his father.

"Come on, Kubu. Let's sort out the bill at the guesthouse, pick up my vehicle, and head back to Gabs."

As Kubu drove them back to the guesthouse, Dow smiled. "Well, Kubu, you've come up with really useful ideas. Well done."

"Thank you, sir. But I don't think the director is too pleased with me."

"So he said before I came down. But the main thing is that the dead man is very probably the witch doctor who was helping the robbers, and we may know the identity of the man behind all this. Also, it's very likely he has the diamonds."

"How do we know that, sir?"

"They got a Debswana geologist in this morning to help them. The gravel that they found in the box brought back from South Africa wasn't the same as the gravel in the two decoy boxes. But it *was* the same as the samples from the sack you found in the house. Almost certainly this Vusi made the switch when those men stayed with him overnight."

That made sense to Kubu. "I see... He probably did it to fool the robbers into thinking the box was still full of diamonds. They wouldn't try to open it with the fetishes covering the locks." Then he had another thought. "And maybe he also leaked false information about the robbers to the informer—that they were gunrunners with lots of money hidden in the seats. All he had to do was tell the informer when they'd cross the border, and he tipped off the Motswedi police to set up an ambush. He got them to do his dirty work for him."

Dow nodded. "You may be right about that."

Both detectives felt that they were finally getting to grips with what had happened. In fact, it looked as though the man who'd murdered the witch doctor was the kingpin in the whole Debswana robbery. All they had to do now was catch him.

Chapter 77

When he left the Jwaneng police station, Mabaku headed straight to the mine to talk to Chamberlain. After going through the various security checks, he eventually ended up in front of the major's PA.

"Assistant Superintendent Mabaku from the CID." He showed her his police card. "I'd like to speak to Mr. Chamberlain, please."

"The major doesn't want to speak to anyone today," she responded. "He's in shock. As you know, one of his senior men committed suicide last night."

"That's why I'm here. Please let him know."

The PA hesitated.

"I'll give you five seconds. One…"

She picked up the phone. "Sorry to disturb you, Major. But Assistant Superintendent Mabaku is here to see you."

Mabaku couldn't hear the response.

"I know, sir," the PA continued, "but he insists. It's about Rra Tau."

After a few more seconds, she put down the phone. "Please go through."

Mabaku marched into the major's office and sat down.

"I can't believe it," the major said. "I never suspected that

Eddie was involved in the robbery. We've worked together for several years, and I thought he was completely loyal to me and to Debswana."

"Mr. Chamberlain, in your statement to the police, you said that you spoke to Tau last night after work. Tell me about that."

The major described how he'd received a call from Tau around dinner, pleading with him to go to his home to talk about the robbery.

"You stated that he confessed to leaking information about the backup plan and that he put something in the box with the diamonds."

"Yes."

"And that you tried to persuade him to turn himself in immediately."

"Yes. I thought he could make a deal—provide information in return for a lighter sentence. But he said he'd do it in the morning. He wanted to explain everything to his wife first."

"Did he seem suicidal?"

"Not at all. If he had, I'd never have left him. He must have realised he could go to prison for a long time. Or maybe he couldn't stand the thought of looking his friends and family in the eye, knowing that they knew what he'd done."

"I've read your statement, Mr. Chamberlain. You must have been in shock when you made it. I just want to make sure that you put down everything that Tau told you. Maybe you remembered something more when you got back to your office."

The major hesitated, then pulled a piece of paper out of his desk drawer.

"I didn't forget anything, but I purposefully left a couple of things out of the statement because the local police are totally incompetent. I didn't want them to make a complete hash of the investigation and lose the culprits and maybe the diamonds."

Mabaku took out his notebook and waited for the major to continue.

"The most important thing he told me was how they were

going to get rid of the diamonds. The robbers are meeting a fence in Johannesburg in four days."

"Do you know where and when?" Mabaku asked eagerly.

"The Zoo Lake at four in the afternoon. It's a park in Johannesburg."

Mabaku nodded. "There'll be good views in all directions and probably several roads to leave on. Better than a building, where it's easier for people to hide."

"So, you'll set up an ambush?"

"I don't know what we'll do—maybe nothing if the South Africans don't cooperate."

"Dammit, you have to do something. We need our diamonds back."

"We'll see. Did Tau tell you who this fence is?"

The major shook his head.

"That's a pity. Anything else?"

"Yes, because Tau was suspicious, he arrived early for a meeting with the witch doctor and saw him arrive in a pickup—a white pickup. He didn't pay attention to the make, but he wrote down its licence-plate number." He held up a piece of paper.

"Did you write it?"

"No, Tau did. I asked him to."

"Please put the paper down on the desk."

The major complied.

"Do you have an envelope?"

The major pressed a button on his phone and asked his PA to bring one through. While they waited, Mabaku copied the number into his notebook. When the PA put the envelope on the desk, Mabaku used his handkerchief to pick the paper up and put it in the envelope.

"Need to check for fingerprints. Now you see why it's useful we have yours. May I use your phone?"

The major dialled nine for an outside line and handed the handset to Mabaku.

Mabaku dialled the CID number, and the director's secretary answered.

"Miriam, this is Mabaku. I need to speak to the director."

Mabaku spent the next few minutes bringing the director up to date and asked him to have someone follow up on the licence-plate number. It was a South African number. *Probably stolen anyway*, Mabaku thought.

"Thank you, Director. I'll phone back in an hour to see if you've got any more information."

Mabaku handed the phone back to the major.

"Are you mad? Why didn't you tell him about the meeting in Joburg?"

"I will when I'm ready. In the meantime, Mr. Chamberlain, the local police think Tau died between eleven and one last night. Where were you at that time?"

"Are you insane? Do you think I killed Eddie? He bloody well committed suicide."

"Until his death is officially pronounced a suicide, I have to assume it may be a homicide. It's my job to gather information. Let me ask you again, where were you between eleven and one last night?"

"I was at home with my wife and daughter. She's visiting from Johannesburg. We watched a couple of episodes of a BBC series called *Morse*. And I went to bed about half past eleven."

"Thank you. I'll talk to them later."

"Don't you believe me?"

"Mr. Chamberlain, I don't have the luxury of believing anyone. I work in the world of facts that have to be checked and double-checked. Do you own a firearm?"

"This is preposterous. Of course, I own one. I've a British-Army-issued handgun, a Browning nine millimetre."

"I'll need to get it from you."

"Never! I'll never hand it over. I'll never see it again."

"Mr. Chamberlain, you *will* hand it over, right after we've finished here. And you *will* get it back if it wasn't used in the commission of a crime."

The major was quiet for a few moments. "Why do you need it?"

"We need to eliminate people such as yourself as suspects. We'll fire your gun and see if the bullet markings match with whatever we find in Tau's head. If what you say is correct, there won't be a match and you've nothing to worry about. I'll have a constable accompany you home."

The major sat scowling. "Any more accusations you want to make, Assistant Superintendent? Do you want me to stick out my hands so you can arrest me?"

"Not at the moment, thank you, Mr. Chamberlain. But I do have a few more questions. Do you owe anyone money? Any gambling debts? Anything you would like but can't afford, such as an anniversary gift for your wife?"

"You're a bastard, Mabaku. Digging into my private life. How did you know our anniversary is coming up?"

"I didn't. I just used it as an example."

"Well, for your information, I'm taking her for a couple of weeks to lie on the beach in Mauritius. And it's all paid for."

"When are you leaving?"

"We're going for Christmas and New Year."

"I asked you if you had any debts."

"No, I don't. Except for a little on my credit card."

"Please wait here until I can arrange for someone to escort you home to get the handgun. If your wife and daughter are there, please ask them to come to the station to give a statement about your whereabouts last night. It should only take a few minutes." He stood up. "My condolences for Rra Tau's death. Thank you for your time."

Chapter 78

Mabaku left the major's office and walked down the passage to speak to Goodman. When he got there, he noticed Tau's secretary sitting in the office opposite. Her eyes were red, and she'd clearly been crying. He went across to her.

"I'm very sorry about your boss's death, mma."

She nodded and wiped her eyes.

"May I ask you a question? Was Rra Tau right-handed?"

She looked puzzled and shook her head. "No, he was left-handed. I've seen him sign documents many times. Why do you want to know?"

"I'm just curious. Thank you."

It didn't take him long to be sure that Goodman hadn't been involved in Tau's death. Not only did Goodman have a watertight alibi, but Mabaku believed that his anguish at Tau's death was genuine. In addition, Goodman didn't seem concerned by the phone call he'd received from the deputy commissioner the previous afternoon.

"I didn't know who he could be referring to," he told Mabaku. "I couldn't believe it was the major, and I'd have bet my life it wasn't Eddie. I was shocked when the major told me he had committed suicide. I thought I knew him well."

"You had no indication he was involved in the robbery?"

"No."

"Nor that he might take his own life?"

"I still don't believe he would."

Mabaku thanked him and asked if he could use an office with a phone for an hour.

"Why don't you use the meeting room? There's a phone in there. Dial nine for an outside line."

Goodman showed Mabaku to the room, where he sat down and wrote a summary of his meetings. When he finished, he sat back. He was convinced Goodman wasn't involved. And he was pretty sure the major didn't shoot Tau, even though he enjoyed pulling his chain. He stood up and gazed out the window at the huge hole in the ground.

Maybe, he thought, *the problem is that I just don't like ex-British-Army personnel who insisted on being called by their rank.*

———

Mabaku's next stop was at the mine's infirmary, where he found Mma Tau slumped in a chair, sobbing. He introduced himself and offered his condolences.

"I'm sorry, mma, but I have to ask you a few questions."

She nodded.

"I believe you were visiting your mother last night."

She nodded.

"What time did you get home?"

"About ten o'clock."

"Was your husband at home?"

She nodded again.

"Did he seem normal?"

"Yes." She took a deep breath. "He'd never kill himself," she blurted.

"What happened when you got home? Anything different from usual?"

"Well, he said he had something important to tell me. I could tell he'd been drinking, so I wondered what it could be. He was usually quite private."

"Then?"

"Just as we sat down, the phone rang. When he returned, he said he had to go out for a quick meeting with Major Chamberlain. That he'd be back in fifteen minutes. When he wasn't back after half an hour I went to bed."

"I know what happened the next morning. It must have been a shock."

She choked back a sob.

"Just a few more questions, mma. Do you know of any reason why he would want to take his own life?"

"None. We were happy and lived comfortably."

"And when you saw him last, you had no indication he was so depressed he would do such a thing?"

"I would have known."

"Did he have any debts that you know of?"

"No."

"I have to ask this. Was he having an affair?"

"Impossible. We were always together."

"Thank you, mma. My deepest sympathies."

With that, he took his leave and walked back to his vehicle.

Chapter 79

When he left the mine, Mabaku headed back to the Jwaneng police station.

"What did you discover about the fingerprints?" he asked the station commander.

The man smiled. "His prints were on the gun. And only his prints. Just as I expected."

Mabaku knew how easy it was to fake that. "And the gun?"

The smile disappeared. "It's not licenced. Illegal." He shrugged. "Some people just want one and take a chance. Maybe he got it for the suicide."

"You've been tapping the conversations on the home phones of Chamberlain, Goodman, and Tau. I want to listen to those tapes."

"Why do you need to do that? He killed himself!"

"Dammit, Station Commander. I don't believe he did kill himself. And even if he did, I want to know why. And if he didn't, I want to know who killed him. Now, how do I get those tapes?"

"There's a technician two doors down the corridor on the right. Ask him."

Mabaku nodded and walked out, leaving the station commander fuming.

A few minutes later, Mabaku was sitting in the technician's office with the tapes set up.

"Start with the ones on Tau's line for yesterday."

There were several personal calls to and from Mma Tau during the day, but nothing unusual. Then at 6:48 p.m., there was Tau's call to the major asking him to come around to talk about the robbery.

Well, that agrees with Chamberlain's story, Mabaku thought.

However, the next call was a surprise. It was made at 8:14 p.m. Mabaku asked the technician to play it a second time.

"Gaborone Sun. How can I help you?"

"Room two ninety-three, please."

"I'll put you through."

There was a pause, and then a voice said, "Yes?"

"Call me at the second number in fifteen minutes." Then the call ended.

It was only two sentences, but Mabaku was sure that the caller was Chamberlain. All he could tell from the one word reply from room 293 was that it was a man. But why was Chamberlain phoning the hotel from Tau's number?

"Okay. Go on."

The next call was at 10:35 p.m., and it was interesting too.

"Hello, this is Eddie."

"I have a message for you. From the witch doctor."

"Who are you? Why are you calling me at home?" Tau's voice was slurred.

"Just listen. He needs to meet you. Go to the Pick n Pay parking area right now. He knows how to solve all the problems. Everything will be fine. But you must come right away. It's very important."

"Tell him to fuck off! Look where his visions have led me. Prison! Fuck off."

"If you don't go to him, he'll come to you. You don't want your wife involved in this, do you? Leave now." The line went dead, and that was the last call for the night.

"Do we know where that last call came from?" Mabaku asked.

The technician nodded and checked a spreadsheet on his desktop computer.

"It was a Jwaneng call box, sir," he replied.

"Wasn't a detective supposed to be monitoring these calls every day?"

The technician shrugged. "I was just told to record them and find out the numbers, sir. The station commander said he'd get a detective to go through them when someone wasn't busy."

Mabaku shook his head in exasperation. He grabbed the technician's phone, reached the CID, and told them to get someone over to the Sun.

"Find out who was occupying room two ninety-three last night. If he's still there, keep him under surveillance, but be careful. Don't try to approach him. He may be very dangerous. Call me back at the Jwaneng police station as soon as you have any information. Tell them I'm with the technician."

He turned back to the technician. "Let's listen to all the other calls now."

After about half an hour, a call was put through from reception. The man in room 293 had checked out the night before around 8:30 p.m. even though he was booked in for another night. He was a South African, and they had his name and passport number from the hotel register. Nothing else had been discovered about him as yet.

"Get on to the South Africans and find out what you can about him."

Then they went back to listening to the tapes. It was a long evening, but they discovered nothing else of interest.

SUNDAY
Chapter 80

Although it was a Sunday, almost all the detectives were at the CID. There was a strong feeling that at last they were close to catching the men responsible for the diamond robbery and the murders. No one wanted to miss out.

Kubu and Dow went to the director's office and spoke to Mabaku from there. After they'd related what they'd discovered at Otse, and Kubu's theory about Tuelo, there was a long pause on the line. At last Mabaku said, "Well, Bengu, it looks like you came up with some valuable information and even managed to avoid getting yourself killed. But if you keep pulling those sorts of stunts, you'd better have good unemployment insurance. And a funeral policy."

"Yes, sir," Kubu said, hoping the valuable information cancelled out the unemployment.

"It's an interesting theory about Vusi Tuelo. He seems to fit the profile we're looking for pretty well. Get his fingerprints from the South Africans and take them to forensics. With luck, we'll know if your theory makes any sense very soon. At the same time, try to match the fingerprints of the man you found murdered with the ones we found on the package that was given to the pilot and the partial we found behind the fetish on the diamond transport box."

"I'll follow that up right away, sir."

"What about Tau?" Gobey asked.

"I'm doubtful about the suicide theory," Mabaku replied. "But I'm pretty sure the Jwaneng mine managers aren't involved in his death. If he was murdered, then it was probably the man who was staying at the Sun. We need someone to follow up there with Tuelo's picture."

"I can do that, sir," Kubu volunteered.

"I want you to go to the morgue. The pathologist should be doing the autopsy on Tau this afternoon. We asked for top priority. Get his report. And tell him Tau was left-handed."

"Left-handed? Yes, sir."

"I hope the new pathologist knows his stuff," Gobey put in. "He's just out from Scotland. Probably more used to cold, wet bodies than hot, dehydrated ones." Dow chuckled.

"Bengu, get on with all that," Gobey instructed. "Ask Neo to follow up at the Sun. Mabaku, stay on the line. You can give us a more detailed report. Then head back. I need you here."

Kubu left, disappointed not to hear more about what Mabaku had discovered but enthused by the urgency of what he needed to do.

Chapter 81

As soon as Kubu had received Tuelo's faxed prints from South Africa, he went across to forensics. He wasn't sure if anyone would be there on a Sunday, but he met a technician, who called the head of the division, who was in his office. He was an elderly and imposing man and not impressed about being disturbed by a detective sergeant. However, once he'd heard the story, he became interested.

"Let's take a look," he said.

Kubu was surprised. He hadn't expected the head of forensics to do the work himself. The head sent the technician off to fetch the file of fingerprints that they'd lifted from the Otse house. While they waited, he asked Kubu what he knew about fingerprint matching. Kubu tried to recall the details of what he'd learnt at university but was worried that he might be confusing whorls and spirals. Nevertheless, the head seemed to be satisfied by his response.

When the technician returned with the file, the head took a magnifying glass from his desk drawer, polished it with his handkerchief, and started looking through the prints, checking each one in the file against the set of ten prints received from South Africa. It took him less than a minute to find a match.

"Take a look," he said.

Kubu took the magnifying glass and examined the prints.

"You see that tented arch?" the head asked, pointing to the ridge patterns with a pencil. "Now look at the index finger on Tuelo's right hand."

Kubu did so and picked out the peaked feature right away. Then he compared the surrounding structures. They were similar, but not identical.

The head nodded. "Remember that the prints often have smudges and distortions in practice. And these faxed ones aren't as clear as they might be." He frowned. "Ask them to send an image by email next time."

They found four more good matches, and the head said they didn't need to check any further. "No doubt about it," he said. "This man Vusi Tuelo was definitely in the house in Otse. And he was also at the secret hole in the border fence—his prints were on the cigarette found there."

They went through a similar process for the dead man Kubu had found at Otse and decided that the witch doctor who'd been involved in the robbery and the man whose throat had been cut were the same.

Kubu thanked the head and left greatly encouraged. His theories had been proved correct, and he hoped that Mabaku and the director would be suitably impressed. However, when he reached Gobey's office, Miriam told him the director would be out for some time, and when he went to Mabaku's office, the assistant superintendent hadn't returned yet. Since he had to follow up on the autopsy of Tau right away, he scribbled a message and left it on Mabaku's desk.

———

As Kubu drove to the Princess Marina Hospital, he was a little apprehensive. He'd never been to the morgue before and had a feeling that attending an autopsy was likely to be more gruelling than looking at the overhead slides that had been used to illustrate one in lectures.

He needn't have worried. By the time he'd reached the morgue behind the hospital, the pathologist had finished and was removing his gloves and lab coat.

He greeted Kubu with a smile. "Good day to you," he said with a broad Scottish burr. "I'm Dr. Ian MacGregor. I just started here this month. And you are?"

Kubu smiled back. "I'm Detective Sergeant David Bengu, but everyone calls me Kubu. And I'm also new."

MacGregor washed his hands and arms, dropped the towel in a laundry basket, and then shook Kubu's hand.

"Kubu? Does that name mean something?"

Kubu laughed. "Hippopotamus."

MacGregor's eyebrows raised. "I can see the similarity, but don't you mind? I mean..."

Kubu shook his head. "I'm used to it."

"Well, apart from their size, hippos have some other characteristics that are pretty impressive. So Kubu it is. Call me Ian. Now how can I help you?"

"Assistant Superintendent Mabaku wanted me to be here for the Tau autopsy and to get your report."

"Well, I just finished the autopsy, but I can show you the cadaver if you like. Or shall I just explain my findings?"

Kubu was relieved to settle for the latter. "What the assistant superintendent really wants to know is whether it was murder or suicide."

"I believe it was murder, but I can't be sure. Sit down and I'll explain." He pulled out a sheet of paper and drew a sketch of a skull from the front. Then he spent the next few minutes describing the trajectory of the bullet through the brain and the damage it'd done. Tau had died instantly.

"There may be some doubt about who pulled the trigger, but

no debate about the cause of death," Ian concluded. "There was powder burn and stippling around the wound, so I'd say that the gun was two or three centimetres from the head. That's unusual for suicides. They tend to put the gun against the skull. Stops it shaking."

Kubu was impressed by how much could be deduced from analysis of the injury. He took another look at MacGregor's diagram, and said, "Isn't it surprising that he shot himself in the right side of the head? The assistant superintendent found out that he was left-handed."

"Ah! Well, in that case, I'm confident it was murder. He couldn't have used his left hand to hold the gun to inflict that wound. It's physiologically impossible with that wound angle. And if he used his right hand, why didn't he support the gun on his head? Makes no sense. And another thing is that he was verra drunk. That actually supports suicide—alcohol is a depressant, ye ken. But shooting himself that way when he was that drunk?" He shook his head. "I don't believe he could do it."

He glanced at his watch. "Will that keep your boss happy till I get the full report to him? I need to do another autopsy now. This one had his throat cut. It's been quite a busy weekend already."

Kubu thanked him and took his leave.

"Nice to meet you, Kubu," MacGregor responded. "When the dust settles, maybe we can compare our impressions of our first weeks on the job. Maybe have a dram together?"

Kubu wasn't too sure what a dram was but agreed without hesitation. Not only would it be useful to be on good terms with the pathologist, but he had taken an immediate liking to the wiry Scotsman.

As he walked out of the morgue, he made a mental note to look up the other impressive characteristics of hippos.

Chapter 82

When he returned to the CID, Mabaku picked up Kubu's note, talked to Neo, and then headed for the director's office. When he arrived, Gobey was talking to the deputy national commissioner of police in Johannesburg. He motioned Mabaku to a seat, and then finished his conversation.

As he hung up the receiver, he sighed. "Well, it's all set up. The South African police will be at Zoo Lake in full force on Tuesday afternoon. I hope it's not a bloodbath. Apparently, there'll be a lot of people there—jogging and picnicking and just enjoying the park at this time of year."

"It's really our best chance to catch him," Mabaku responded. "It's Tuelo all right. Not only did the fingerprints from the Otse house match his, but one of the staff at the Sun recognised his picture.

"What puzzles me is the call to him from Tau's house. I'm convinced it was Chamberlain, but he denied it, of course. The voice recognition people will take a look at it, but they're doubtful. The whole conversation was less than a dozen words."

"Is it possible Chamberlain shot Tau?"

Mabaku shook his head. "I don't think so. Both his wife and his daughter were with him that night after he came home from

Tau's. I don't think they're lying. The wife's a bit of a battle-axe. I doubt she'd lie for him anyway. And she was at pains to tell me how well she was connected with the Oppenheimers at De Beers. No doubt the commissioner will get a call about it."

"So why would he get involved in something like this anyway? It sounds as though he has it made."

Mabaku shrugged. "I have no idea what his motive could be. I just can't see how anyone else with an English accent would be phoning from Tau's house that night. It's just too much of a coincidence."

"Well, I trust your instincts, Jacob. Maybe everything will be clearer if the police in Johannesburg nab Tuelo. Let's go home and see what happens tomorrow."

Mabaku nodded. It had been a long two days. "Thank you, sir. I think I could use a good night's sleep."

MONDAY
Chapter 83

There was a spring in his step as Kubu walked to work on Monday morning. He was happy that he'd made a significant contribution to the investigation of the diamond robbery. Now he wondered how it was going to be wrapped up.

He was pleased to see that Neo was in his office, so he walked in and sat down.

"Good morning, Neo. How was your weekend?"

"What weekend?"

Kubu shrugged. "I didn't have one either. Any news about the suitcases? What did the airlines say?"

"I have to give it to you, Kubu. Those questions you asked me to follow up on? I had no idea what you were thinking…"

"The tags didn't match the bags, right?"

Neo nodded. "Of the bags that the airlines thought didn't make it onto their final flights, seven still had the tags—three in England and four in France. All of those tags were for the stolen ones."

Kubu grinned with satisfaction. "It took me some time to see what was right in front of us. We assumed that the tags were on their respective suitcases when they were scanned. But then I realised that if they took the tags off the bags they wanted to steal, scanned them, and then switched them with tags that had already been scanned, it would look as though all the bags left Gabs. It was a clever idea."

"I'm still confused as to how they were able to take them off the airport."

"I'm not sure either, but it's sure to be simple. Let's check with the assistant superintendent that we can bring the two baggage handlers in the CCTV back here for questioning."

Chapter 84

Mabaku hadn't had the good night he was hoping for. He'd tossed and turned, trying to put the pieces of the case into order. It could all make sense: Tuelo planned the robbery and used the witch doctor to co-opt Tau, who was the insider supplying information about the backup plan and presumably arranging the fence. But was Tau so naïve that he told Tuelo who that was, making himself disposable? That was possible, but one piece wouldn't fit no matter how he tried it—the phone call from Tau's house to Tuelo at the Gaborone Sun. There was only one arrangement of the pieces that made that fit.

Still tired from the restless night, he went into the CID early to catch the director in his office. After their discussion, Gobey phoned the deputy commissioner.

"Deputy Commissioner, could we have a private meeting with you?" Gobey said. "There are a couple of issues we need to bring to your attention urgently."

The deputy commissioner agreed, and they headed across to his office.

Mabaku kicked off. "Deputy Commissioner, there is one aspect of our investigation that doesn't fit with Chamberlain's information. We learnt from our tap that there was a call from

Tau's house to Tuelo at the Gaborone Sun hotel around eight fifteen p.m. on the night he was murdered. Although I can't be certain, I believe it was Chamberlain. It certainly sounded like him."

"Go on."

"Chamberlain admits he was there that evening. He gave us all the information about the meeting with the fence that Tau supposedly told him. But it could just as easily have been information that he knew himself, because he was behind the whole crime and in touch with Tuelo."

The deputy commissioner frowned. "But it makes no sense! In your scenario, Chamberlain sets up the crime, including the fence, then tells Tuelo to kill Tau, and when it all works out according to plan, he throws it all away by telling you all the details. It doesn't add up."

"That is a big question. My guess is that Chamberlain didn't tell Tuelo to kill Tau or the witch doctor, for that matter. Quite likely he doesn't even know about the witch doctor's murder. I think he was alerting him to a problem. Tuelo decided to solve it his own way, just as he did by tipping off the SA police about the robbers crossing the border. After that, Chamberlain could see he was next. As soon as the meeting with the fence had taken place and they had the money, Tuelo would kill him too, and not only keep all the money but also get rid of the last connection to himself."

"But surely Tuelo and the fence will turn against him when they're captured? Their joint evidence will sink Chamberlain too."

Mabaku nodded. "That's true, but I think he'll have tipped off the fence not to be at Zoo Lake. He probably decided that he'd walk away free if it comes down to his word against that of a known felon like Tuelo."

"This is all based on that one phone call," the deputy commissioner objected. "That's pretty slender evidence and certainly nothing that Chamberlain wouldn't be able to beat in court." He turned to Gobey. "Director, what do you think? At the moment, we have Tau identified by his own admission as the insider at the mine, and if all goes well in Johannesburg, Tuelo will be caught and Debswana will have their diamonds back. Also, Mrs. Chamberlain is closely connected to the De Beers' Oppenheimers. Is it a good idea to go on what could be a wild goose chase that just raises difficult questions and embarrasses influential people?"

Gobey took his time before answering. "Deputy Commissioner, what about the families of those security guards? Would they be happy if Chamberlain was responsible for their loved ones' deaths and we let him go free?"

The deputy commissioner sighed and stood up. "Look into it. Try not to let it drag on, though. You need to have something concrete by the time the South African police spring their trap in Johannesburg."

It was clear that the meeting was over. The two detectives left him and headed back to the CID.

Chapter 85

When Gobey and Mabaku returned to the CID, they pulled Kubu from Neo's office and started brainstorming. Everything the deputy commissioner had said was true. They couldn't afford to accuse the major and have him laugh in their faces and walk away.

They tossed around some ideas, but none seemed promising. Kubu listened to the discussion without commenting. Then, when there was a pause, he asked, "If Chamberlain was behind the robbery, how did he communicate with Tuelo?"

The two senior detectives looked at him.

"Well, Assistant Superintendent Mabaku believes he phoned him at the hotel," Gobey said.

Mabaku understood immediately what Kubu was driving at. "But what about when Tuelo was at Otse with the witch doctor? There wasn't a phone in the house, was there?"

Kubu shook his head. "I didn't see one."

Gobey nodded. "They must have had an intermediary they communicated through."

"That would be another loose end for Tuelo," Mabaku responded. "He wouldn't want someone else in the loop.

"Cell phone?" Gobey suggested.

Mabaku shook his head. "They're so new, the network is only

available in Gaborone. Not even in Jwaneng, I believe. How about a message service?"

Kubu nodded. "I checked. There's only one in Botswana. And it's here in Gaborone."

Again, the senior detectives looked at him. It seemed the young detective sergeant was a few steps ahead of them.

"Go over there and see what you can find out," Gobey said.

"And go right now," Mabaku added.

Kubu was already on his feet heading for the door.

———

When Kubu arrived at In Touch, he expected to see something high-tech looking. In fact, the messaging service was in a small group of ordinary offices near the airport. The receptionist took him to the manager's office past half a dozen young women answering calls and typing at their computers.

The manager introduced herself and asked him how she could help. Kubu gave her a little background, making it clear that a major crime was involved, then asked her how the system worked.

"It's quite simple. You register an account and a password with us. When you want to leave a message, you give an account name. The operator checks it and sends the message to the appropriate mailbox. Alternatively, you can ask for messages received and be brought up to date with any messages left for you. For that you need to have the account password, of course."

"So, if you know the account number and the password, you can leave a message or retrieve messages?"

"Correct."

Kubu felt despondent. It sounded as though it was impossible to trace the person who owned a mailbox. Then he had a thought. "How do you do the billing?"

"Anyone who opens an account needs to provide identification and make arrangements for payment. That can be by payment in advance to cover a certain period, or by credit card or debit order."

That sounded more hopeful. Kubu thought it unlikely that the criminals would open an account in a real name, but he needed to ask. "Do you have an account in the name of David Chamberlain? Or Edward Tau?"

The manager hesitated, clearly concerned about sharing clients' information.

"In strict confidence, this is connected with that diamond robbery from Debswana."

She turned to her computer. After a few moments, she shook her head.

Perhaps Tuelo opened the account, Kubu thought. *But he wouldn't have done it in his own name.*

"What about Bongani Makanya?" he asked, giving the name Tuelo had used to register at the Gaborone Sun.

Again, she queried her database. "Yes, he is a client. He's a South African and gave his passport for identification. He also paid three months in advance."

"Do you still have the messages?"

She nodded. "We keep them for three months. This account has been active for about a month, so we still have all of them."

"I need a printout of them, please."

She hesitated again. "That information is confidential. We have a responsibility to our clients. You need a court order…"

"Five people have died already. There could be more deaths if we don't get the information we need immediately."

She thought for a few moments before she turned back to her computer. Kubu decided to push his luck. "Do you keep a record of the incoming phone numbers?"

She nodded. "They'll be on the printout."

A few minutes later, Kubu was given a computer printout with a list of about fifty entries, each with the date and time of the call, the phone number of the caller, and the message, if there was one. Kubu read through them.

"What does it mean if there's just a date, time, and number and no message?" he asked.

"The caller phoned to ask for his latest messages."

As Kubu scanned the printout, he saw that almost all the entries were of that type. All the calls seemed to come from just four numbers. Clearly, each party checked regularly to see if there was any communication. Only nine messages had content, and even those just requested a phone call at a certain time.

"Would any of your staff remember these callers?"

The manager shook her head. "We have dozens of messages every day. All the operators do is check the account is paid, and then type the message or ask for the password and read out the stored messages. Then on to the next call."

Kubu thanked her for her help and left. As he drove back to the CID, his first reaction was one of disappointment. There was nothing in the messages that identified the callers or what they were planning. But there was information there. The telephone numbers could be used to fix the callers at a certain place and time.

Chapter 86

Back at the CID, Kubu established that all the numbers were call boxes—two in Otse and one in Jwaneng—except for the number 588-1100, which was the main number of Jwaneng mine.

He went to see Mabaku, and together they worked through the list of calls. Kubu started.

"The first message was 18/11/1998–16:34–539 4281. That's an Otse call box. It reads: 'Here. All good. Call number B tomorrow three p.m.' That must have been Tuelo confirming that he was set up at the witch doctor's house. Only two call boxes were used in Otse, so they must have agreed to call them A and B."

Mabaku nodded. "Then the next morning there was a call from the mine with no message. So, let's assume it was Chamberlain who picked up Tuelo's message, and presumably he made that call at three p.m. We need to trace that. Maybe it came from a phone we can link to him."

Kubu agreed, but he wasn't optimistic.

The next message was a week later from a different Otse call box: "Ngaka to Jwaneng tomorrow."

"That will have been when the witch doctor started working on Tau," Mabaku commented. "The man was an idiot and paid for it with his life."

There were a few more messages to arrange calls, and then on the Saturday before the robbery, there was a message: "It's on." After that, there was nothing until the Thursday after the robbery. Then there was a call from the mine in the morning with an urgent request for a call.

"Thursday would have been the day when Chamberlain discovered that the diamonds hadn't been recovered in South Africa after all. Before that, he probably thought Tuelo had been killed with the others in the SA police stakeout," Mabaku noted.

The final entry was later that morning, and no message was left.

"After he picked up the message, Tuelo will have phoned the mine and told Chamberlain that he would be at the Gaborone Sun," Kubu said. "That's how Chamberlain knew to phone him at the hotel."

Mabaku nodded. "Let's get printouts of the calls to and from those call boxes. We can try the mine too, but they'll have hundreds of calls to go through. The problem is that if Tuelo was calling the mine, he could have been calling Chamberlain or Tau, and we can't distinguish between them this way."

"I'll go through the printouts for the call boxes with Sergeant Neo. It'll take us a bit of time."

Mabaku nodded and pointed to the printout from the messaging service. "This is a good start, Bengu." He frowned. "Chamberlain has been very careful, but he made a mistake when he called Tuelo from Tau's house. He must have made others. We just have to find them."

Kubu stood up. "One more thing, sir. Neo and I think we've solved how the suitcases went missing. They were stolen here in Gabs. We need to bring in some baggage handlers for questioning."

"Interesting. You'll have to tell me about it later. And I want to be there when you talk to them. I'm sure I know a few tricks you weren't taught at university."

Kubu headed for the door, certain he didn't ever want to be interrogated by Mabaku.

TUESDAY
Chapter 87

Mabaku obtained an order from a helpful judge, and to Kubu's surprise, the details of calls to and from the phone boxes in Jwaneng and Otse for the previous month arrived the next morning. He was also surprised by the length of the report when Miriam gave him the printouts. More people used call boxes than he'd realised. He immediately headed to Neo's office.

"Mathew, I need your help. The assistant superintendent wants us to match these numbers." He dumped the printouts on Neo's desk.

Neo frowned. "Why am I always helping you? I'm the senior detective here. But you get to go to meetings with the director, and I get to go through printouts. Do your own dirty work."

Kubu was amazed by the reaction. Only last week, he'd been struggling to be accepted by the CID detectives. Now it seemed they were jealous of him.

He thought it through. It was true he'd been assigned to investigate around Otse—an important assignment—and Mabaku had asked for him to join the meeting to brainstorm with the director. He'd thought that the other junior detectives were equally involved in important work, but now he realised that wasn't the case. He'd been singled out. Mabaku might be gruff and demanding, but he must have been impressed by his work.

"Nothing to say? That's unusual," Neo added.

Kubu realised that Neo's feathers were ruffled, and he needed to make an effort to smooth them.

"We're all doing important work, Mathew. I've been lucky to stumble on a few useful things. And a dead body! But the deputy commissioner made it quite clear at the meeting that this has been a team effort—we all contributed. I don't think my work is any more important than yours. We're all working together on this. And I need your help."

Neo hesitated, trying to evaluate Kubu's response. At last he said, "Okay. What do you need?"

The next hour was spent going through the printouts. A few calls had come in to the phone boxes, but almost all were outgoing. By matching the agreed-on times from the messaging service list with calls between phone boxes, the detectives were able to spot the two conversations that had taken place between Tuelo in Otse and the insider at Jwaneng. Both were lengthy. One was a week before the robbery and presumably covered the details of what was going to happen. The other was after the robbers had been killed.

Neo slumped in his chair. "So what? We've still no idea who was calling from Jwaneng."

"Let's check the other calls. Maybe we can pick up something."

They went on working.

Suddenly Neo sat up. "Here's something odd. Immediately after that second call from the Jwaneng call box to Tuelo, there's a call to a cell-phone number. There's only one other call to a cell phone over the whole three weeks, and it was to the same number several days later."

Kubu walked round the desk to take a look. Neo was correct. Immediately after one of the calls to Otse, whoever had been in the phone box had called the cell number.

Kubu scratched his head. "It can't be another person using the phone. It's too soon. Just seconds between the end of the Otse call and the start of the call to the cell phone."

"And here's the second call to that number from that box. On the fifth of December."

Both detectives stared at the printout. "That was after Tau was killed," Kubu pointed out. "If this is the same caller who was speaking to Tuelo in Otse, then it definitely wasn't Tau."

Kubu grabbed Neo's phone and dialled the number. There was some delay, and then he heard a recorded message.

"This is Lucas Letsa. I'm travelling out of the country at the moment. Please leave a message, and I'll get back to you when I return." There was a beep, and Kubu hung up.

"There was just a recorded message. The man's name is Lucas Letsa."

"Who's Lucas Letsa?"

"I don't know, but I think we need to find out. If Letsa has a cell phone, I bet he has a landline too. Do you have a telephone directory?"

Neo dug around in one of his drawers and produced it. He flipped through the pages till he reached L, and then ran his finger down the list of names.

"Here it is. There's only one Letsa. Letsa, L B. It has two listings. One must be his personal line. The other says Debswana and then gives a different phone number. That must be where he works."

Both of them sat and puzzled about what this latest loop back to Debswana could mean.

Kubu climbed to his feet. "Come on. We need to tell Assistant Superintendent Mabaku about this."

Chapter 88

Kubu told Mabaku what they'd found out, taking care to give Neo credit for spotting the cell-phone connection.

Mabaku listened attentively and then nodded. "It all hangs together. It could only be Chamberlain who made that second call. We need to look into Lucas Letsa and what he does at Debswana. Maybe he's the link to the fence. If so, I'll bet that call was to warn the fence of the police trap, and the fence won't be at Zoo Lake."

Kubu told him that he'd called the number, but Letsa's cell phone went straight to voice mail.

Mabaku considered that for a few moments. "Letsa will never admit to a connection with a fence. I'll check if he's being investigated for anything, but it's a very long shot. It's convenient that he's away, isn't it?" He paused. "We really don't have enough evidence to take it further. Tuelo was very helpful to Chamberlain by bumping off Tau and the witch doctor. They might have known something that pointed to him. Probably Tuelo and Chamberlain met at some point, but they would've been careless to do it in public. And they're not careless. As for the witch doctor, probably Chamberlain never met him at all. Why would he?"

"Maybe he doesn't even know that the witch doctor is dead,"

Neo put in. "The man hasn't been identified yet. We're still waiting for input from the SA police."

Kubu sat up. "If that's true, we could…" He trailed off. His idea seemed too way-out to be worth mentioning. *Mabaku will laugh at me,* he thought.

"Well, what's your idea?"

Kubu shook his head. "I just thought of something, but it's silly."

"Sometimes Kubu's silly ideas work out," Neo said.

"Spit it out then," Mabaku said

"Well, I was just thinking that if Tuelo is caught and out of the way, and Chamberlain thinks that the witch doctor is still alive, maybe we could use the witch doctor to make him incriminate himself."

"But the witch doctor is dead!" Mabaku snapped.

"It wouldn't be that witch doctor. I know someone who might help us…"

Neo looked uncomfortable and drew back a bit. "You know a witch doctor?"

"He helped me find the murdered witch doctor. He would be very convincing."

"Why would Chamberlain even talk to him?"

"Perhaps he could say that he knows Chamberlain was involved. Pretend to blackmail him," Neo suggested.

Mabaku shook his head. "He expects Tuelo to point to him. He'll just say they're in it together to try to shift the blame."

"If Chamberlain is behind the robbery…" Kubu began tentatively.

"Well, we're working on that hypothesis," Mabaku interjected.

"Then it was for a share of the value of the diamonds."

"But if we catch Tuelo, there will be no share. And the diamonds will have been recovered," Neo said, obviously puzzled.

"But Chamberlain doesn't know that," Kubu added. "We could say the diamonds weren't recovered even though they actually were."

Neo was shaking his head. "This is like the suitcase business again," he muttered.

However, Mabaku was looking thoughtful. "So, your witch doctor could show him some diamonds and say he knows where the rest are."

"And then when Chamberlain tries to find out and goes along with the witch doctor's instructions, we grab him."

"There's a problem," Mabaku objected. "He'll just say he was going along with it to try to recover the diamonds for Debswana."

"I think we can do something a bit more dramatic," Kubu suggested. "Something that Chamberlain will find hard to resist. And it'll require his input. Something he could only know if he was working with Tuelo."

They spent the next half hour working it out in detail. Then Mabaku went to try to sell the whole plan to Gobey.

"Wish me luck," he said as he headed for the director's office. "I'm going to need it."

WEDNESDAY
Chapter 89

Senior Superintendent Buthelezi was very nervous. He was sitting in the back of what looked like a delivery van in a parking area at Johannesburg's Zoo Lake on the basis of a tip-off from the Botswana police. The man he'd been tasked to capture, Vusi Tuelo, was wanted for murder and armed robbery by both the South African and Botswana Police Services.

It wasn't the fact that he would almost certainly be armed that worried Buthelezi. He was used to that sort of danger. It was that the exchange of stolen goods for money was going to take place in a public park with plenty of civilians wandering around. Every one of them could be in danger if they couldn't arrest Tuelo without a firefight.

He was also nervous because so much was unknown. All he'd been told was that an exchange was going to take place. He didn't know who the fence was or what he looked like. Or precisely where it would happen. After all, the Zoo Lake area was large, comprising both the lake and substantial park land. It was quite possible that they could miss the exchange completely.

He wasn't sure how both parties would arrive. Would they arrive by car? On foot? Or, as he expected, by motorbike, which would make escape much easier in the snarled traffic of a

Johannesburg peak period? He'd planned for the latter because it
made the most sense and had strategically stationed four motorcy-
cle policemen several blocks away from the park in each direction,
keeping out of sight until needed. He also had three policemen
and one policewoman in civilian dress in different locations. He
prayed that they looked like normal citizens and not policemen
dressed as normal citizens. Finally, in the back of the van with
him were four top members of the police SWAT team.

The final big unknown was when the exchange would take
place. They'd been told four o'clock, but that was just a point in
time. Both Tuelo and the fence would be checking and double-
checking that the situation was safe. He didn't know how they
would do that. Would they sit far away and check everyone
with binoculars? Would they send surrogates? If they did that,
the operation was certainly doomed. Did each know what the
other looked like? One had to assume that at least one knew
what the other looked like. Otherwise how would they make
the connection?

Buthelezi hated it when there were so many questions.

As he thought through his plan, he felt very uneasy that it was
based on only two pieces of solid information. He knew what
Tuelo looked like, as did all the policemen and policewomen in
the operation. And Tuelo would be carrying about twenty kilo-
grams of diamonds—a heavy load that would impair his mobility.
So Buthelezi's plan was flexible. As soon as Tuelo was spotted, he
would be informed and only then decide how to proceed.

Buthelezi picked up his microphone. "Rowboat, everything
okay?"

Constable van der Merwe was an added worry. He didn't
like putting women in danger, and she'd be on a rowing boat in
the middle of the lake posing as a birdwatcher. It was the best
vantage point but made her a sitting duck if Tuelo suspected her.
He winced at the metaphor. However, she was the least likely to
catch anyone's attention.

He checked in on all the rest of his people, and they all acknowledged they were in position.

He clicked the microphone. "Now we have to wait. Try to act normal."

———

It was four thirty-five, and Constable van der Merwe was at the end of her second lap around the island. Every now and again, she raised her binoculars, ostensibly to look at the colonies of cattle egret and sacred ibis roosting in the trees, but in reality, to check out newcomers to the area. A movement caught her eye, and she saw a man pushing a motorbike over the grass towards the lake from the Bowls Club side. He was walking slowly, constantly looking around.

She casually moved her hand to the switch under her blouse. "Ndlovu, come in for Rowboat."

"Go ahead, Rowboat," Buthelezi responded quietly.

"Man with bike approaching from the south."

"Roger. Camera one, did you copy?"

"Roger. Stand by."

At the far end of the lake, an older man briefly dipped his 600mm lens and photographed the man and his bike. Then he quickly adjusted it back for photographing the roosting birds. At his distance, it was unlikely the man would have noticed. The photographer looked at the image on the screen at the back of the camera.

"Ndlovu, it's him."

"Thank you. Rowboat, move away now. Bikers, all move closer into your position two. All others, continue as before."

Buthelezi slid open a small panel on the side of the van and used his binoculars to scan. It took some time before he was able to see Tuelo and his bike.

"Suspect is wearing a coat, probably concealing a weapon. And has a backpack. I assume it's the stolen goods but don't know for certain. Old Man, he's approaching you. Let him pass and wait until I tell you."

As Tuelo approached, Old Man looked up from his book and nodded a greeting. Then he returned to reading. Buthelezi could see Tuelo hesitate, but then he moved forward again.

"Ice Cream, approach."

A young man on a tricycle with an ice-cream cooler on the front started moving slowly along the path next to the lake in Tuelo's direction. "Ice creams, Eskimo pies, lollipops," he shouted, ringing his bell. "It's hot. Cool off. Get your ice creams here."

Buthelezi saw Tuelo stop and look around. *He's worried that someone's moving towards him,* he thought.

"Ice Cream, stop at that couple on the grass to your right. Offer them a free ice cream each. Then talk to them."

"Roger."

Buthelezi decided it was time to move. "Old Man, follow the suspect."

"Roger."

Just as Old Man stood up, Buthelezi saw a dog bounding in the direction of Tuelo, followed by three children. Tuelo stopped again and looked back.

Buthelezi grimaced. "Old Man, call the dog. Talk to the children."

He watched as Old Man tried to help the children catch the dog, which appeared to take delight in approaching, then running away.

Tuelo watched for a few moments, then continued walking.

"Damn that dog!" Buthelezi growled. "Camera one, pick up your tripod and move closer."

"Roger."

At last, one of the children grabbed the dog and gave it a couple of smacks. Buthelezi could see Old Man say something, then continue walking.

"Get ready, Ice Cream."

"Roger."

Tuelo stopped again and looked back at Old Man shuffling towards him thirty metres away. He looked at Ice Cream, forty metres ahead.

He's beginning to feel trapped, Buthelezi thought. He took a deep breath.

"Old Man, do it!"

Chapter 90

Old Man pulled an automatic from his shoulder holster. "Police. Put your hands up." Tuelo whipped around, pulled a gun from under his coat, and fired at Old Man, who collapsed to the ground.

"Drop your gun!" It was Ice Cream, now running towards Tuelo, who fired a couple of shots in his direction.

Tuelo jumped on his motorbike, kicked it into life, and headed away from the lake directly at a group of picnickers, who scattered in terror as the bike approached. Ice Cream held his fire for fear of hitting the bystanders.

"Bikers, suspect is headed towards Westwold Way and Jan Smuts Avenue. Report contact."

A few moments later he received confirmation that Biker Two had Tuelo in sight.

"Suspect headed north on Jan Smuts. Following."

———

Biker Two had never been so frightened as he followed Tuelo along Jan Smuts Avenue. It was peak period, and the northbound two lanes were bumper to bumper. When there was no oncoming traffic, Tuelo roared down the wrong side of the road. When traffic came towards him, he swerved between the lines of cars, barely missing them on either side. A couple of times, he even used the pavement. Biker Two thanked God there were no pedestrians.

There was no point in trying to close the gap. There were far too many civilians around. All Biker Two hoped to do was keep Tuelo in sight until an opportunity came to engage.

Tuelo moved onto the wrong side of the road again. Biker Two followed, a hundred metres behind. He hoped Tuelo would turn up one of the side streets where there was little traffic. Instead, as a car came towards him, Tuelo shot through a narrow gap between two cars and accelerated between the two ribbons of cars. Biker Two followed, terrified that someone would change lanes or open a car door.

A few moments later, Tuelo was on the wrong side of the road again, then between the lanes of traffic. Then back on the wrong side.

"What's your position Biker Two?"

"Still Jan Smuts northbound," he gasped.

Just then Tuelo cut back between the lines of traffic as a bus came towards him. Biker Two followed. Suddenly a minibus taxi changed lanes without indicating. Tuelo braked but was too late. He crashed into the side of the taxi and was thrown into the air, hitting the top of the taxi, causing him to somersault several times before hitting the ground.

Biker Two screeched to a halt, pulled his handgun, and screamed at the people getting out of their cars. "Police, police. Get away. He's dangerous."

As the people scattered, he ran up to Tuelo, who was lying motionless on the ground, bleeding profusely from his head. He held his gun to Tuelo's head and grabbed the gun from under his jacket. He stuffed it into his belt. Then he unclipped the buckle of the backpack and pulled the pack roughly off Tuelo's back. He twisted one arm behind Tuelo's back and snapped on a handcuff, then did the same with the other arm. After what

Tuelo had just put him through, he wasn't inclined to be gentle. Finally, he unzipped the backpack's flap and gazed at hundreds of glasslike stones, but he didn't know if they were diamonds. He just hoped they were.

He closed the flap, picked up the pack, and ran back to his bike. "Ndlovu, this is Biker Two. Suspect is down near Bompas Road. Need an ambulance. Urgent. And I have the stones."

Chapter 91

It was nearly six o'clock when the deputy commissioner's phone rang. He grabbed the handset. "This is the deputy commissioner."

For the next few minutes, he took notes as the voice at the other end of the line explained what had transpired. At the end, he asked a few questions, then offered his thanks.

"Thank you, Deputy National Commissioner. The South African Police Service has been a great help. I look forward to your updates and will get back to you when I've briefed the people here. We realise it'll be impossible to prevent reporting of the incident because it's so public, but it would help us if the details can be kept quiet for a few days, such as who the fugitive was and why he was being sought. Also, it's critical that there's no announcement of the recovery of the diamonds. We still have some work to do here."

After he hung up, he phoned the commissioner to bring him up to date. Then he called Director Gobey and asked him to bring Mabaku, Dow, and Bengu to his office for a meeting in fifteen minutes.

"You're going to like what I'm going to tell you."

———

The deputy commissioner addressed a full meeting of the CID detectives. Everyone was keen to know what had happened at the Zoo Lake, and there was enthusiastic clapping when he announced that Tuelo, the ringleader of the robbery, had been captured. Furthermore, the police were sure that Tuelo was the person who had murdered Tau, his accomplice inside Jwaneng. Tuelo was currently in intensive care under heavy guard. The diamonds hadn't been found yet, but the South African police were confident that they soon would be.

"On behalf of the commissioner," the deputy commissioner concluded, "I'd like to thank you all for bringing this case to a successful conclusion. Any questions?"

"Was the fence captured?" Dow asked.

The deputy commissioner shook his head. "The South African police closed the park and interviewed bystanders, but there were no suspects. Somehow he must have realised there was something very wrong."

Mabaku nodded. That was what he'd expected.

Kubu put up his hand. "Deputy Commissioner, has Tuelo said anything to the SA police yet?"

The deputy commissioner shook his head. "He's unconscious. We're not sure he'll survive. But that's confidential."

After a few more questions, the deputy commissioner closed the meeting. On his way out, he pulled Mabaku aside. "Assistant Superintendent, this obviously isn't important now, but for your information, I checked the director's finances carefully. Everything is in perfect order."

"Of course, sir. I'm sorry—"

"Don't be. You did the right thing."

With that, he turned and headed off to his office.

THURSDAY
Chapter 92

Major Chamberlain liked an early start at the office, but there were usually a few people around before him. However, on the morning after the trap had been sprung at Zoo Lake, the office block seemed deserted when he arrived. He hardly noticed. His mind was on the future.

One thing that still puzzled him was why Tuelo had hidden the diamonds. What was the point of going to the rendezvous without them? Apparently, he'd been wearing a heavy backpack, but it'd turned out to be full of gravel yet again.

He'd spent the night wracking his brains over where the diamonds could be, going through every possible scenario that Tuelo could have followed. But in the early hours of the morning, he came to the conclusion that there was nothing he could do about it. He knew he'd have to fight off the suspicions of the police and the disdain of his wife, but he was confident he could handle both, provided he was careful. So, he'd resigned himself to the failure of his plan.

One consolation was that perhaps the contribution he'd made to the arrest of Tuelo would help him with future promotion, help him escape from the dusty nothingness of Jwaneng and the constant nagging of his wife.

He walked through his PA's office—she'd make his first cup of coffee when she arrived at 8:00 a.m.—and started to unlock his door but discovered it wasn't locked.

I must've forgotten to lock it when I left yesterday, he thought. *There was a lot on my mind.*

He opened the door and walked into his office. Then he froze, staring at the man seated behind his desk.

"Who the hell are you, and what are you doing in my office?" he spluttered.

The man sitting in his chair was wearing a leopard skin over his otherwise bare shoulders, and a necklace of bones around his neck. He'd placed the head of a crow on the desk in front of him, and it was oozing blood over the major's papers.

"I am Katlego. Everything that was done was done by me. Everything that was undone was undone by you."

"Get out! I'm going to call security right now." He started backing towards the door.

Katlego picked up the crow's head and pointed its beak at the major. He laughed when he ducked. "Call them if you like. They will not come."

He didn't want to, but the major believed him. "Who are you?" he asked again.

"I told you who I am. I destroyed the plane to block the runway. I wove the spell over Tau so that he would help us. I bewitched Kenosi to hijack the security vehicle. And yet you ask who I am?"

"You're Tuelo's witch doctor?"

Katlego shook his head. "I belong to myself. And the spirits."

The major bristled. "That's all nonsense. He hired some confidence trickster to pretend to be a witch doctor. What do you bloody well want?"

"Is that what he told you?" Katlego laughed. "He probably thought you wouldn't believe the truth and made up that stupid story. As to what I want, I want you to help me sell the diamonds. You know how to do that."

For the first time, the major saw a possible advantage to himself. "The diamonds? You have them?"

Katlego was silent.

The major pulled himself together. "I don't believe you. Are you from the police?"

Katlego laughed again. "The police? Am I from the police?" He stopped laughing and stood up behind the desk. He was an imposing figure, and the major took another step back.

"You betrayed us!" Katlego thundered. "We had won, and even though you did nothing, you would have got your share. But you betrayed us!"

"No! It was Tau, not me. He—"

"You told them! He knew nothing about the arrangement with Letsa. It was you!"

"But Tuelo killed Tau when I told him he was going to the police! He would have killed me too. And you!"

"You believe he could have killed *me*?" The witch doctor sneered. "Tuelo is nothing."

Katlego had come around the desk and was walking closer. He had a knobkierie in his right hand.

"You are supposed to be a soldier, but when you smell danger, you run like a girl child."

He was getting closer.

At last the major stood his ground. "All right. It doesn't matter what you think. Tuelo killed a lot of people. That was never supposed to happen. He can rot in jail for all I care. I had a perfect plan, and he ruined it with his greed and violence!"

The witch doctor was now standing in front of him.

"We can work together," the major went on. "I'll contact Letsa. He can set up the deal again. If Tuelo hadn't had the robbers killed, the diamonds would already have been safely sold. He's the one to blame for this mess. Not me." He paused. "You have the diamonds?"

Katlego reached into his pocket and took out a handful of raw gems. He let them trickle to the floor.

The major suppressed the urge to pick them up. He looked Katlego in the eye. "Fifty-fifty. Same as the deal with Tuelo before he double-crossed me."

Katlego reached forward and wiped his bloody hands on the major's shirt. Then he walked out of the office without another word.

The major turned to follow him but found the door blocked. The man standing in the doorway was Assistant Superintendent Mabaku. He was holding a set of handcuffs.

———

Katlego walked next door, where Kubu and a technician had the sound-recording equipment.

"Well, young Bengu," he said as the technician relieved him of the microphone and small transmitter from under the leopard skin, "I hope you enjoyed the performance."

Kubu jumped up and shook his hand, ignoring the red dye on it. "You were brilliant! You could be a professional actor."

Katlego laughed. "There's no money in that. But every successful witch doctor has some talent in that direction. It's not enough for people to get what they want; they need to feel its value also." He smiled. "I'm going to change into some proper clothes. I don't believe I'll meet you again, but I foresee a bright future for you. Greet your father for me."

He left to get cleaned up.

Kubu wondered about his comment. A bright future? Was that just a compliment, or was it a prediction? He shook his head to dispel such nonsense.

He went into the passage in time to see Chamberlain being led away by two constables.

Some Weeks Later
Chapter 93

Kubu drove up to a small block of flats not too far from where he was staying. He was so excited that he was fifteen minutes early. He parked the Land Rover and thought back on the events that had brought him there.

He still couldn't believe he'd accepted Joy's suggestion that they go out for a Saturday lunch. He'd been returning the map he'd borrowed, thankful he'd been able to erase the marks Constable Murewa had made when he was in Otse, when she'd sprung the idea on him. He was so surprised that he'd blurted out that he'd take them to The Palms. She'd just laughed and said that she knew he couldn't afford that. She'd suggested a restaurant that she'd found to be of good value.

"And," she'd insisted, "we're going to share the cost."

Kubu had just stood there speechless for a few moments, his emotions in turmoil. He wanted to be the perfect gentleman but had to acknowledge she was right about his finances. Going to a more modest establishment than he'd suggested was fine, but splitting the costs? That was going too far.

"No, it's my treat," he'd protested.

She'd just laughed again, her eyes twinkling. "When you're

an assistant superintendent, you can treat me. Until then, we split the bill."

Kubu was smart enough to know he wasn't going to win this battle with a woman whose soft smile seemed to belie an iron will.

"Well, if you insist," he'd demurred. "But I'll pick you up if you're willing to ride in an old Land Rover that needs to be driven occasionally."

"I'd like that. How about a week from Saturday at noon? I'll write down my address. I'd give you my phone number, but I don't have a phone. They're too expensive."

"I don't have one either," Kubu had responded, thankful they were on a less challenging topic.

He remembered walking back to his office, heart pounding, mulling over what had just happened. On the one hand, he'd felt elated that she'd taken the initiative. That was a great relief because he wasn't sure he would have had the courage to do it. On the other hand, he'd felt a little embarrassed to be asked out by a woman. Invitations were a man's job, he'd thought.

And it seemed that Joy was possibly thinking that this may not be the only time they would go out. After all, she'd said he could treat her when he'd become an assistant superintendent, which was obviously years ahead.

When he'd reached his office, he'd shut the door, sat down, put his feet on his desk, and let his imagination take over.

————

Kubu walked up the two flights of stairs and paused on the landing to catch his breath and pat down the wrinkles in his shirt.

Well, here goes, he said to himself.

He walked along the passage to Flat 14 and knocked. As he waited, he had a horrible feeling that he should have brought flowers. He felt his stomach tighten.

He knocked again, now worried that Joy had decided her

suggestion had been a mistake. Then the door opened. Kubu took a step forward and smiled, then stopped. It wasn't Joy at the door, but someone he didn't know.

"I'm so sorry. I must have the wrong flat. I'm looking for Joy Serowe. Do you know her?"

The woman smiled. "Come in. I'm Pleasant, Joy's sister. You must be Kubu. Nice to meet you." She reached out to shake his hand. Kubu responded, feeling overwhelmed. He was on his first date, and already other people knew about it. He'd hoped to keep it under wraps in case it didn't turn out well.

"Joy will be out in a few minutes. Can I get you a glass of water or a cup of tea?"

Kubu declined, then felt embarrassed as Pleasant mentioned that she'd heard that Kubu was new to the CID and had been instrumental in solving the department's biggest case.

"No, it was a team effort. Everyone made an important contribution."

"Anyway, congratulations."

Kubu mumbled his thanks and stood, feeling decidedly awkward. "Have you lived here long?"

Pleasant was about to answer when Joy walked into the room. Kubu thought his heart had stopped. He couldn't take his eyes off her. Her dress was casual, yet stunning, with an abstract pattern of muted, typically African colours. And her smile! Happy and warm. He wanted to take her into his arms and give her a big hug.

"Hello, Kubu. Ready for the big adventure?"

Kubu stuck out his hand to avoid answering. "Nice to see you again, Joy."

She shook his hand, then pulled him towards the door. "Let's go."

"Don't do anything I wouldn't do," Pleasant warned as they left.

Joy rolled her eyes. "Younger sisters! Come on, Kubu. I'm hungry."

Chapter 94

"I hoped this was the restaurant you had in mind," Kubu said as they sat down. "I've heard it's very good."

"I've been here a couple of times. I like it."

Kubu was thankful that the waitress arrived with menus because he wasn't sure how to continue the conversation. "What would you like to drink?" she asked.

Kubu looked at Joy. "Just a glass of water."

"And you, sir?"

Kubu wondered whether he should order what he really wanted—a glass of wine—but decided that Joy may disapprove of drinking alcohol at lunch. So, he opted for a safe alternative. "A diet cola, please. But no ice."

What if she's completely against alcohol? What will she think when she finds out I like wine?

He took a deep breath, trying to find something to say.

"Tell me about your family, Kubu. Are you from Gabs? Do you have brothers and sisters?"

This was a safe topic, so Kubu opened up and talked about his upbringing in Mochudi and how lucky he was to have loving parents who'd sacrificed so much to ensure he'd receive a good education.

"They even managed to persuade our local priest to approach Maru-a-Pula School to give me a scholarship."

"You went to Maru-a-Pula? That must have been difficult— with all those rich kids."

"Actually, it was wonderful. The teachers were very good and helped me a lot. And even though it took quite a long time, I did make some friends, mainly through sport."

Joy looked at him quizzically. "What sports did you play?"

"Oh no. I didn't play, but I was the scorer for the cricket team. I liked that." He paused, wondering whether he should say what was on his mind. "Actually, it was there that I got my nickname. One of the boys, Angus Hofmeyr, called me a kubu, for obvious reasons."

"That wasn't very nice, calling someone a hippo."

"I was hurt at first, but he didn't say it to hurt, but more as a term of affection, I think."

"You should have flattened him."

"Anyway, I got used to it. Now I hardly know that my real name is David. Everyone calls me Kubu."

———

Kubu was thankful when the food arrived because he had a respite from Joy's gentle probing. As he chewed on his lamb burger, he realised he'd done almost all of the talking so far, without feeling at all embarrassed.

She's so easy to talk to, but I don't know anything about her.

They both passed on dessert, and when the coffee arrived, Kubu started asking Joy about herself. He discovered that her childhood had been very different from his. She'd grown up in Francistown and was a middle child with an older brother, Sampson, and sister, Pleasant, who was two years younger. Her mother had been a teacher, and her father had owned a small but successful shop. Joy was fifteen when their mother died from tuberculosis.

"It was the worst moment of my life. We were very close." Kubu could see Joy's eyes tear up.

"What did your father do?"

"He was devastated and threw himself into making his shop even more successful. We hardly saw him. Fortunately, both my grandmothers were still alive, and they took care of us."

"When did you come to Gabs?"

"Two years ago. My father had a massive heart attack and died."

"I'm so sorry."

"Thank you. None of us knew anything about running a shop, so we sold it, probably for less than what it was worth. But we ended up with more money than we'd ever had. Pleasant and I decided to come to Gabs and find work. Sampson stayed in Francistown and works for the government."

"What does Pleasant do?"

"She's a travel agent."

"Why did you join the police? It's seems an odd place for a woman to work."

Kubu could see Joy bristle. "What do you mean by that?"

Kubu blushed and stammered an apology. "I mean..."

"I joined the police service so I could find a husband. A strong man who would protect me."

Kubu didn't know what to think. Why had she asked him out then? He hardly fit that image. He sat there desperately trying to find something to say.

Then she burst out laughing. "I was working for an agency that provided temporary staff. I was assigned a few times to the police records department, and they liked what I did, and I enjoyed the people I was working with. When they offered me a full-time job, I accepted."

———

"So, tell me how you like being a detective."

Kubu signalled the waitress to bring two more coffees.

"I love it! Other than the paperwork, of course. I get really bored filling out forms, so I make mistakes. Then I have to do it again. Otherwise, it's even better than I expected. My first case was really intriguing. Let me tell you about it."

Kubu then told her about the suitcases that apparently went to their destinations, only not to arrive there.

Joy frowned. "That doesn't make sense."

"That's why it was so interesting." He then went on to explain how the tags were switched. "So, in fact, although their tags reached their destinations, the bags didn't. They never left the airport here."

"But how did they take them from the airport? It would've looked suspicious for baggage handlers to walk out of the terminal carrying fifteen bags."

"That puzzled us also, but when we grilled them, they eventually told us. Very simple, actually. After taking the tags off, they returned to the terminal with the bags and put them onto the same carousel as the bags they'd just taken off the plane. Since that was what they did the whole time, nobody had a second thought about it. Then an accomplice who worked for a travel agent just took them off the carousel and put them in his tour bus. Nobody was suspicious because that was his job, something he did every day. Quite clever."

Joy laughed. "It's amazing what people will get up to."

"It was a very small case, but very intriguing. Very different to the diamond heist."

"Tell me how you solved that one."

Chapter 95

The waitress returned and put down the cups of coffee. Kubu took a sip. "First, I didn't solve it. We did. Everyone played a part. And second, for me, the most important thing I learnt was how little I know. After university, I thought that I knew a lot, but now I realise that the most important learning comes on the job. Assistant Superintendent Mabaku has a reputation as a tough taskmaster, but I have to say, I've learnt a lot from him. He is tough, but he's fair."

"Please tell me about the case."

For the next fifteen minutes, Kubu described his role in the case, from being a note-taker in meetings to being responsible for locating a witch doctor who seemed to be heavily involved in the robbery.

"It's interesting," he continued. "One of the things I learnt at university is that most criminals are not that bright, that they make mistakes. But this lot was pretty careful. I was lucky to spot a simple mistake the so-called witch doctor had made. He gave a fetish to a white man. I thought anyone who was a real witch doctor would have known that most whites are not worried about fetishes and spells. That it wouldn't have any impact. That got me thinking that maybe this witch doctor was in fact a person just pretending to be one. That opened our eyes to other possibilities.

"Then I had a second piece of luck. The day I joined the CID, I browsed through a folder of APBs. One of them was of a safe-breaker wanted by the South African police for murder and armed robbery. I remembered the face, which was unusually narrow. So, when a woman described a person at a place we were interested in as looking like a jackal, I thought there may be a connection. It turned out there was."

"Was he the brains behind the operation?"

"We thought so initially, because he systematically got rid of anyone who could identify him. He ordered the armoured-car guards murdered, including the one who hijacked the armoured car with the diamonds. Then he tipped off the police in South Africa to set up a stakeout where all the robbers were killed, and he slit the throat of the man who was pretending to be a witch doctor.

"Then we picked up another mistake." Kubu explained how Chamberlain said that the mine's head of security, Eddie Tau, told him that he was going to confess to his involvement in the crime. Tau was murdered shortly afterwards on the same evening.

"But it turned out that Chamberlain made a call from Tau's home to the Gaborone Sun hotel right after speaking to him. The hotel confirmed later that the person who received the call was our jackal-faced suspect. Now we had Chamberlain linked with the robbers. But jackal-face realised Tau could identify him and drove to Jwaneng that night and shot Tau, trying to make it look like a suicide. I think the only thing that saved Chamberlain that night was that he was the only one who knew the fence in Johannesburg who would exchange the diamonds for hard cash."

Kubu stirred his coffee and took a big mouthful. He wasn't used to talking so much and needed to catch his thoughts. Joy said nothing.

"So, we were pretty sure of who'd been involved—jackal-face for the robbery and murders, and Chamberlain for the brains. But knowing all of this doesn't amount to much without hard evidence, so we had to work out how to catch them.

"Fortunately, Chamberlain gave us jackal-face on a platter. He told us when and where the diamonds were going to be given to a fence. At a park in Johannesburg, in fact."

"How would Chamberlain know a fence?" Joy interrupted.

"He didn't. But he knew someone who did—a Lucas Letsa who works for Debswana. It turns out he's a con man who conned his way into Debswana using false credentials. He'll be met by police when he returns to Botswana—if he does."

Kubu drained his coffee cup, then continued. "So, the South African police set up an ambush at the Zoo Lake to catch both jackal-face and the fence."

"But why did Chamberlain do that? He lost his share of the diamonds that way, didn't he?"

Kubu nodded. "We think that Chamberlain had realised the situation was deteriorating rapidly and decided the best way to save his own skin was to get rid of jackal-face. So he set him up. As you've probably read, the South African police caught him, but he was seriously injured. He's now conscious, but there's brain damage. He's confused, and he's been raving about the major and the witch doctor and the robbery. Maybe one day he'll be able to tell us a coherent story."

"And how did you catch Chamberlain?"

"Well, he'd covered himself well, except for that one mistake of using Tau's phone the night of the murder. We didn't have enough to convict him, so we had to set a trap for him."

"I didn't know police set traps. Isn't that against the law?"

"It depends on how it's done. The trap we set was designed to get the major to admit what he'd done."

"Why would he do that?"

"Well, we threw him off balance. One of my father's friends is a real witch doctor. We asked him to dress up in leopard skins and so on. When Chamberlain came to work the first day after jackal-face had been captured, the witch doctor was sitting in his office chair. Of course, we'd primed him with all the relevant information."

Kubu smiled. "Maybe I was too hasty about white people being immune to witch doctors. Initially, Chamberlain told the witch doctor he was a fake. But when the witch doctor started recounting information that only the witch doctor involved in the robbery would know, he started to wonder and became pretty scared. Anyway, the witch doctor made Chamberlain think he had the diamonds. He even dropped a few on the carpet. Chamberlain couldn't resist. He took the bait and implicated himself in the whole affair."

"I read he was arraigned the other day on charges of theft, accessory to murder, and several others I can't remember."

"Yes, he's going to be a guest of the government for a long time."

"But why did he do it? He was the head of the mine! He must have had plenty of money."

Kubu nodded. "He's refused to say anything other than denying his involvement. But the recording of his meeting with the witch doctor is very incriminating—apart from anything else, he mentioned jackal-face's real name. How would he have known that if he wasn't involved?

"As for motive, that's harder. We've been digging around and discovered that all the family money comes from his wife, who is related to the De Beers owners. Probably he got his job that way too. He wasn't popular at the mine and was likely to be replaced by a Motswana soon. Then he'd have been out of a job and stuck with his wife. They don't get on, and she's now filed for divorce. From what we've heard, they are a real pair of losers. And deserved each other."

"It seems that however much someone has, it's never enough," Joy commented.

Kubu nodded. "I don't have much money, but I do have a job I love, several good friends, and wonderful parents."

"Well, congratulations, Kubu. You've certainly had an amazing first few weeks."

———

It was mid-afternoon before Kubu drove Joy back to her flat. When they arrived there, he parked and climbed out of the Land Rover.

"You don't have to come up, Kubu."

His lack of confidence kicked in immediately.

Is she giving me the brush-off?

But her next words allayed his fears. She took his hand. "I had a delightful afternoon. Let's do it again next Saturday."

"That would be wonderful," he stammered.

She leant forward and kissed him on the cheek.

"Thank you."

She turned and headed for the steps, leaving Kubu standing next to his Land Rover at a total loss for words. His whole body felt full of...

What is it I'm feeling? Excitement? Fear?

Both, he concluded. And also impatience for the following Saturday to come around. He smiled and climbed back into the Land Rover.

"Joy," he said out loud. "What a beautiful name."

———

"Well?" Pleasant asked as soon as Joy came through the door. "How was it?"

Joy didn't answer.

"Come on. Tell me. What's he like?"

"He's wonderful." Joy smiled. "And he doesn't know it."

THE END

GLOSSARY

Asseblief: Please (Afrikaans)
Bakkie: Pickup truck (Southern Africa)
Batswana: The Tswana people (see Motswana)
Botho: The idea of gaining respect by giving it (Setswana)
Debswana: 50/50 partnership between De Beers and the Botswana
　　government
Dikgobe: Setswana word for a mixture of beans and samp (see
　　below)
Dumela: Hello (Setswana)
Dram: Shot (of whiskey)
Fundi: Expert (Southern Africa)
Gabs: Short for Gaborone
Gou-gou: Quickly, quickly (Afrikaans)
Highveld: Southern African plateau above about 1,200 metres
Ja: Yes (Afrikaans)
Jislaaik: An expression of surprise (South African slang)
Jong: Young man (Afrikaans)
Kêrel: Bloke, fellow (Afrikaans)
Knobkierie: A short club made from hardwood with a knob on
　　one end, used as a weapon (Afrikaans)
Koffee: Coffee (Afrikaans)

Kraal: Small traditional village (Southern Africa)

Kubu: Hippopotamus (Setswana)

Lekker: Nice (Afrikaans)

Lobola: Bride price (Southern Africa)

Mense: People (Afrikaans)

Mma: Respectful term when addressing a woman. Mrs., madam
     (Setswana)

Motswana: A Tswana person. Singular of Batswana

Muti: Medicine (Southern Africa)

Nee: No (Afrikaans)

Ngaka: Doctor (Setswana)

Nyama: Meat (Setswana)

Oke: Person (slang)

Pap: Dry corn porridge (Southern Africa)

Pula: Botswana currency = 100 thebe

Rra: Respectful term when addressing a man. Mr., sir (Setswana)

Samp: Southern African food consisting of dried corn kernels
     that have been stamped and chopped

Setswana: Language of the Batswana people

Seswaa: Traditional Botswana dish made from beef and goat meat

Shake Shake: Brand of sorghum beer in Botswana

Sjambok: Heavy leather whip

Skelm: Bad person

Thebe: Botswana currency (See pula.)

Tsotsi: A bad person; a criminal (Southern Africa)

Veld: Grassland, field (Afrikaans)

Vrot: Rotten (Afrikaans)

Ye ken: You know (Scottish)

ACKNOWLEDGMENTS

Many people have given us their help and encouragement with this book.

We thank our agent, Jacques de Spoelberch of J de S Associates, for his continued support.

We are delighted to be published by the Poisoned Pen Press imprint of Sourcebooks, and thank Barbara Peters, Diane DiBiase, Anna Michels, Beth Deveny, and the rest of the team for their input and enthusiasm for our stories.

We benefitted greatly from the valuable input of the Minneapolis writing group—Gary Bush, Barbara Deese, and Heidi Skarie. Also, Steve Alessi, Linda Bowles, and Steve Robinson read the completed novel and gave us very helpful feedback. With all their comments, it's hard to believe that the book still has mistakes, but it probably does, and we take responsibility for any that remain.

We're also very grateful for the support and patience of our partners, Patricia Cretchley and Mette Nielsen, without which we'd never have reached THE END.

ABOUT THE AUTHORS

Michael Stanley is the writing team of Michael Sears and Stanley Trollip. Both were born in South Africa and have worked in academia and business. Stanley was an educational psychologist, specialising in the application of computers to teaching and learning, and is a pilot. Michael specialised in image processing and remote sensing and taught at the University of the Witwatersrand.

On a flying trip to Botswana, they watched a pack of hyenas hunt, kill, and devour a wildebeest, eating both flesh and bones. That gave them the premise for their first mystery, *A Carrion Death*, which introduced Detective David "Kubu" Bengu of the Botswana Criminal Investigation Department. It was a finalist for five awards, including the Crime Writers Association Debut Dagger. The series has been critically acclaimed, and their third book, *Death of the Mantis*, won the Barry Award for Best Paperback Original mystery and was a finalist for an Edgar Award. *Deadly Harvest* was a finalist for an International Thriller Writers Award.

They have also written a thriller, *Shoot the Bastards* (*Dead of Night* outside North America), in which investigative journalist Crystal Nguyen heads to South Africa for *National Geographic* and gets caught up in the war against rhino poaching and rhino-horn smuggling.

Visit their website, michaelstanleybooks.com, and follow them on Twitter @detectivekubu and on Facebook at facebook.com/MichaelStanleyBooks.